CRYO

BLAKE FISHER

First edition

Editing by *Dylan Garity*

Typesetting by *Natalia Junqueira*

Cover Design by *Liam Relph*

For my mom,
who has been my editor and biggest supporter
since I learned how to read and write.

CONTENTS

PART 1

CHAPTER 1

"What happens after death?"
The room was silent.

"For all of recorded history, people have attempted to deal with that very question, and likely far before that too. It's not hard to imagine that when our distant ancestors first were able to conceive of death, they immediately became consumed by the idea. I am sure that some of you know that chimpanzees and elephants have been known to bury their dead just like we do. Even though these animals can conceptualize death, there is still one very key difference between them and us in how we approach it. We preoccupy ourselves with the idea, almost every day. Some more than others—the lucky few can go so far as to *overcome* their fear of death, but for many of us, it is a notion that we cannot help but to preoccupy ourselves with."

I reached over to grab the remote to the slideshow that was being projected in the dimmed lighting at the front of the lecture hall. *Click.* A picture of a chimp and a man scratching their heads with red question marks scattered around the screen stood about ten feet tall, towering behind me to my left. Damn, why hadn't I changed that picture? I'd have to remember to do that before next semester. So lame.

"As you can see from this picture, we, like our primate relatives, collectively do not understand the meaning of life and death. We know that we are alive, and we know that we die, but we do not know the meaning of this, if there even is any. In my class, we will explore that one paradoxically simple question: what is death? I know some of you are thinking, 'But Professor King, this is supposed to be a class about the history of religion,' and I will tell you to shut your mouth because that is singlehandedly the most important concept in every religion throughout history. That being said, I strongly advise students who cannot handle the subject matter to drop the class, because although I think many of you will find it interesting, it is quite the opposite of a feel-good course."

There were a few chuckles, as well as a very audible scoff.

"Tell you what, since it's beautiful out and all we're going to talk about from this point on is syllabus bullshit, I'll let you guys go, and when you come back on Thursday we'll start the course by discussing Paleolithic Religion and how it relates to the religions that followed. Thank you, and see you guys on Thursday."

A couple students in the first few rows gave meek smiles, then got up quickly with the rest and rushed out the door. Three students stayed, asking a couple dumb questions they obviously already knew the answers to in order to have that leg up when grading time came around. I had to give them credit, though—their strategy definitely worked. But the last kid—he asked a question that actually made me stop to think.

"Without death, would there still be religion?"

I thought for a second and then tried to answer. It had crossed my mind once or twice before, but I'd never come up with a cohesive answer. "Well, on one hand, there have been plenty of gods that have been worshiped that have nothing to do with death. Almost every polytheistic religion has numerous gods devoted to a variety of aspects in their respective societies. But I honestly don't know. Death absolutely appears to be the necessary keystone for any religion to function. That really is a great question. What's your name?"

"David"

"David. Nice to meet you. I'm Louis King. Keep asking questions like that. I'm going to think about it and see if I can give you a more direct answer next lecture."

"Sounds good, Professor. See you then."

David exited out the door at the back of the multi-tiered lecture hall, and I was left to myself. The first day of class was always stressful for me. A light flickered toward the back of the lecture hall. These halls always seemed too bright, like I was on stage in the spotlight, and I hated having all eyes on me. It therefore surprised all of my family when I told them that teaching was what I wanted to do, especially at this level. To an extent, it surprised me as well, but after the first nerve-wracking couple lectures each semester, I always seemed to get my bearings. Year by year, the fear subsided more and more.

I sighed in relief and went to gather my papers off my cheap particle-board desk off to the side of the stage I was standing on. Then I strode off toward the door with the dimly lit exit sign hanging over it. Through it, I was met with the soft woosh of the wind and a darkened sky.

CHAPTER 2

On the drive home, the clouds far off in the distance to my right formed together to make a darker, more ominous Tuesday. Slivers of sun pierced through the clouds, illuminating portions of the ground and making the countryside look like it was going through a rapture where the pure souls were ascending to heaven, while the rest of us were left to deal with the impending gloom, soon to engulf us all. Good thing I didn't believe in any of that, or the apocalyptic-looking storm would have been pretty frightening. I flipped the radio on and was thrown into the middle of Blue Oyster Cult's "(Don't Fear) The Reaper." I turned it up and sped down the highway home. It would be a suitable race to try to beat the storm, if that was even possible.

"Beep. Beep. Beep. This is a test. This station is conducting a test of the Emergency Broadcast System. This is only a test."

The song resumed. Well that was dumb—why the hell couldn't they just wait until the song was over to test their system? I glanced back over at the storm. Since they'd ruined the best cowbell part already, I switched it off and called my wife. The phone barely rang once.

"Hey."

"Hey honey bear," she replied, "are you on your way home?"

"Yeah, I am. There's a pretty nasty-looking storm that looks like it's coming in over Staplehurst. I should be able to beat it, though."

"Alright speed racer, you just get home. I have a surprise waiting for you." There was a subtle almost wink in her voice that implied it was the sort of surprise you wouldn't find at a child's birthday party.

"Alrighty then, I'll put the pedal to the metal. See you in sixteen minutes and forty-two seconds, give or take. Love you."

She laughed. "I'll start my stopwatch."

I turned the radio back on and glanced over at the darkness again that was slowly engulfing the almost-perfect fall sunset. Simon and Garfunkel were just beginning to elucidate how silence sounded, and I pushed down my foot a little harder to work the Chevy Cruze up to a comfortable 82 mph down I-80. The perfect seven over the speed limit to continue my journey, but remain under the radar of most cops prowling in any of the highway turnarounds. The song had just ended when I took the exit onto 379 toward Seward, where my destination lay only about six minutes away. Nine-and-a-half if traffic was bad. That was always the best part about living just on the outskirts of the city—no dealing with the assholes who thought they were the most important people on the planet and that their business was worth almost running you off the road to get one car length ahead of you.

Don't get me wrong. I love the city. Always have, always will. But having lived there my whole life, traffic is one thing I will never miss. The clouds began rolling in overhead. Damn, that storm was moving fast. Just then, rain started splattering the windshield like Jackson Pollock working overtime. I slammed the windshield wipers on as fast as they could go, and they barely did the trick. I could still see only about twenty feet ahead of me, so I slowed the car down to a reasonable 30 mph. Once or twice, I thought about stopping the car completely, but that seemed foolish as I was only about seven or eight minutes away now due to my significantly reduced speed. I clicked the flashers on to warn any daredevil drivers out there that I would be setting my car to the "Driving Miss Daisy" speed for the remainder of my trip.

The rain started to get denser. Or perhaps blurrier? I had never seen rain that looked so strange. It fell and splattered on the windshield, but before it was wiped away by the blades, it started stretching and shrinking. I decided to slow down a little more, but as I looked at the speedometer, I saw that it was also contorting into unfamiliar shapes. *Okay? What the fuck is going on?* I thought coherently. But that was the last coherent thought I had. My left arm quickly lost control of itself, and the dead weight of it pulled down hard on the steering wheel. What coherence I had left was no longer there, and nothing in my body told itself to veer back onto the road. Then—black.

CHAPTER 3

Flashing red and blue lights filtered in through the cracked windshield. I felt cold. Reaching down into my pocket, I tried to retrieve my phone. Only immediately I realized that I was actually reaching upward. Groggily, I stretched my arm around my side to click the seatbelt. The unlatching of the belt was followed by an audible thud and a pain in my shoulder as I fell into the ceiling of the car. Through the windshield, which I could now see was slightly wedged into the muddy earth, two paramedics were approaching. I rolled myself uncomfortably until my stomach was touching the roof of the car. My briefcase, coffee cup, and other small items had joined me in resting on the ceiling. Instinctively, I reached for my briefcase as if I had just arrived at my destination and was ready to go about my daily business.

"Sir," a voice called into the car. "Can you move?"

"Yeah, I'm fine," I called back out. Remarkably, I did feel fine.

"We're going to have to break the window now. Please turn away for a moment."

"Sure thing." I turned my head and looked out the other way toward the woods. Rain pattered on the ground, soon interrupted by a surprisingly quiet shattering of the window. I turned back toward the paramedics, one of whom was now peering in at me. His thick mustache reminded me of a young Burt Reynolds.

"Besides the damage to the car, it looks like you're actually in pretty good condition," Burt's doppelganger told me.

"Mint condition," I half-laughed as I crawled my way out through the window. I didn't remember crashing. Didn't feel any pain. Had I been dreaming? Or was it the adrenaline coursing through my body? Either way, everything felt surreal. I got to my knees and then up to my feet to survey the scene. Behind me, dozens of cars' headlights were slowly moving past as an officer waved them by. I looked back down at the car. The little Chevy Cruze was lying belly up, its windshield wipers still flapping back and forth. The car may have been unsalvageable, but those wipers weren't going down without a fight. Rain sloshing rhythmically from the passing cars filled my ears.

"Excuse me..." Bert interrupted, as I was listening to the symphony of the rain.

"Oh, sorry. Yes?"

"It's alright. I asked what your name was and if there is any emergency contact we can call?"

"Louis," I responded. "And no, I'm capable of calling my wife. Thank you." I pulled the phone out of my pocket, went to recent calls, and called Violet back. Immediately I was met with her voice.

"Louis?" She sounded panicked. "Where are you? Are you okay?"

I must have been out for a little longer than I thought.

"I was in a little accident. I'm okay."

"Okay." I could hear her take a deep breath through the phone. "Where are you?"

At first, I honestly didn't know, but after a moment, it came back to me.

"Just got off the exit," I told her. "If you want to come down here, I think the red and blue flashing lights might give away my hiding spot."

"I'm already on the way," she assured me. "What happened?"

All at once, I remembered how I had crashed. It was so confusing, and frankly scared the hell out of me. I had never had anything like that happen before. Sure, I'd felt woozy from dehydration or from standing up too fast. But randomly blacking out? My heart started beating fast, and I was either sweating or simply getting drenched by the rain. I took a deep breath and responded.

"Oh it was nothing," I tried to say calmly. "Just got into a little fender bender trying to save a pack of baby deer from a burning car. Forgot to put the car in park when I hopped out."

"That is the stupidest thing I've ever heard you say," she told me. "And that's a lot coming from you."

We both laughed. It felt good. But I felt a deep uneasiness in the pit of my stomach.

"I'll see you soon then?" I asked.

"Yeah, be there in a minute."

I talked to the police for a bit while they took down my statement. For some reason, I lied to them and said a deer was crossing the road and I swerved. I lied, hoping that whatever had just happened to me was some type of anomaly. That ignoring it would somehow make it not real.

Maybe it really hadn't been anything that bad. People pass out all the time. It happens.

I saw the familiar Subaru blue of Violet's Crosstrek pull off to the side of the road. The hazards flashed on. She hopped out and ran over to me, pulling me into her arms. I could feel her heart racing against my chest as she squeezed the life out of me. "Don't ever do that to me again, you jackass," she said lovingly. The rain was starting to let up a little, as off in the distance the sun started to break through the clouds.

"It was an accident. Like I said, those helpless baby deer..."

"Oh shut up," she kissed me. We waited there a long while dealing with the cops, waiting for the tow truck, and handling all the standard post-accident protocol. The paramedics asked if I wanted to go to the hospital to check for any injuries. Violet insisted that I should, but I adamantly declined. I felt fine now, besides a minor headache. I had always been prone to headaches, and although they seemed to be happening more frequently recently, it was nothing to concern myself or Violet over. She was always a worrier. It was always best not to fill her in on mildly concerning matters, because she always went overboard on the research. One time I had a random bruise on the side of my knee, and she went full-on Wikipedia doctor and came to the conclusion that I had leukemia. Which obviously wasn't the case, but it still forced me to go waltzing into the doctor to get it checked out. Although this random episode was more than mildly concerning to me, now wasn't the time to tell her about it. If ever. I was an open book with her, but some things for both of our sanity were better left unsaid.

Once everything was said and done, I got into the car with her. The moon was starting to rise in the sky as the wind whooshed in through the open window. That pleasant smell that comes after a rainstorm that can only be described as fresh and earthy filled my senses. I lay my head down, exhausted from the day's events, and felt the wind caress my face. The whole ride was silent, but Violet had her one free hand gently placed on my knee. That was one of the most beautiful things about her. We could be completely silent and just feel each other's presence. Say a thousand things without saying a word.

When we pulled into the driveway, the house looked like it always did. It was waiting there for us like every other day, but something seemed off about it—like returning home from a long trip and not knowing if something had happened inside while you were gone, or if someone was inside waiting to thoroughly ruin your day. But inside, everything was the exact same as always. The light maple wood near the front door still had the massive gouge in it from when Violet came rollerblading in through the front door and went ass over heels, clipping one of the wheels on the threshold. The familiar smell of an apple-cinnamon candle wafted through the air, mixed with the also-familiar smell of slightly burnt chicken. Violet hadn't been the best of cooks, but she tried relentlessly to fix that. Everything was palatable at least, but generally, if I was home first, I was the cook. Although I was far from a Gordon Ramsey myself.

"I made us some broccoli chicken." Violet broke the silence as we walked in, and I sat my briefcase on the breakfast bar that broke up the kitchen from the living room. "Although, it kind of tasted like burnt trash." She gave a meek smile.

"As appetizing of a description as that is, I think I'm going to have to pass tonight. I'm exhausted. It's been a day and a half."

"That's fine, love, I understand. I'll box it up and we'll see if you can keep it down tomorrow." I gave her a one-armed hug and turned around to head down the hallway toward our bedroom. Falling face-first into the bed, I lay sprawled out, breathing into the mattress, until Violet opened the door and came in. She rubbed my back, which still all these years later made my heart feel a funny warmness. She then proceeded to tell me how happy she was that I was back safe at home with her. One thing led to another, and we did what two consenting adults do behind closed doors. Or not behind closed doors—to each their own. As we lay together afterward, I felt the anxieties of the day melt away and fell asleep with my head gently rested on her chest.

CHAPTER 4

I opened my eyes and awoke to a pounding headache. The smell of bacon wafted through the air, and I could hear Violet quietly singing to herself in the kitchen. The crash must have rattled me up a bit, because I couldn't remember the last time my head felt this way. Recently, the headaches were a little worse than normal, but nothing this bad. Getting out of bed, I stumbled a bit to catch my footing before standing up. My vision blurred from the head rush, but once I was up everything seemed to return to a sense of normal.

The sun pierced my eyes as I walked out of the bedroom, bringing the headache back into full tilt. I squinted them and closed one like a drunk trying to read their texts to see if their late-night message was going to pay off. The room felt unstable, but I shook it off and walked over to the kitchen.

"Morning, Evil Knievel." Violet smiled as she walked over to give me a kiss. "Planning on crashing any more cars today? Or are you going to stay home with me and finally get back to work on your book? I promise I won't distract you." She winked.

"Distract me all you like, that garbage fire is never going to get finished anyway," I yawned.

"Would you shut up? Just because one single person who read it said that it was convoluted and unfocused doesn't mean a damn thing." The bacon made its satisfying popping noise, and she turned back around to start taking them out of the pan.

"Well he is my editor, so it kind of does mean a damn thing. I'll get to cleaning it up, I think I just need some fresh air first. My head is killing me."

"Flipping a car tends to do that. Maybe you'll think twice before trying to get a career in stunt work next time."

"Piss off," I replied with a sly smile, and headed out to the back yard. The morning air was crisp and felt cathartic on my face. The soft singing of the birds in the trees echoed into the perfect blue sky. As I was walking to take a seat in my chair, which matched Violet's beside it, I felt the earth slightly turn to the right, and stumbled a little over my feet. I looked back to see if Violet saw, but she was plating up the bacon and eggs. Quickly, I walked over to the chair and fell down in it to avoid giving her any worries about my newfound lack of balance. I heard the sliding glass door open, but didn't turn around, feeling that the glance over my shoulder would somehow send me into another dizzy spell. She sat down next to me and held both plates in her lap.

"I was going to make you one," she said as she shoved a piece of bacon into her mouth off of one of the plates, "but..." She took another piece off the other plate and shoved it into her mouth. "If you're not going to write, I guess I'm going to be the breadwinner of the family," she said with exaggerated chewing. "I'm going to need all the energy I can get." She tried keeping a straight face but eventually choked back some laughter and sent bits of bacon flying into the grass.

"At least you can make yourself laugh," I scoffed with a grin. She handed me over the plate and I greedily took it. I was starving. Shoving the bacon in my mouth, I chewed it. And chewed it. And chewed it. But it didn't want to go down. Eventually, with a hard swallow, I got it down. It was painful—another thing I could add to the list of things that had never happened to me before—but my stomach was turning over on itself, so I tried for a bit of the eggs. Same thing. Violet paid no attention; she had her head tilted back looking at the sky and was feeding herself like a baby bird.

"Louis," Violet said, still looking at the sky. "You're a wonderful writer. Just get the book to a point you're happy with. If people don't like it, to hell with them. You do happen to have a professorship to fall back on." She turned her head over to look at me sideways, and I didn't hide my discomfort quickly enough. She sat bolt upright and stared at me. "Louis, what's wrong?"

"Just worrying about the book," I lied.

"No," was all she said. She could read me like a book no matter what—it was impossible to lie to her. That would get me into trouble from time to time when I would tell her I got something done around the house, or mailed a package I forgot to mail, or anything of the sort. "What's wrong?" she repeated, grabbing at my hand softly now.

"It's nothing, I'm just having a hard time swallowing this food." Being the pseudo-nurse that she was, she began asking other questions.

"Is anything else going on? Are you dizzy? I know you said you have a headache, but is anything else feeling off?" Her usual playful tone was now stern and alarmed.

"Vi, I'm fine," I assured her. "Just feeling off after the accident."

"I'm going to call the doctor—maybe you have a concussion or something. We should get it checked out."

"Seriously Violet, there is nothing wrong. Just a bit off today."

"I'm still calling," she protested. Her misgivings seemed to always turn her into an amateur hypochondriac. It was not my favorite quality of hers.

"Okay, fine," I consented. "If it'll make you feel better, call away." Before I could even finish the sentence, she was already going back into the house to grab her cellphone off the table. Luckily, I hadn't mentioned why I crashed in the first place, or I would probably have been halfway to the hospital in the back of an ambulance, Violet planning my funeral as she drove behind. She always jumped to the worst-case scenario. Always. It was much better keeping her in the dark in places where she didn't pry too much. I could hear her describing the symptoms over the phone as I stared at the lonely cherry blossom tree in our backyard, its leaves getting ready to start falling in the next couple of weeks.

"Okay," she said as she came back outside. "He said that it isn't abnormal to be feeling off after an accident, but to monitor any of these new symptoms, and if they don't recede to come to the hospital. So you're off the hook for now, but just please keep me in the loop. Don't want to wake up next to your corpse," she half-laughed, but I could see real worry in her eyes.

"I promise," I said, and stood up. The dizziness was no longer there at the moment, so I took this chance to rush inside and grab my laptop. Unfolding it, I set it on my lap as I sat down on our old torn-up leather couch. I didn't know why we couldn't get rid of it—it wasn't like we couldn't afford anything nicer. But Violet insisted it had sentimental value because it was the first couch we bought together. A picture of Violet and me beaming like idiots from our trip to London brightened on the screen, and I went down to click on the "Why am I writing this?" doc.

The last year-and-a-half's worth of research and writing opened up on the screen, and I was met with the impending dread that precedes writers block. When I first started writing it, I thought that a book about death traditions around the world would essentially write itself—the subject matter was relatively interesting and deeply disturbing. But, *Obscure Death Traditions* was far from that. My editor was right—it was convoluted and unfocused. I tried tying them together, but it ended up being a boring overview on the countless traditions cultures have, with no real connections or through lines. I stared at the Sati section, but my mind kept drifting.

When their husbands died, wives in India were forced onto the funeral pyre with their recently deceased spouse. I looked up at the ceiling and the dizziness reappeared. *Wives in India were ...* The ceiling was slowly shifting to the left and right. I shook my head. *When their husbands...* I inhaled deeply and closed my eyes; it felt like when you get off of a merry-go-round and the world spins for a moment while you're still planted firmly to the ground. But this spinning didn't stop. *Forced onto the funeral pyre... deceased spouse.* I slammed the laptop shut.

Taking a deep breath, I stood up to go to the kitchen. The water splashing through the closed door as Violet took her shower sounded entirely too distant. I opened up the cupboard and grabbed for my ironically favorite 'I Love Lincoln' mug. My arm felt heavy, and my hand was trembling. Walking over to the fridge felt like a mile. I pushed the mug up to the water dispenser and waited. The slow fill was an eternity. Bringing the mug up to my mouth, I took a sip, and my vision started to fade to black. My legs gave out, and I heard a shattering noise.

CHAPTER 5

Slowly, my sight came back to me. I was staring underneath the refrigerator. Shards of broken ceramic were sprinkled all about. The peaceful sound of the shower trickled off in the distance. I propped myself up on one elbow and slid my back up against one of the espresso-colored cabinets. It took a moment before I realized what had happened. My heart started to beat fast. Something was seriously wrong. Yet I still decided to hold out hope that it was something related to the accident.

I got my footing, stood up, and stumbled over to grab a broom. The shower squeaked off as I started sweeping the fragments into a pile. I could hear the curtain rings rattling on the bars , and I hurriedly walked over to the dustpan to clean up the remaining evidence of my fall. With the click of the doorknob, Violet strode out of the bathroom and into the kitchen. She was wrapped in a pink towel that covered down to the middle of her thighs.

"I see you abandoned the book idea," she said as she held her head tilted to the side, wringing out her hair with a matching pink towel. "That must be record time."

"Writer's block is a bitch," I told her. My eyes drifted down to a piece of mug I had missed on the ground.

"I bet," she said as she came to give me a hug. The warm wetness of the towel mixed uncomfortably with the cold contrast of her hair resting on my neck and shoulder. "It's okay—inspiration will strike you soon. I know it." She pulled back and gave me a loving smile.

"Yeah," I halfheartedly agreed.

"Oh, quit sulking," she insisted. "You know you're not going to get me to feel bad for you."

"Not even if I do this?" I put on my best puppy-dog face, which was admittedly terrible.

"Especially if you do that," she laughed. "You look like a constipated turtle."

"A what?" I laughed hard. Violet always came up with the most obscure descriptions, and I loved it about her.

"You heard me, Koopa Troopa." I momentarily had forgotten about my troubles, until the ongoing laughter sent me into another light dizzy spell. Violet took notice. "Seriously Louis, are you sure we shouldn't take you in?"

"No, I'm fine, I promise—maybe we should go for a walk?" I was a little frightened by the prospect of walking far, but the fresh air couldn't hurt.

"You know I'm always down," she said, and went to go get dressed. I went over to the little nook by the front door where we kept our shoes and sat down on the fold-out bench, inside of which we had optimistically planned on keeping our frisbees and other outdoor equipment. But years later, it only contained one baseball—strange, because neither of us fessed up to putting it in there. Probably found on one of our drunken adventures out. I laced up the dirty black Nikes and sat, waiting for her to join me.

Moments later, she came and sat down next to me, where she slipped on her light grey Pumas. She never tied her shoes. I always joked to her that she probably didn't even know how. A lame joke, but it always got a pity laugh. "Ready?" I asked.

"Ready as I'll ever be." She smiled and dramatically whipped the front door open and started jogging in place. I made some exaggerated arm stretches and then slipped my hand into hers. Her stationary jogging caused our hands to jostle around vehemently. Then, all of a sudden, she stopped and exhaled deeply. "Okay, that's enough of that."

We walked out down our walkway toward the quiet street that we lived on. As we strolled along the edge of the road given the absence of sidewalks, the soft breeze felt remarkable on my face. It was a night-and-day difference. Our hands swung as we walked in perfect silence.

Our neighbor was out trimming his bushes. We both waved with our free hands. He smiled politely and waved back. The sun was beginning to be covered by light wispy clouds, causing the light on the ground to dance. My mind wandered back and forth between trying to figure out how to fix my book and trying to figure out if there was anything actually wrong with me, or if it was just the after-effects of the crash. I'd never been in one before, so I really had no idea. Violet was looking around, smiling at the little corgi that was always out in the yard in the house on the corner of the street. She was making baby noises its way, and it was wagging its little stump of a tail ferociously.

I took a step, and all of a sudden the world shifted, like unknowingly stepping onto a trampoline. The feeling reverberated through my body, a shock to my system. All at once, my vision teeter-tottered until darkness started to veil my eyes. Quickly, I tried to blink it away, but with each blink it got darker and darker, until I felt my knees give out and heard Violet scream.

CHAPTER 6

I couldn't tell where I was. Lying prone, but clearly still moving, I could see the sky. Over my shoulder was an unfamiliar face, wearing a symbol I must have seen a hundred times before but couldn't seem to recognize. The sound of a small dog barking filled my ears, but behind that I could hear people talking indistinctly.

"Snokay hapsbital," the voice seemed to murmur in my direction.

"What?" I tried sitting up, but my body didn't seem to want to listen to simple commands.

"It's okay, Louis," Violet's familiar voice broke through. "We're heading to the hospital. You're going to be just fine." I felt her hand squeeze mine. I squeezed back as I started to gain a bit of lucidity accompanied by a heavy dose of fear. Everything hadn't been alright. It hadn't been alright at all. Suddenly, I felt my mind racing to figure out anything else that had been out of the ordinary recently. With limited mental capacities, it was hard to think of anything except the repeating thought that something was wrong. Something was very wrong.

With every passing moment, greater clarity returned. I was in the back of an ambulance by this point, that much was clear. The symbol I had seen earlier was that of a paramedic. They were asking questions—questions I probably could have given the answer to without much thought normally, but my mind was miles elsewhere.

"Sir, can you tell me who the current president is?" one of the paramedics asked.

"Where's Violet?" I asked, completely ignoring the question. I needed her next to me. To hold her hand, and have her tell me everything was going to be okay. Not surrounded by unfamiliar faces. The inside of the ambulance was sterile, and well lit. I felt like an extraterrestrial on an operating table. By the way that the paramedics were looking at me, I must have looked like one too. As the thought of what ET must have felt like was crossing my mind, the ambulance stopped and the back doors opened.

CHAPTER 7

Violet and I waited impatiently in a small examination room for the doctor to come in. She was completely silent, nervously stroking the back of my hand with her palm to the point where it felt like she would rub my skin off completely. I didn't mind; at least she was there now. With my one free hand, I was nervously tapping at the side of my leg. There were no longer any problems with my vision. The downside of that was that the bright lights in the room were seared into my brain. It felt like King Kong had his hands around my head and was trying to use it as an accordion.

"You'll be okay," Violet whispered, trying to sound sincere, but it fell flat. I could see real fear in her eyes, a fear that I had never seen before. I guess that was a side effect of seeing your significant other drop out of nowhere like a piano in an old cartoon. "You'll be okay," she repeated, but this time it sounded like she was trying to convince herself.

I focused down into my lap, where the light wasn't projecting directly on me.

Soon the doctor walked in, clipboard in hand.

"Good morning," he said. "I'm Dr. Seaton, and I'll be taking care of you." I almost had to laugh. Even though it was pronounced 'sea-tonne,' the striking likeness to Satan was hard to ignore. Maybe he should have changed his name or thought of a career in the mortuary sciences instead. Either way, it couldn't be a good omen. "I understand you had a fall this morning?"

That was an understatement. More like fell out of the land of the living momentarily.

"Yes," I replied.

"Have you been experiencing any irregular symptoms? Dizziness? Headaches? Vision problems?" He sat down in his chair and leaned forward. Check, check, and check. His long, neatly trimmed beard bounced with the movement of his questions.

"Yes sir," I replied. Violet turned to me quizzically, knowing now that I had been hiding some pretty major details from her.

"I see." He jotted a few notes down on a clipboard. "And when would you say this started?"

"Well..." I paused to look over at Violet for a moment, knowing that she wouldn't be happy with the next response either. "My headaches have seemed to be getting more severe and frequent over the last couple months. But I never had any other issues that I can think of until last night, when a dizzy spell caused me to pass out and lose control of my vehicle." Violet squeezed my hand hard. I knew it wasn't out of anger, but that her fear had just increased tenfold.

"I see," he said again, and wrote down a few more things on his clipboard. His face was stern and serious. But that wasn't exactly a departure from how he'd walked in, either. He didn't seem like the friendliest of doctors. I hoped that his lack of affability was made up for by professionalism. "Can you hop onto the table for me?"

Without saying a word, I placed my hand on top of Violet's and stood up, the air blowing an uncomfortable breeze up my gown. I stumbled a little on my way to the table and heard Violet let out the faintest gasp.

Once I was up, Dr. Seaton pulled out a stethoscope and had me breathe in and out several times. "Everything seems normal on that end," he told me. I looked over at Violet, but that didn't ease her fear in the slightest. "I'm going to test your reflexes now." He hit me under the kneecap, and there was a slight delay before my leg decided to jerk. He did it a couple more times, and it was the same thing. "Hmm," he muttered under his breath. Then he proceeded to pull out a pen and told me to follow it with my eyes. I did the best I could, but the pen seemed to blur a bit as I followed it, like during the comedown from an acid trip.

"So?" Violet asked impatiently.

"These symptoms alone don't necessarily trigger any alarms," the doctor said as he returned his pen to his pocket. "However, with the symptoms you've been experiencing, Mr. King, I would like to refer you over to a radiologist to get an MRI."

"Okay," I said with a slight tremble in my voice, trying to keep it as normal as possible for Violet's sake. I could already picture her running through a thousand different scenarios in her head, all leading to my death. Looking into her eyes, I saw that my assumption was correct. She looked dazed, staring off into nothing. Her gaze met mine momentarily, and I gave her a meek smile. She tried to return it, but her lips were trembling.

"It's nothing to concern yourselves over yet, just proto-col." Dr. Seaton gave a reassuring smile. But my mind drift-ed, thinking about all the people he had given that smile who'd indeed had a hell of a lot to concern themselves over.

"Okay," I repeated.

CHAPTER 8

After ensuring the radiologist that I had no metal plates or anything else that could become a major issue while in the machine, they laid me down on the table and slid me in head first. I could feel my heart beating out of its chest as the machine whirred on and I was left completely alone with my thoughts. Through the dulling of the earplugs, I could hear what sounded like an oscillating fan, but it was soon followed by a rapid beeping that at first I had mistaken for my heartbeat. Thinking I was getting ready to flatline, I squeezed hard. Violet's soft hand molded into mine from the pressure, but she didn't seem to mind. I could feel her heartbeat through her fingers, and it was easily going faster than mine. Our heartbeats together probably sounded like the pattering of two Olympic runners getting ready to cross the finish line. By the feel of it, she was going to take first place.

My mind drifted off to our first Christmas together. It was a comforting memory. Almost without exception, every memory with her was comforting. But as we sat in front of her father's fireplace drinking lukewarm apple cider together and feeling the warmth on our faces, I could feel the comforting feeling in my chest, and the sounds of the machine soon dissipated. Snow fell gently outside the window as her dad lay snoozing away in his favorite chair, his new lower-end Seiko watch that I had got him wrapped around his wrist. It was all I could afford, but he didn't care. He knew the way his daughter and I felt about each other, and that was more than enough for him to be perfectly content.

Her hand delicately wrapped around mine, our fingers dancing together while we stared into the fire. "I think I love you," she said out of nowhere.

"Well, I hope so," I replied. "I'm madly in love with you." I had been too nervous to say anything before in fear of scaring her off.

She turned to look away from the fire and half-scoffed. "Well why didn't you say anything sooner? I'm over here trying to play coy. I love you so much, Louis. You have no idea." The perfect blue-green pools of her eyes flickered with the fire.

"You make me a better person. The person I've always envisioned myself being." I felt a tug in my chest. She truly did. She was always there to be my cheerleader, as I was hers, and as we would always be for years to come. I'd thought about dropping out of college to get a job because money was too tight a few months after we met, and she told me that if I wasn't going to follow my dreams there was no point in living. Life is too short. We could struggle for a while, but at least we would be struggling together.

"You feel like home to me," she told me with a reserved smile. I wrapped my arm around her back, and she placed her head gently on my shoulder. Her dark auburn hair brushed up against the stubble on the side of my cheek. Then the whirring stopped and I was pulled back into reality.

CHAPTER 9

"So what should we do now?" Violet interrupted the silence on our drive home.

"I don't know," I said honestly, not knowing what was normal to do after an MRI of that scale. I thought people probably tried to go on with their day like normal, so that was what I suggested. "Want to go out for some ice cream?"

"Are you sure you're going to be able to eat it?" The question hurt me, but it was a valid concern. Even something as normal as eating ice cream was up in the air at that point. She sensed the hurt in my eyes. "I'm sorry," she said. "I know that was a bad question. Let's try." She smiled and put her hand on my knee as she drove. The radio was softly playing "Mirrorball" by Taylor Swift through Violet's phone with the very noticeable crack down the center of the screen, from the time she decided it would be a good idea to test her tree-climbing skills with her phone in hand.

I stared at the crack a long while, not thinking about anything until I felt her squeeze my knee. "If this is anything,
we'll catch it soon enough."

"Huh?" I said stupidly, coming out of my daze.

"We're going to get you the help you need if this turns out
to be anything," she said, and squeezed tighter, reassuringly.

"Oh yeah, of course." I smiled back at her. It was awkward—the first time since we met that neither of us really
knew what to say to each other. We exchanged weary, sup-
portive glances, but I couldn't bear to look into her eyes
for too long. It hurt far too much thinking that someday I
might not be able to look into them again. Someday soon,
possibly. A lifetime with her was too short, and my hands
started getting sweaty thinking about inevitabilities.

The rest of the day was filled with the same awkward
instances of us not knowing what to say, or how to console
each other. Wordlessly, we would lock in long embraces
while our thoughts both revolved around the same thing.
At night, we both lay in bed, staring at each other. It was
easily the most silent we had ever been around each other. The silence hurt, but it was inescapable. It was the un-
certainty that hurt us both the most. The point when your
mind races alongside all possibilities, but can't pinpoint a
single one. Everything out of your control, and nothing to
be done at that point. No saying "I'll change my diet," or
"I'll exercise more," or "I'll change up my whole fucking life
if I have to." The only thing to do was plead with a god that
I knew probably wasn't there to give me more time with
the woman I loved so much, while staring at her while she
tossed and turned.

That night I fell in and out of sleep, dreaming of things
that would disappear the moment I would wake up—the
types of dreams that leave you with a looming sense of fear

and anxiety, but you can't remember why. Violet had finally fallen into what appeared to be a deep sleep. The birds were softly chirping along outside. It was 8:47 when my phone rang, and she shot straight up in bed to watch me as I answered.

"Good morning, this is Dr. Shafer from radiology. We need you to come in right away," the voice on the other side of the line resonated.

CHAPTER 10

"We can make you comfortable for your final weeks, but unfortunately there is nothing we can do with tumors at this aggressive of a stage."

The doctor's mouth kept moving, but I couldn't make out anything besides a faint ringing noise and the sound of my thoughts washing back and forth like waves in my head. Was this really it? Now? Over and over, like a record player that can't help but replay the final moments of a song.

Violet didn't cry. She just stared. But through that stare, it was easy to see that something had shattered inside her. It hurt even more. I could handle dying. Everyone dies. But the knowledge that I would be leaving her alone in the world was almost too much for one person to bear. When I would predictably leave the world, it would all be over for me. The pain, the hurt, the love, the joy, the feelings that make life beautiful would all be gone. I wouldn't know any of them anymore, but that was okay with me. The realization that she would have to carry the burden was the only thing that made my entire body go numb. It was a numbness that I would carry with me into my grave.

CHAPTER 11

A week went by. Violet did everything she could to find alternative medicines that could potentially help. For the most part, all she found were some godawful-tasting drinks. She even went so far as to take me to a 'healer' that whacked me with some leaves a couple times, which was meant to shrink tumors I guess. At least her heart was in the right place. And at least I still felt fine, for the most part.

Another week went by. The powerful oxycodone that I was prescribed made everything better for a little while, but that didn't stop the relentless vomiting. I had taken to doing research of my own, not for treatments, but to plan for what I wanted done with my body. My body that would still look like me, but no longer contain anything about me. At least I wasn't bed-ridden yet.

Another couple days passed. After doing extensive re-search on burial options, I decided all of them sucked immeasurably. Violet broke down whenever she saw what I was searching for. Then, ultimately, things began deteriorating rapidly. My left arm quickly lost what functionality it had left, and almost every time I stood up I could make it only a couple feet before losing my balance completely. Everything that I said either didn't come out right, or I would lose my train of thought immediately. By that point I was too far gone mentally to understand myself, let alone anyone else. There were still periods of time where my thoughts were coherent, but even in those times my mind prevented me from saying anything accurately.

I wanted to tell Violet every feeling I'd had for her since we met sophomore year in college; I wanted to tell her that every moment spent with her was how I wanted to live my life, and I would do it a hundred times over if I could. I wanted to let her know that she was my everything, and always would be. All that came out was, "Violet. Love we more?" Fuck, if only my writing could have been more lucid than my speech, then I would've been able to let her know. I had hoped she already knew—I think she did. "Tree," I told her.

"I'm sorry love, I don't know what that means," she said with tears slowly trickling down her cheek. I typed in "biod-," but the weakness in my arm was too much to bear. Fortunately, my recent searches popped up, and it brought up the website of biodegradable burial pods that let your body decompose to help the growth of a new tree. I had thought that having a physical living thing would be nice for her to visit sometimes. However, when she did see the page, she adamantly shook her head. Tears streaked down her face, and I could feel a couple land on my neck as she peered over me. "What about this?" she asked through quiet sobs.

With the little remaining strength I had in my arm, I tried to grab at her hand but got her wrist instead as she typed "Cryolabs, cryopreservation and cryogenic freezing" and clicked enter again to open the page. I looked back at her, and her face had the faintest hint of hope in it. I didn't even need to see what was on the page before I nodded. Nodded knowing that nod would be the metaphorical nail in my coffin. Nodded knowing that this was still the end. But if this somehow made her feel more at peace with the fact that I was gone, that was enough for me. Even in death, I would do anything for her, and this was the last chance I would ever get to do that for her.

CHAPTER 12

The day Violet drove me to the lab was a complete blur. Although, I vaguely remember snow blanketing the ground. She was speaking to me as tears were falling down her face, but I couldn't comprehend any of the words. Just the feelings. It felt like the air was forcibly being sucked from my lungs, and nothing would bring it back. I started feeling like this wasn't the right idea. But it was too late by now—there was nothing I could do to reverse my impending fate. Even if I wanted to protest, no one would know what I was trying to say.

The whole day flashed by in what felt like seconds, and before I knew it they were hoisting me up into a futuristic-looking tube with a small window in it. The pristine white room around me faded away as they hooked me up. The door was already closing as I started violently shaking my head, watching Violet stare at me with sympathetic sorrow. I remember hearing the doctor tell her not to worry and that the solar panels would ensure that even in power outages, I would still be safe. Then, suddenly, an air-tight hiss plugged my ears, and I was left in silence. Outside the window I saw Violet mouth what must have been 'I love you.' I tried to lift my arm to the window and say the same thing, but before I could, it was all over. Every moment that Violet and I had shared together. Every laugh, every smile, every tear, every memory. Sealed away with the quiet, air-tight hiss of machinery. Like placing the lid on a sarcophagus, blackness enveloped me.

CHAPTER 13

"Wow, you look like shit. What in the hell's wrong with you?" I heard a voice ask as I struggled to open one of my eyes. I couldn't feel any part of my body. Through blurry vision, I managed to make out a silhouette standing in front me. The room was mostly dark. Artificial lights pulsated in large, cylindrical tubes. Slowly, it started coming back to me. I was in one of those tubes too. I moved my head down with what felt like all the strength in my body. My fingers shifted slightly, but felt wholly disconnected from my body. Dazed, I found no words to explain what actually was the hell wrong with me. Not that I could annunciate anything even if I did find the words. So I bent my head down a little more and turned my forefinger up on my right hand and pointed.

"Oh, you're braindead. Bummer," he said with good humor, but also a hint of discontent. I shook my head. Pointed again. His brow furrowed, searching for another answer.

"Well shit, I'm no good at charades." He paused. "Cancer?" I nodded. "Well I'll be damned; I guess I'm not half bad." I tried to force a smile, but nothing probably came out except maybe a half-assed, creepy smirk. "Well luckily for you, I happen to be your savior." He went over to his suitcase and unlatched one of the latches, and it popped open with an impossible amount of compartments hovering at different levels up to my shoulders over the suitcase. Without saying another word, he reached into one of the compartments on the bottom, grabbed a syringe, slid off the cap, and neatly stabbed it into my neck. "Now, you might be feeling pretty under the weather still for the next couple of days, but then I promise you'll be feeling right as rain." He laughed and turned his back to me. What was going on? Where the hell was I? "So I take it you have absolutely no idea what's going on here, huh?"

"No," I managed to muster. He grabbed my arms and pulled me out of the chamber. I expected to tip over immediately, but my legs somehow kept me standing upright.

"Figures. You damn Cryo Kids keep popping up in labs all over, and it's almost always the same as your case. A last-ditch effort to save one of your insignificant lives. Now don't get me wrong, my life is just as insignificant as yours, I'm just not stupid enough to care about living on past my predetermined expiration date." He pulled a flask from his jacket pocket, unscrewed, it took a sip, and passed it my way.

"No. Thank you," I said with surprising clarity. *What. The. Fuck.*

He laughed. "Sounds like that little mystery syringe is working its magic." I turned my head and really looked around for the first time. The room I remembered going into was no longer pristine and white. The walls were faded to a yellowish hue, as if an everyday smoker had a field day in here for the last couple years. But it hadn't only been a couple years, had it? Water spots marked the ceiling all over, and a thick layer of grime and filth covered the windows. I realized that the only light was being illuminated from the few cryogenic chambers around me, and a small orb hovering behind the young man.

"I don't know if you guys are geniuses or the dumbest bunch of fuck-ups this side of the Deadwoods. Something tells me the latter. On one hand, you did kind of beat death. But I hate to break it to you, friend, we still have a whole lot of that shit here." The smile on his face faded. "Now I'm going to have to tell you something that you won't want to hear." He turned and walked toward what I realized was a completely grimed-over window. Next to it, he grabbed a chair, and threw it into the glass. As the pane shattered, a ray of light poured in. The sky was a perfect blue, with only a few clouds lazily floating by, the air crisp and sharp as it blew in. "Come here," he requested as his short, curly blond hair ruffled slightly in the wind.

I shuffled my feet, expecting to stumble, but my feet moved with surprising lucidity. What the hell did he inject me with? As I approached the window, my stomach dropped. The ground contrasted the sky with a disgusting juxtaposition. Below was littered with the ruins of what had once been a beautiful city. Some buildings still stood, proud, in a desolate wasteland. But for the most part, they were collapsed as grim reminders of what once was. I peered out, looking to see if I could still see the capitol piercing the skyline, but it was nowhere to be seen. The entire city looked like a graveyard long forgotten.

"Now from what I'm reading here, it looks like you were turned into an icicle sometime around the early twenty-first century. Is that correct?" His brow furrowed.

"What? What year is it?"

"We'll get to that. Can you please answer my questions? I have to do my job." He smiled sympathetically. Something behind that smile worried me more than the new world I was looking at.

"Yeah, yeah that's correct. 2024 to be exact."

"Thank you," he shifted. "And what would you say your skillsets include?"

"Like what my job was?"

"Sure, that's a good place to start." I quickly began to realize that him waking me up wasn't out of the goodness of his heart. I looked out the window to see how far the jump would be, and concluded that the five-or-so-story drop would likely relinquish my pass from the land of the living.

"Well I was a professor at the University of Nebraska–Lincoln, so I guess that my strongest skill would probably be critical thinking?" I paused to read his face. "What is this for?"

"Ouch, hate to break it to you again buddy, but that is not going to suit you well in this day and age." His blank face turned to a frown. "Now I'm not going to sugarcoat it for you. You're in a bad place. A real bad place. From what I've read of your time, things seemed to have been relatively free and peaceful. Here we at least have one of those things, as long as the cogs keep running smoothly. I'm afraid to say you're just as much of one of those cogs as I am." He pulled out what looked to be a pack a cigarettes and took one out. As he brought it to his lips, the ember flickered on by itself and he took a long drag. The smoke poured out of his nose. "You'll figure out everything soon enough. Now I suppose the question you're asking yourself now is not where am I, but when am I?" The cigarette let out a faint crackle. "I'll save you having to ask—it's 2231. Now before you panic, I'll also save you having to ponder the typical questions. Yes, all the things you knew about your past life are essentially no longer relevant. The country you knew as the U.S.A. is gone. No, this world has no place for a professor like you. And yes, everyone you ever knew is now dead, unless they were dumb enough to freeze themselves too."

My heart dropped. Violet. The only person in the world who made life worth living in the first place. Suddenly, the realization hit that a leap from the window would be quite easy. Blissful in fact. I had foolishly hoped that the cure was only a few years out and would be able to return to my life in semi-normalcy. Even if Violet had found a new husband and started a beautiful family, I would have loved to be around to see that. Now there was the heart-wrenching fact that I'd never know. Was it better this way? I could at least imagine her surrounded by friends and family, taking her last breath as those around her smiled on, knowing the wonderful things she was able to accomplish in her long and beautiful life.

"So what now?" I whispered.

"Follow me."

CHAPTER 14

The cold, hard ground seemed to buckle under my weight. Outside, the air was a strike contrast to the bleak gray mess that sprawled out in the visible distance. As the new world spread before me, it was hard to think that anything had changed. Besides the obvious devastation that had happened here, the birds still sang to each other; the wind still caressed the grass growing out of every crack in the pavement.

"Come on, we don't have all day, let's go." The man impatiently waved me on.

"Can you at least tell me who you are?"

"Oh shit, where are my manners? I'm Augustus." He reached out his hand to shake mine. "Seriously though, I know you're groggy, but you have to hurry the fuck up— we have a train to catch. Even if I am the conductor, I still have to find some more people before we return." Briskly, he began to pick up his pace, checking over his shoulder to make sure I was playing his shadow.

"So Augustus, I'm inclined to believe that this"—I gestured to the ruins as he looked back—"isn't only in Nebraska?"

Augustus let out an audible chuckle. "Man, there is no more Nebraska, as I said. There's no more United States either." He reached back into his pocket and pulled out another cigarette, put it to his lips, and gestured the pack my way again. This time I caved. I hadn't had one in years; Violet and I had made a pact to quit together, and after over six years of not having one, lung cancer was clearly the least of my worries. Plus, Augustus would probably have another magical syringe to stab me in the chest with even if I did get it. I pulled one from the pack and brought it up to my lips. Heavier than I remembered. The coffin nail sparked up immediately, and I took a long pull. Holy shit—this wasn't a cigarette.

"What the"—I coughed—"fuck"—another cough—"is this?" Immediately, my lips went numb.

"That, sir, is some Wax," he snorted. "Don't worry, your lips will only be numb for a couple seconds." I put my index finger to my lip and poked. The numbness reduced, and then all of a sudden the day became clearer. Birds chirped impossibly loud all around, and I could hear my heart pounding in my chest. I threw the stick to the ground, and it made a loud pop. "Shit, my bad—I completely forgot that Wax is relatively new. I seriously didn't mean to scare you man. But don't worry, it's harmless."

"Harmless? I'm about to have a fucking heart attack." I grabbed at my chest and suddenly didn't feel my heart beat at all. The birds began to whisper, but the rest of the world was so vivid.

"It came about at the beginning of World War 4, when the powers that be realized it made soldiers hypersensitive. In a couple hours, you'll be completely back to normal. Well, I guess as normal as you can be."

All at once, the feeling was cathartic—my heart began beating at a slightly elevated rate, but nothing too abnormal. I kind of wished I hadn't thrown it on the ground now. "So that was some sort of drug?"

"Man, everything is a drug—that's how a lot of people get by around here. Like I said, everything will make more sense soon enough. I don't have the time or patience to give you a full history lesson right now." A park off to the left had a slide that was still remarkably intact. I guess plastic does essentially take an eternity to decompose. In fact, everything in the park looked normal besides the overgrown grass and debris from the surrounding buildings. The metal fencing was contorted in different ways, and an abandoned car was crashed through the middle of it. Inside, the skeleton of a man or woman lay hunched over the steering wheel. It was a weird feeling not even being fazed in the slightest. I didn't really feel any shock at anything at this point. It was strange, absolutely, but I guess part of me had known that the cure wouldn't be close to my time and had mentally prepared myself with what little capacities I had. I'd always been open to trying new things, but my lack of shock, or even care, was likely overshadowed by the knowledge that Violet was gone. Nothing really seemed to matter anymore, and this was the new world, I had to remind myself. There was nothing else I could do, anyway. Augustus stopped. "Shit, I could have sworn I came this way."

"You're lost?" I laughed.

"Damn right—I never cared to learn my way around this shithole before. I'm all over the place. Plus, the car normally does the navigating for me." I thought to ask about the car and where it was, but honestly didn't care at that point. From the short encounter I'd had with Augustus already, I figured I wouldn't even get a straight answer.

"Well the train station, if it's still there, is right down this street." Augustus looked over at me with a waning smile.

"Thank you. I'm glad one of us here knows what the hell is going on." This time we both laughed, but his died quickly. His pace increased, and all of a sudden we were there. The train station itself had completely collapsed, but behind it was an immaculately white train. It looked so odd, kind of like the slide, but in a way that made everything more confusing. Scrawled along the side of the train in perfect black letters was *West Empire Transit*.

Augustus reached into his pocket and pulled out a tablet, then pressed a couple buttons. The door hissed open and slid down to form a staircase. Inside, everything was just as sterile. Perfectly white fluorescent lights illuminated an impeccable interior. Benches lined the walls, with gray leather cushions. There were no windows, but the air inside had a pleasant faint scent of lavender. "Take a seat anywhere," he directed. "There's a bathroom at the back of the cabin that I'm sure you'll want to use as well." I hadn't used the facilities in hundreds of years, and realized it was decidedly a great idea. I opened the door to the restroom, and it was surprisingly familiar. A toilet and a sink, but no mirror. I guess not much had changed in regards to bathrooms. After taking the longest pee of my life, I washed my hands and splashed water on my face.

After leaving the bathroom, I sat down, and the bench slid out sideways on its own to point me in the direction the train must be heading. Abruptly, the vehicle started to move, and the motion made my stomach turn. It was clear Augustus could see my discomfort.

"Here, take these—you'll need some rest." He pulled out a couple pills from his suitcase, which this time didn't open up into the air as it had before. "I promise, these ones you'll be accustomed to. Sleeping pills haven't really change for hundreds of years."

I took them from him skeptically, but hey, when in Rome. Suddenly, the thought made me laugh, as I wondered if Rome was still around or if the rest of the world looked just as bad as Lincoln. I tossed them into my mouth, and he handed me a bottle of water that came up through the floor. After downing the whole bottle like a freshman at their first frat party, I lay down on the bench and put my arm under my head to act as a pillow.

"Here, press that top button," he said. I looked over and saw three buttons on the wall next to me. I did as instructed, and a distinct hiss sounded as the bench slid back toward the wall while a section of the wall came down on top of me, enclosing me in a strangely comfortable coffin. The noises of the train completely dissipated, and I was left alone with my thoughts, of which I had surprisingly few. As far as being tossed into a completely new century, I felt I was taking it remarkably well. It was as if I were on autopilot, or like walking through a strange dream, trying to take things in without asking too many questions and getting on Augustus's nerves. He seemed friendly enough, but I didn't want to push my luck. After all, there was nothing I could have done anyways—it was the new world, and I didn't have the ability to change a thing about it.

CHAPTER 15

A steady rumble woke me, and groggily I remembered who, where, and when I was. The button above my head pulsated a low, red light, and I pressed it. The top of the coffin hissed open and brought me back to lying forward.

"Hey, you're awake," Augustus called over. "Hope you slept well. Care to go for a walk?" My eyes were still fuzzy with sleep as I stood up and stretched like a cat who had just awoken from its fifteenth nap that day. There was a soft ringing in my ear, but to my surprise the shot that I had been injected with the day before continued to work its magic, and I felt better than I had in years. At least physically better. The knowledge, or lack of knowledge, of where I was still held a heavy weight on my heart.

"Where to?" I asked in a half-yawn. The compartment was still completely empty except for Augustus and me.

"Looking for more friends for you to play with," he said cheerily, but there was something hidden behind the tone in his voice that I couldn't quite place. "Generally, we're supposed to not take any newcomers with us, but I'm bored, and quite frankly, fuck them. This is one of our few chances to take in a bit of freedom, so I suggest you take it." It was the first time that I actually was in complete fear of what was to come. Knowing that I knew nothing gave a bit of a romanticized notion of what I was being led toward. But with that one phrase, and more particularly one word, that romantic idea was quickly replaced by dread.

"Freedom?" I asked stupidly, as if I had never heard of the word before. And then even more stupidly followed with, "Shit, I forgot to grab the rest of my belongings out of the cabinet next to my cryogenic chamber." But I already could predict what the next words to come out of Augustus's mouth would be.

He laughed sympathetically. "You won't be needing those anymore. The only thing you are allowed to bring is you and yourself. I can explain more while we walk, but I have a schedule to keep, as I'm sure I've already made clear to you." He got up and walked toward the train door, fidgeted on his tablet, and the door hissed open again. The fresh air slapped me in the face and woke me up the rest of the way. The sun appeared to be just going down. Or was it coming up? I really had no idea how long I was asleep in the pod.

"I'm guessing you're wondering where we're at?"

"Not really." I paused. "A little bit more concerned about where we're heading at the moment." I followed Augustus down a cracked sidewalk next to chain-link fences that clearly had houses in them before, but were now reduced to piles of rubble or completely returned to the earth, sprouting trees and overgrown grass.

"That's a hard one to explain to you at the moment." He paused as he turned back around to look at me. "But

I'll try. The people in charge won't like me explaining it to you, so just be woefully ignorant if anyone asks you any questions." I nodded as he surveyed my face, and seemed to come to the conclusion that I could keep a secret. Of course, I doubted he would tell me anything truly important that could get him in trouble, because I had only met him for a brief period of time the day before, or earlier that day, whichever it was.

The wind whirled around us and kicked up some leaves that were scattered around. "We're heading into the capitol city of the West Empire, which is probably best de-scribed as what's left of North America. At first, the city might look beautiful and grandiose, but I promise you it is far from that. There's a reason that you aren't allowed to bring any of your belongings. The one and only rule that reigns supreme there is order." He stopped talking, and ran his hand alongside one of the fences as it clanged along its rusting supports. As he took a deep breath, he conceded, "I'm not taking you anywhere that is enjoyable. But you might be important to the city someday. If you want to turn around and leave right now, I fully support that decision. You might be able to survive out here in the wastes, and some days, dying out here might be preferable to living in the city." I could see in his eyes that every last word that he was saying was completely truthful, and it scared the living hell out me.

"So you think I should make a run for it?" I asked, not knowing a damn thing about surviving off the land, let alone a broken, desolate piece of land like this.

"I'm saying you're stuck between a rock and a hard place, my friend. Both options suck, but each has its own sets of cons that make it suck more. They have a strict re-gime, and any breaking from orders is met with severe punishment. Which is why you can't say anything I told you, because our orders are strictly to bring you in with no deviation. But at least if you come with me, you'll have a roof over your head, plus food and drink." Suddenly he paused and doubled over to laugh. "Whoops, here you go," he said as he handed me a small capsule. "Something to tide you over—forgot you haven't eaten in a while."

Debating whether following orders to a tee or starving was preferable, I turned the pill over in my hand and was completely shocked that he thought a tic-tac was going to tide me over. He did seem to have my best interest at heart so I popped it in my mouth. The overwhelming taste of potatoes and gravy shocked my taste buds, but soon after, my hunger dissipated. "Weird."

He laughed again. "Yeah, this is what you'll be eating from now on."

"It's a good thing I don't hate potatoes and gravy then."

"You'll be able to get different ones when we get to the city, I just love potatoes. Must be the Irish in me." He did a goofy little jig.

"So are you from the past too?"

"No," he said without looking back. "I'm a born-and-bred Arcadian. Like all my ancestors before me since the founding of Arcadia and the soon-after formation of the West Empire. Before that, I can't really say. I just like telling people I'm Irish on account of my orange hair and freckles. Most people don't understand the joke though, seeing as they probably don't even know what Ireland is. But I honestly have no idea who my people were before the founding."

"Anything's possible—you can be an Irishman in my book." We both laughed this time. My laughter died as I looked at a metal post in a yard and a chain that led to an

CRYO

empty collar. Underneath the collar were the bones of what must have been a dog, some half-buried in the dirt. My stomach turned as I looked away. Whatever happened here must have happened quickly, because no one but a monster would have just left their dog like that. I started to feel the breath leaving my body as I thought about the dog patiently waiting for his master to come back and feed him while he slowly lost hope. Or maybe he never lost hope until he took his last breath, and that thought hurt even more. "So you mentioned the people in charge?" I asked, trying to erase the thought process from my mind.

"Oh yeah. There is a long list in the chain of command. All routes lead to the emperor though. He is in charge of everything—no big or small changes come about without his say-so."

"And where are you in this chain?"

"Oh, I'm small potatoes," he laughed. "Or I guess not that small. I'm a faction leader with the Scouts. You'll learn about factions soon enough, but it's not too important to concern yourself over until you find out which one you're placed in. But hell, we're all small potatoes in the emperor's eyes. Even the counselor and the chancellor, who are his two right-hand men and would take over in the case of his untimely death if he doesn't name a successor, are still small potatoes. Like I said, everything goes through him. You'll probably see the bastard from time to time in some bullshit propaganda videos."

"Sounds like you don't like him too much," I laughed.

"Eh." He rolled it over in his head. "I guess he isn't any worse than the previous ones, from what I've been told. But he's been emperor my whole life. I'm just living in his shadow." He stopped talking suddenly. A noise rattled from inside a brick building that we were passing. The front windows had been boarded up, though seemingly sometime not too long ago, because although they were rotting away, they were still intact for the most part.

"Hello?" Augustus called out. There was another clatter as he reached toward his side and pulled out what looked to be a gun straight from Star Wars. He then reached down into the suitcase he had been lugging around and pulled out the white orb, which floated over his left shoulder as he started approaching the building. "You better wait out here," he said, then crossed the threshold into the building.

"What am I supposed to do if you die in there?" All I could hear was laughter as the echoes trailed off. I sat down next to the building and waited. Far off in the distance, the sounds of dogs barking and howling pierced into the wind, and I realized that the sun truly was setting and not coming up. The sky faded to an orangish hue and was starting to be replaced by darkness when Augustus came back out. His gun was already holstered, but the orb still floated over his shoulder. "So?" I asked.

"It was some kid. Not a pretty sight. He was lying next to his parents, who looked like they died from Hedon knows what. Maybe a virus, maybe an infection. Could have easily been starvation from the sight of it. Either way, he chose to stay here, and I don't blame him. Kid's grown up out here his whole life; he should be fine." Augustus looked truly troubled by the encounter. I put a hand on his shoulder, and he nodded and turned around to walk the way we came. "I think we better get back to the train actually. It wasn't a great idea me bringing you out here without anything to defend yourself. Just wanted a little company for a bit."

As we walked back to the train in silence, I made good effort not to look back at the post that now served as a grave marker for the dog, and tried to imagine the scene Augustus had walked in on. It must have been heartbreaking, but I also knew that wasn't the first nor the last time he would have such an encounter. I would probably be having my own encounters like that trying to survive outside the city. Wherever I was going couldn't be worse than it was out here.

Once back on the train, he handed me another pill and gestured toward the pod that I had taken my nap in earlier. "I'll see you tomorrow." He tried a smile, but it was clear that the kid was weighing heavily on his mind.

"See you then," I said as I lay back down.

"It never gets any easier," I heard him mutter to himself before the silence of the pod engulfed me.

CHAPTER 16

When I woke again, the train compartment was filled with other pods squeezed up against the wall. A couple of people were seated in the rows around me. A girl with fire-red hair sat directly across. A small tattoo of a dove directly below her jawline on the left side of her neck stared at me while she looked blankly at the wall. Beside her was another scrawny blond girl with her hair put up in a bun.

"Oh hello, sweetheart!" she said with all the enthusiasm of someone who just won the lottery. "You're a real cutie, ain't ya!" A saccharine smile broadened across her face. She reached out her hand to shake mine. "I'm Lydia, and you are?"

"Louis." I shook back. "Do you know what's going on here?"

"No, I don't." She smiled back enthusiastically. "Augie took me out of one of those cramped little chambers, and here I am!"

"So you're not from this time either?"

"I was born in 2042, frozen in 2063, just before the third world war, I'm told! Guess my intuition was correct." She let out a soft chuckle. "The world was really starting to go to hell when China started swallowing up the countries around it, and I figured once India went, it was only a matter of time before all hell broke loose. I'm surprised the great war didn't start earlier, honestly—I guess everyone was too afraid for the nukes to start flying."

"So..." I tried to interject.

Without taking notice, she continued. "They weren't wrong, though. I'm sure wherever you were from was one of the lucky places that got bombardments over nukes. Otherwise, we wouldn't be having this pleasant little chat right now!" She giggled. "Or I suppose it isn't really a chat, because I've been doing all the talking. Sorry, I've always had a bad habit of running my mouth. I'm just so excitable! This is cool, don't you think? We get to see a whole new world. It's all just so exciting I can hardly contain myself. This here is Rose, sitting next to me. She don't talk too much though, quite mysterious, I think I like her!"

"Yeah," Rose said.

"See, she may look a little older than me, but she was born twenty years before me! Isn't that interesting? She's really twenty-six, but time is crazy, isn't it? Ah, I'm just so excited! I'm sorry, I'm sorry. Now how old are you, sweetie, and where are you from?"

"Thirty-two, and I was frozen in 2024," I replied. "But I—"

"Oh my gosh! That is so exciting. So that would mean that Rose was born before you were ever frozen! You guys were in the same place at the same time for an instant, that is sooooo cute." She let out a little squeal of excitement. "Now where do you think we're headed? Augie said that he couldn't tell me, but I'm sure if I badger him enough he'll let us all know! He really is quite sweet too, don't you think?"

Augustus let out a loud laugh. "Lydia, respectfully, will you please shut up? The man just woke up."

"Oh golly, I'm so sorry, I really have to learn when to keep my old trapper shut. I'm sorry Louis!" She frowned.

"No worries," I laughed, "it's actually quite refreshing. Old Augie here isn't the most cheerful." Lydia giggled and let out a meek smile.

"Jesus, if you guys keep calling me Augie, I'll push you out of the train right here." He smiled, a comforting smile this time. "Call me August if anything."

"Cuuuute!" Lydia exclaimed. "That's when my birthday is! I'm like in love with that name. Ah, it's just so cute. You know, when my parents had me, they—"

"Lydia." August smiled gently.

"*Okay!* I'm sorry, I'll keep quiet now." She pressed her thumb and forefinger to her lips and slid them across, twisted them, and let out a smile.

"Okay, good, because we're almost there, and I need you guys to listen to me. When we get out, you have to listen—do not speak unless you are spoken to. I cannot stress that part enough. Do not speak. I know it will be hard for you, Lydia, but please just trust me." Lydia nodded. "Good, just listen to whatever they tell you, and follow directions, and you will all be just fine."

I hadn't noticed that the other pods had opened up, and there were now three other people behind us listening in—an older couple who looked to be in their sixties, and a kid likely in his late teens. Tears were flowing freely from his eyes. "Now, I'm going to have to ask you all to put these on." August opened up his tablet again and pressed a button, and toward the front of the compartment, ten black suits dropped down. "It's one-size-fits-all, so grab whichever you like."

Everyone stood up and walked toward the front of the train car, and I suddenly realized that we were now stopped. August fiddled with his tablet again, and ten box-like compartments dropped from the ceiling into the aisles between the seats. "When you get the suits on, put your thumb up to the front of your suit where a breast pocket would be," August continued. "I'll see you all momentarily—try to hurry. It's best not to keep them waiting."

One by one, each of us grabbed a suit off the hook and walked back to one of the individual changing rooms. I flipped back the curtain, and inside was a small light illuminating the cramped room. Crouching down, I took off the unassuming shoes that they had given me at the cryogenic lab before I had been frozen, and pushed them off to the side. Then, struggling to maintain balance in the tiny room, I shuffled off the rest and slid the jumpsuit on. It seemed like it was at least fifteen sizes too big. Looking like an emcee from the '90s, I brought my thumb up to my chest and held it there. Swiftly, the nylon-type material began shrinking until it was comfortably plastered to my body. God, that couple must be having a hell of a time getting theirs on if I struggled this much. On the front of the suit, opposite to where I pressed my thumb into were six numbers: 101023. Just below that was a red line with two diagonal, parallel slashes through it.

One at a time, everybody started coming out of their dressing rooms, all shoeless.

"Whoops, forgot to give you these." August picked up a pair of comically large black tennis shoes and handed them to me, and continued the process until everyone had a pair. "Same drill, just step into your shoes and they'll shrink down to the size of your feet. If you guys would please not say anything about forgetting them, I would really appreciate it." August took a deep breath and turned around. "Alright, follow me please."

CHAPTER 17

The door hissed open. A flash of sunlight struck me in the eyes, but after my eyes refocused, the scene before me was breathtaking. Pure white skyscrapers flooded the horizon in varied geometric shapes. Other buildings looked to be made of clear glass, many with trees growing on the first levels. Drones zoomed along the skyline in every direction. It looked like something straight out of a science fiction movie. In all fairness, it seemed like even in my day, a lot of technology first appeared because it was dreamt of in a book or movie. But this was something else entirely. The whole scene was extraordinary and when I looked to my left and right, it was easy to tell that everyone else was thinking the exact same thing. I glanced over my shoulder and saw a hole in the wall that the train must have come out of. My eyes followed the wall—it looked like it went on forever, though the slight curve had to mean it surrounded this place.

My eyes narrowed forward, having missed the twenty or so people all dressed in black standing in front of us. The woman at their forefront was wearing an all-red three-piece suit with the same symbol as on our uniforms, but in black.

"Welcome to Arcadia," the woman in red said monotonously. "I'm sure you all have questions. Be silent while I speak—there will be no questions. You all have come from different times, so I will not waste my breath on explaining to you why you are here. The only thing you need to know is that you will follow orders. Order is the mortar that keeps society from crumbling around us. If the mortar is weak, the walls fall. That is how it is." She paused and looked everyone over. "Replacing faulty mortar is not easy, but it is necessary in keeping a strong foundation and keeping the horrors of the old world out there." Gesturing at the wall, she continued, "You will all be given jobs. You do those jobs. And you do them well. If not, you have no place here. Make sure that you..."

"Wow this is kind of scary," Lydia whispered without moving her head.

"101025, please step forward," the woman in red demanded without skipping a beat. Lydia's face went ghost white, but she stepped forward while the rest of us stayed perfectly lined up behind her. The whole thing looked like the Sharks and the Jets lining up waiting for a rumble. I almost could have laughed except for the pure terror on Lydia's face.

"Yes?" Lydia gulped.

"Now, did I ask you to speak?" A small smile formed on the woman's face. "I should hope that your handler would have briefed you on how we feel about speaking when not spoken to." My eyes shifted toward August. His face was blank, but the look in his eyes said everything. Her head nodded forward, and two of the people dressed in black walked swiftly toward us in lockstep. One pulled out a black sack. August didn't flinch, even as they placed the sack over his head. The other pulled out a tablet and punched in a couple of numbers. Suddenly, both of August's arms jerked behind him and plastered themselves to the small of his back. They quickly led him down the street behind the wall of people in black.

"Please, no! He did tell us, he really did. I promise he..." Lydia trailed off. Tears quickly began forming in her eyes.

"Oh, he did?" The woman in red's eyes pierced into Lydia as her mouth formed a sickening grin. "So you mean to tell me that you are unwilling to follow orders. That is not good. Not good at all." She let out a *tsk tsk.*

"No, I promise I can. I'm sorry, I'm really sorry!" The tears flowed freely now.

"Did I ask you to speak?" Her smile looked like that of a tiger who finally found its prey. Lydia shook her head. "Good. It looks like there may be some hope for you after all." Her grin widened as she shifted back to look at a small drone hovering above the group behind her, almost as if she were putting on a show for whoever was watching through the drone. "Unfortunately, I don't think a simple oral reprimanding will be enough for you to learn. Too bad. It is quite unfortunate, really." She nodded her head forward again. The same process ensued—two of the people in black rushed forward, and Lydia's arms locked behind her back. She shook her head vigorously, tears rolling down her cheeks, and took a couple steps back. One of the men linked his arms around her back and held her in place while the other grabbed her by the face, his black-gloved hand pressing hard into her soft, rosy-white cheeks. "Now stick your tongue out, dear."

Lydia tried to shake her head, but it held in place. Her eyes darted back and forth rapidly. The rest of us were all looking at her, except Rose. Rose's eyes were fixated forward. What the hell could she be looking at? This poor girl was about to get her tongue ripped out, and somehow she was unfazed. "I won't ask you again," the woman said coldly. Lydia slid her tongue out between her lips, and the man grabbed it and pulled. He then retrieved a switchblade from his pocket, the tip of the blade glowed a dull orangish-red.

He looked back at the woman in red. She nodded. He placed the knife at the edge of Lydia's tongue. She let out a whimper, but stood still. "If anyone else has anything to say, now would be a good time," the woman in red conveyed to the rest of us. No one moved or said a word. "Good." She nodded again.

Slowly, the man slid the knife into the edge of Lydia's tongue. She tried to wail, but her tongue being held made it come out as a sickening *unghh* sound. Her shoulders rose and fell as she began to sob. The knife slid further into her tongue. I couldn't take any more, and looked away. "101023, don't you dare look away," the woman in red commanded.

I forced myself back. The knife was about a third of the way through by now. "Okay," the woman in red said. The man halted immediately. "Luckily for you, 101025, I am feeling quite exultant today. It's not every day when we have such worthy contenders in the games, and I would quite like to get back in time to not miss anything." The man dropped Lydia's tongue, and she let it hang out for a moment, slightly sloped to the left because of the incision. She quickly brought it back into her mouth and fell to her knees. Her arms unlocked from behind her, and she grabbed at her tongue. There were small trickles of blood on her fingers, but not nearly as much as there should have been. Tongues bleed a lot—I remembered accidentally slicing into mine with a Coke can when I was a kid and thinking I was going to bleed to death. This was immeasurably worse, yet barely any blood at all. The only thing I could think of was that the knife had cut and cauterized the wound in one motion. "The lot of you, take them to processing," the woman commanded, and strode off. The people in black approached, as a solid mass.

CHAPTER 18

We marched forward into the closest skyscraper, and the enormity of the building shocked me. I could only compare the feeling to when I was in Chicago as a child with my parents and stood with my chest to the Sears Tower and looked up. The feeling of vertigo takes hold, and suddenly your knees begin to wobble and your stomach drops to your feet. I hadn't had that feeling since I was a child, but here it was again. Only worse. Not knowing what was inside was absolutely terrifying. Huge white doors roughly thirty feet tall slid apart to reveal a cathedral-sized lobby. Massive windows on either side of the lobby let in beams of light. Directly in the center there was a half-circle desk with a woman sitting behind it.

"Hello, welcome to admissions, please take a seat any-where that is available," she said in a monotone, almost ro-botic voice. We all took our seats and the doors behind us shut, and with that all the people dressed in black were gone. It was only the six of us sitting in silence. Lydia still had her hand to her mouth and the tracks where her tears were would occasionally let one or two roll out. I turned to console her when all of a sudden a massive hologram formed at the center of the room. An older man stood there, with a neat haircut and a clean silver suit carrying the same symbol everyone had, but his was a deep purple. He was standing in a room with a large glass wall behind him. The backdrop was of the city skyline, and it gave him an even greater grandiose feeling. As if the twenty-foot hologram wasn't enough.

"This, my friends, is Arcadia," he spoke with a welcoming and calm demeanor as he gestured out the window. "I am Emperor Olysseus, and I can't begin to express my gratitude that you are all here with us today in this fine city. I hope that you had no troubles getting here, and I trust that you are all ready to become part of what makes this city so great. For hundreds of years..."

"Why are we here?" the kid spoke up, but Olysseus kept talking unphased. It seemed highly unlikely that this was any more than a prerecorded message. "This is bullshit."

"Please. Keep it down," the woman at admissions smiled politely. I missed what Olysseus had been saying, but he kept on talking.

"... it was a miracle. We live life here in a perfect oasis. Where all your wildest dreams will come true—once you have paid your dues. Our ancestors forged this land out of nothing. A sullen waste. We rose like a phoenix to come back better than ever. With your help, we will continue to be the greatest community on Earth. Welcome home." The hologram fizzled off into the air. The old woman scoffed, and the man next to her gave out an amused chortle. I didn't know what to think about what the emperor had said. Honestly, I didn't really care either—it seemed like a bunch of hokey nonsense anyways. I diverted my attention toward Lydia, who was still silently crying.

"I'm so sorry, Lydia. I wish we could have done something," I whispered to her. She nodded. "You know there was nothing any of us could have done, right?" She nodded again. I put an arm around her shoulder to comfort her and she buried her face in my chest, hand still over her mouth, and started sobbing again. The silent room echoed her quiet sobs. Sure, she was kind of annoying, but she was just a kid still. The contrast between her expectations of what would happen and the reality were clearly heartbreaking.

"It's okay, sweetie," the woman in her sixties sighed, and leaned forward to pat Lydia on the knee. "Back in my day, people would pay to get their tongues split, and I'm sure you'll look quite nice—you're a pretty young girl." Her husband gently tapped her with the back of his hand. "What, Harold? I'm just saying it could have been worse."

"Oh hush, just leave the poor girl alone," Harold replied.

"We're going to die, aren't we?" the teenager said in a low voice.

"Of course not," the older woman said gently. "If they wanted us dead, we would have been dead already. Just keep your head up and do what they say."

"Well, no one's here besides her." The kid tilted his head towards the receptionist. "What's stopping us from leaving? I would rather take my chances outside the wall than in here."

"And how do you plan on getting past the wall?" Harold asked.

"I don't know. I figure if I can get to the train tunnel, I could pass through that and just run."

"Run to where exactly?"

"I don't know, but with that welcoming party, I have a hard time believing that out there is any worse than in here," the kid mused. "I think I'm going to make a run for it. I know I'm faster than all of them."

"Kid, even if you hold the world record in track, you're not going to outrun a bullet," Harold cautioned.

"I didn't even see them with guns—maybe they have been outlawed."

"Please don't do it," I chimed in.

Lydia nodded.

Without another word, the kid stood up and walked rapidly toward the door.

"Sir, I would highly advise against leaving," the receptionist said with a false smile.

"Fuck you," he replied. The massive doors opened again for him, and he peered outside. "See, there's no one out here," he told us.

"Please come back and sit down," Harold's wife suggested.

"No. You guys can wait here to die if you want; I'm not taking my chances." He walked forward a couple more feet, then stopped. A faint *woosh* sounded in the lobby, and the kid fell to his knees. He paused for a second like he was praying and then fell backward. A neat red dot on his forehead began leaking blood down over his right eye. Everyone screamed, except Rose, who was still blankly staring forward.

"Oh my god! Harold!" his wife screamed. Harold vomited onto the pristine white floor. Lydia kept sobbing. The receptionist kept typing away on her computer.

"Shit," I whispered to no one.

A man in a white lab coat walked in, and glanced over at the kid. "Well that's unfortunate," he noted, and scribbled on his clipboard. "Will 101020 follow me please?" Harold shakily got to his feet and looked back at his wife. "Don't worry—no matter where you get placed, you will still be able to see your wife," the man assured Harold. "Now please, follow me."

The two of them walked to the left of the receptionist desk and into an elevator. I stared back over at the kid again. My heart pounded, thinking of how easily that could have been any one of us. If the incision in Lydia's tongue didn't make me realize how important following the rules was, this sure as hell did. The poor kid looked like David, the student who had asked me the final question of my career. "Without death, would there be religion?" And the only thing I could think of now was that there would never be a world without death. Even if science made it possible to live forever—and judging from the magical syringe they gave me, they must be pretty close, if not already there—there would always be instances like this. A pool of blood was now forming behind his head, while his eyes stared blankly at the ceiling.

Thirty minutes or so passed as these thoughts looped in my head, and then the man reappeared without Harold. "101021, please follow me."

"Where is Harold?" his wife demanded.

"Don't worry, he is well. He's been placed," the man said.

"How do I know that? How in holy hell am I supposed to believe anything that you say?"

"Ma'am, follow me." The man flashed his eyes at the kid. Reluctantly, she got up and followed.

Another thirty minutes passed.

"101022, please follow me." Rose got up immediately and headed with him into the elevator.

"Pea o eave me," Lydia whispered to me. "I'm o care."

"It's going to be alright," I assured her, but I could only muster a half-assed tone. Her little blue eyes looked up into mine.

"You on't owe at," she protested.

"I know, but we just have to put on a brave face and try to get through it."

"I owe, pea cuh find me if you ca." She grimaced at the pronunciation of find, and brought her hand back to her mouth. "I on't wanna be aone."

"Of course I will—we're in this together." I smiled at her. She smiled back and put her arms around my neck for a hug. Then she lay her head back on my shoulder, and we sat in silence until the man reappeared. I stood up and reassuringly squeezed Lydia's hand.

"Okay 101023, please follow me."

CHAPTER 19

The inside of the elevator was also pure white. I was getting really fucking sick of all this white already. No buttons were anywhere to be seen. The man in the lab coat flipped a page on his clipboard and slid his finger up the page. The elevator began rising at a smooth speed; I almost couldn't tell it was moving except for the numbers above the door rising—20, 30, 40, 50, 56, and the elevator stopped. The doors slid open to reveal a room filled with glass cubicles. Some were tinted for privacy, and clicking keyboards were the only sound besides a faint *hiss* of air being pumped into the room.

"This way," the man directed, and held his hand out toward the right. I followed him into a small room with one glass wall, the other three light gray. "Here." He pointed at a chair on the other side of a steel table. I sat down as he flipped to another page on his clipboard tapped and the glass wall went dark. "Now I have a couple of questions for you, and be very careful to answer them as truthfully as possible."

"Okay," I replied, and shifted forward a little in my seat.

"First of all, what did you do in the past as a career?" he asked.

"I was a professor at the university of..."

"Professor," he noted. "Please keep your answers brief, a couple words will suffice."

"Okay," I replied again.

"If your friend was dying from blood loss, would you: A) Put him out of his misery, B) Attempt a transfusion, C) Call for help, or D) Walk away?"

"Call for help," I answered.

"Just saying the letter will do."

"C."

He jotted down on the clip board and continued. "If you receive an item that is beneficial but you know would result in the pain of others, would you: A) Politely refuse the item, B) Report the person to the authorities, C) Use the item, or D) Walk away.

"A."

The man licked the tip of his pen and scribbled down a couple words, but I didn't dare try and look over at what he was writing. Although, I did see the handwriting morph slightly into perfect penmanship, following his hand. It must not have been a typical pen and paper after all.

"When you die, would you rather: A) Donate yourself, B) Be buried, C) Take others down with you, or D) Walk away.

"Walk away?" I laughed. His eyes narrowed, but he smiled.

"It's not impossible, you know," he said calmly, "so please answer the question."

Somehow, picking A or D seemed like a grave mistake. And besides this question, it surprised me how relatable most of them had been. Perhaps society wasn't as different now as I'd thought. Either that, or they had personalized tests for people coming from different time periods. The whole thing was surreal. Less like an aptitude test, and more like a random quiz you would take on the internet to see which television character you were.

"B."

"If you do not agree with killing, but your superior requests it and he is following protocol, would you: A) Just do it, B) Report your superior, C) Protest, or D) Walk away." The fact that they put that in the test frightened me to the core. It seemed as though if I answered A, murder might be in the future. But I quickly realized that I should answer this one less honestly and make sure to tell them what they wanted to hear. Who knew what would happen if it came down to that? I certainly wasn't capable of killing anybody, but that was a situation that I would have to face only if it was presented in front of me.

"A, of course." I smiled. He jotted down another note.

"If your family member came to you with criticisms of the Empire, would you A) Hear them out, B) Report them, C) Kill them, or D) Walk away.

My mind flashed back to Violet. I would have burned the whole city to the ground before I willingly let anything happen to her. No way in hell would I report any of my family, for that matter. But I answered "B" anyway. He nodded and continued asking random ethical questions for the next twenty or so minutes, and I continued my rote recitation of letters in response.

"Okay, thank you for your time. Your results will be processed momentarily, and you will be placed." He dropped the clipboard into a box in the back of the room. "She will escort you to your results." A pleasant-looking lady in her forties stood in the doorway with another clipboard. The man got up, grabbed the clipboard from her, and walked back toward the elevator.

"I'm Delphine." She smiled. "If you would please follow me, we can get you out of here." I sighed and stood up. Nothing would make me happier right now. She held the door open for me and walked next to me, gently guiding me where to go. "Now, wherever you get placed, just know you are of vital importance to the city of Arcadia and the West Empire as a whole. I hope you can take solace in that." She smiled again.

I faked a grin. "Of course."

"Good!" she said cheerily, and continued walking. We turned and strode toward a large window, the only one that appeared to be on the entire floor. The skyline of the city was magnificent. But I couldn't help but think of what other terrible things lay underneath the spectacular façade. As I pondered the thought, the window slid open into thin air. I expected to be blasted by a gust of wind, but there was none. "After you," she smiled, and gestured me out.

"What? My test results couldn't have possibly been that bad!" I panicked and backed up a little.

"Oh my." She giggled and stepped forward. "We're not trying to kill you. Where would be the utility in that?" She appeared to be floating fifty-six stories off the ground. "Please, let's go—I have a schedule to keep." Timidly, I put one foot out and dipped it down like I was testing to see if the pool water was warm enough. My foot hit something solid. Now why would this even be a thing? Who the fuck thought this would be a good idea? I laughed to myself and put my other foot out and looked down. The window closed, and we began falling.

"Shit!" I yelled. She laughed again. Well, I guess I was going to die with a crazy suicidal lady—this was fun.

We were falling extremely fast, but I could still feel the platform below my feet. There was no wind resistance. Before I could think anything else, the rapid drop began to decrease, eventually slowing until we were completely stopped, our feet hovering inches off the ground. I walked forward to lean over and catch my breath and smacked face-first into an invisible wall.

"Here, let me open that for you," she giggled. Her hand reached over and pressed a button on her watch, and two black, parallel, vertical lines formed in the middle of the air, then parted until there was about eight feet between them. "Okay, let's go." She gestured forward.

"Please, after you." I gentlemanly gestured forward. I wasn't falling for that again. Whoever invented this shit needed a good ass-kicking. She smiled and walked out as I followed. The breeze touched my face with sweet relief.

"We're just going over here." She pointed at a small glass building down the block, with a massive concrete monstrosity behind it. "They'll tell you where you're going to end up."

"And where is that?" I asked.

"Well, there are six different positions you can be placed in. There's Medics, Scouts, Administrators, Enforcers, The Assembly, and Donors. I myself am in administration. I'm quite happy here, in fact." She smiled assuredly. "I would love to be able to explain to you what each of the positions entails. But unfortunately, we're already here, and if I did explain them to you that might actually get me in some trouble."

"It's okay. I appreciate you being the only one since we got off the train who actually treated me like a human."

"I'm sorry about that—it's a tough world we live in, but they do what they have to. Try not to take any offense from it." The door on the glass building slid open, and we both walked inside. "So this is where I leave you. Good luck, and I hope to run into you again someday."

"Thank you. Me too." She nodded and exited.

A cherry blossom tree stood proudly in center of the lobby with a waterfall running behind it and a small river surrounding it. There were six doors at the back of the lobby, three on either side of the waterfall. Roman numerals from I through VI were engraved on each. To the left were dozens of empty chairs, and on the right a man was seated behind a desk.

"Over here, sir—please take this." The man held out an envelope. "Enter through the number inside." He looked down at the envelope and muttered, "101023," then looked back up at my number and held his hand out again. I grabbed the envelope and ripped down one edge of it, and slid a coin-shaped piece of metal out of it. Engraved on it was a small *II*. I flipped it over in my palm; the other side displayed the same symbol as on my jumpsuit—a line broken up by two diagonal, parallel slashes. Striding back toward the second door, I gazed up at the cherry blossom. It looked identical to the one Violet and I had in our backyard. My heart dropped.

CHAPTER 20

"Honey?" I heard her call from the backyard. The ice cubes in my drink clanked on the side of the glass. I put my phone face-down on the granite countertop and looked out the window. She was sitting under the cherry blossom tree that we had planted together when we first moved in four years ago. Her bright blue-green eyes stared back at me through the window, and she let out a goofy little wave. Walking toward the sliding door that led to the backyard, I let out a heavy sigh, and slid it open.

"Yes Vi, are you in need of assistance?" I smugly grinned at her. She let out a little *hurumph*. The cold bristles of grass brushed my bare feet as I strode toward her.

"Yes you little smartass, get over here." She smiled, perching her head up for a kiss, and I obliged. I sat down in the worn-out wicker chair next to her. Her hand leaned out over her chair to grab mine, and she looked up at the perfect pink petals looming above us. "You remember the day we met?"

I thought about her face peering at me through the crowd. The same eyes that I fell in love with looking directly at me, or at least I thought they were. "Space Song" was echoing from the speakers on the stage, while Beach House serenaded the crowd. I walked over to her and was about to ask her name. Without even acknowledging my presence, Violet said, "Have you ever thought about how you can always see your nose, but your brain chooses to ignore it?" Her eyes were narrowed down at her nose. "Can't say I have," I replied, and she handed me a joint she'd been holding down at her side. Somehow, we ended up going to every concert at the festival together after that. The rest was history, as they say. It's amazing how two hearts can find each other so quickly in any type of situation.

"Do you?" she repeated with a smile, still looking at the tree.

"Yes, of course," I replied. We both laughed, but my smile quickly died.

"So what's wrong?"

"I stopped in today."

"Oh." Her smile also faded.

"Yeah."

"It's okay," she reassured me. "Maybe we aren't ready to start a family anyways."

"There is nothing more in the world that I want than to create some beautiful little monsters with you. But, Dr. Yates said there was absolutely no possible way." I pulled my hand away and looked down into my lap.

"So that would explain the day drinking, huh? I thought we were trying to relive our college days." She grabbed my hand again. "You know I'll always love you, no matter what."

"Yeah," I replied. Tears started flowing freely from my eyes. Violet caressed my head, and laid it on her shoulder, then rested her head on mine. We sat there in silence for a great while, just staring into the trunk of the tree where we'd cheesily carved *V+L*, surrounded by a heart. "I love you, Cherry Blossom," I whispered to her.

"I love you too."

Through my blurry, tear-streaked eyes, the heart began to morph. The shape broke apart, and a red line violently slashed through the middle of the letters, and then two more slashes crossed over the line.

CHAPTER 21

With the coin grasped firmly between my fingers, I slid it into the slot to the right of the door marked *II*. The door dropped down from the ceiling into the floor and revealed a hallway with a string of lights in the upper corners, and more large, rectangular lights embedded in the floor every few feet. At the end of the hall, a man stood with his arms crossed. He remained there until I reached him, and when I did, he turned without a word. I followed. We reached another door, and he put his thumb up to a button next to it, and this door also slid down from the ceiling and vanished into the floor.

Inside the brightly lit, white, cavernous room was an arsenal of weapons that were hardly recognizable. I couldn't recognize any of the guns on the shelves that lined the walls; they looked more like tranquilizer guns than anything else. The only really recognizable weapons were katana-looking swords that also had the faint orang-ish-red glow like the knife used on Lydia. The man fell back through the door and it closed again. I was left with my-self and one man sitting and typing away at a computer. This time, the computer had images floating in the air. He clicked a button and all the backward images reversed to show me what the image said. An image with a circle and an arrow through it appeared with '101023:Scout' written directly underneath it.

"Can you please explain to me what that means?" I half asked, half demanded. The man had a clean-shaven face and a small scar under his right eye. He pressed another button and the images all disappeared into the air.

"Yes." He stood up and walked over. "Here." Walking over to the wall with the katanas I saw that he had a severe limp. His eyes scrolled through the swords and picked one up and handed it to me. Then he walked over to the wall with the guns and handed one over.

"You're really just going to hand this to me? What if I was a little out of my mind and decided that I wanted to use them on you?"

"I assure you that you would not be the first. You cer-tainly won't be the last. However, I promise you that is not in your best interest if you're intent on living." He eyed the ceiling momentarily. "Now let me show you how to use these before you accidentally get yourself killed." He grabbed the sword back impatiently and flipped it with the hilt up. "Now, all you have to do is press this button with your thumb." I grabbed it and pressed it, and it floated out of my hand and behind me. With a *clink*, I felt it secure itself to my back. I looked at the gun, and underneath the bottom of the grip was the same button. He nodded. I pressed that too, and it securely holstered itself at my hip. "In order to unfasten them, simply grab the hilt or the grip on either of them and they will unlock. Otherwise, they will stay fastened even if a building collapses on you."

"Huh," I replied. "Neat."

"You may leave now." He went back to his computer, sat down, and clicked another series of buttons. Part of the wall behind him fizzled and became translucent. Jesus, these guys couldn't have decided on one type of door? This all seemed so unnecessary. At least one thing you could say about this new world was that even though there were a lot of questionable construction decisions, they were all extremely efficient at processing. In and out like a fast-food restaurant. Behind the now-translucent door was a room with several people in it. All of them had the same black suits on, but their insignia was a forest green instead of the red that we all had on. I wondered how Lydia was holding up. As I passed the threshold, I came into full view of what this colossal room had in it. Behind the three people was an enormous, lush forest. Spruce, pine, oak, maple, and countless other tree species lay spread out throughout the massive expanse. The ceiling mimicked the sky with a beautiful red orange sunset. Sounds of rushing water and birds chirping filled my ears. The three people stood on a brick terrace, where lush green grass met on the other side.

"Welcome, scout 101023," the man in the middle spoke up. "I'm Nero, and this to my left is Philomena." He gestured to a tall, muscular brunette woman with her hair tied back into a ponytail.

"Call me Na," she smiled to me.

"And the gentleman on my right is Nikola."

"Call me Nikola," he laughed. His wiry orange hair stuck out in all directions, and the freckles scattering his face gave him a very friendly appearance.

"We're happy to have a new recruit from outside the city limits—normally it's just kids from Arcadia. It seems new blood like you are becoming fewer and far between as we grow. The retention rate is also slightly lackluster. However, as long as you listen to us and use what you've been taught correctly, you'll do just fine. Unfortunately, your handler, Augustus, we've been told is indisposed at the moment, but we're all hoping that he makes a full recovery." Nero's eyes looked down, clearly saddened by the August situation. "Well there's nothing we can do now—he's in Hedone's hands." He shifted on his feet. "Now, what you're looking at is a precursor to the training grounds we will be entering whenever you're cleared to begin."

"So this is all for show?" I asked.

He laughed, "Yeah, Arcadia is certainly not known for its humbleness. I think it's more a façade for showing the beautiful things you could see in the world. Sure, we come across some nice landscapes from time to time, but most of where we go is dirty and desolate. So don't get your hopes up too high."

"Wait, so we're not stuck inside the city?"

"Eh." He turned the question over in his head. "For the most part, yes, we're stuck, but when we're given retrieval duties, then we're allowed outside the city. Augustus was on retrieval when he found you. I guess we're luckier than most of the other factions in that regard, but our line of work is not for the lighthearted."

"What happened to August?" I asked.

"I'm not at liberty to say, but word travels fast around the factions. He is recovering now with the Medics." He cleared his throat. "Anyways, that is nothing to concern yourself with at the moment. We just always introduce ourselves briefly to new recruits, and we've received word that you're the last one for the day. Generally we're supposed to wait around for the recruits to find their way out as a first sort of pre-test, but I want to get out of here to go see how Augustus is doing." He spun around along with Na and Nikola. They strode over to where a river cut through a clearing in the trees and headed toward a fallen tree downstream to the right. All three hopped on and swiftly walked over it without changing pace. I hopped on, my knees wobbling, and I shot my arms out to retain my balance. Slowly I shuffled my way along the tree and hopped off on the other side. I had to sprint to catch back up to them.

A waterfall pumped crystal clear water with fish dashing back and forth in a pond below it. Nero disappeared into the water first, followed by Na and then Nikola. I followed, and the water wicked away to either side of me. I came out into a cave completely dry. A solid steel door stood menacingly at the end of the space. Nero pushed on the door, and it slid open easily, revealing a beam of sunlight and fresh air. Outside, a car hovering a foot off the ground was waiting. No one was inside.

"Alright, hop in. We'll see you tomorrow," Nero requested. He pulled the handle up on the back door and it slid up. I entered into the back seat and the door whirred shut.

"Okay, but how do I know where..." I tried to say, when the car started accelerating.

CHAPTER 22

Outside the car window, we passed what must have been thousands of people all walking around, sitting in cafes, coming out of shops, playing with their kids in parks and surprisingly doing all types of familiar activities. Cars floated by, most driverless, but some people still sat in what should have been the driver's seat; none actually had steering wheels from what I could see. There were no stoplights, or any type of street signs for that matter. Markers floated as holograms around the corners of the blocks to let people know where they were going. The car drove for what was probably about twenty minutes, stopping to let people cross the street periodically. Saying the city looked magnificent would be an understatement—it looked wholly unearthly. Each building stood tall to the point where I couldn't see the tops when I leaned my head into the window. The lights were vibrant. I could only imagine what it must look like in the nighttime. The only thing I thought of that could be even close to comparison was a futuristic Tokyo. Although I'd never been to Tokyo, I imagined that was what it looked like from the pictures I'd seen.

The amount of freedom shocked me. Everything up until this point had led me to believe that we would be stuck laboring for the city. But these people were out walking around and laughing with each other. The whole atmosphere felt hopeful and cheerful. Some people were walking around with holograms floating from their wrists as they talked back to faces that floated in two dimensions. The car stopped at a corner, and there was a couple eating a bowl of noodles as they smiled at each other, lovingly holding hands.

People walked around with their dogs and cats not on leashes. Some people even walked with what looked like little foxes, and others with reptiles or birds on their shoulders. Although it was only probably one in twenty who had a pet with them, the amount of people outside in general was staggering.

We rounded a corner and it seemed like everyone was high off of something. People sat in lavish booths outside, slumped back in them, giggling. Others wandered out into the road, also laughing, which caused the car to come to frequent stops as people stumbled around. It was easily the most bizarre scene so far. I suddenly realized what Augustus had said about the prevalence of drugs for some people in the city. It was like a new-age Mardi Gras. But everything was so clean and spotless.

The same scene was sprawled out for the four or five blocks until the city changed back into people walking around, going about their daily business. People were walking in and out of shops with bags floating silently beside them. Farther down, there was a park where kids were playing on a number of unfamiliar objects. The only semi-recognizable one was a merry-go-round that hovered off the ground as kids twirled around on it. There was also something that looked like a slide, but the kids would lie down at the bottom and get sucked up to the top onto a large platform that they were dancing around on and pushing each other. My jaw dropped as one was pushed over the edge and went hurling to the ground. But no one batted an eye, because as soon as she was about to splat into the ground, she floated for a second and was gently brought to the ground, giggling.

Another ten or so blocks down, the car came to a checkpoint and then hovered through it. On this side of the checkpoint, there were still a great number of people, and it was still beautiful. But the mood seemed to change entirely. Some people still looked happy, but the atmosphere wasn't nearly as jovial. It also seemed like there fewer restaurants or shops, although there were still some coffee shops and other unrecognizable businesses. For the most part, it was large buildings with different symbols on the outside. Each symbol must have represented the different faction buildings.

Eventually, the car came to a stop outside a tenement that must have been at least twenty-five stories. The same familiar forest-green symbol with a circle and an arrow through it was fixed to the front of the pristine white building. Small, circular windows riddled the exterior. "Arrived," the car said, and my door whirred open again.

A couple people stood around talking in the lobby. Thick green lines trimmed around all the doors and windows, along with the reception desk. "101023, welcome home." The woman behind the desk smiled. "I hope that you find your stay to be exceptional—I will handle any and all questions you have. I'm sure you have many."

"My friends," I said, "or the people I came with, am I allowed to talk to them?"

"But of course!" she said happily, and looked at her screen. "You must be talking about 101020 through 25."

"Yes, thank you. How do I get ahold of them?"

She typed a little and looked at the screen. "I apologize, it appears 101024 is deceased. Also, 101020 and 21 are inaccessible at the moment. But you may contact 22 and 25 at your leisure . You'll find a phone in your domicile once you get settled. Now is there any other questions you have?"

"Why can't I contact 20 and 21?" I asked worriedly.

"I'm sorry, I'm not at liberty to tell you that." She smiled politely. "Is there anything else I can help with?"

"No, not that I can think of."

"Splendid," she replied. "In that case, you will be staying in apartment 1114. Just take the elevator to floor 11, and you will assuredly find it promptly."

"Do you have a key for me?"

"No." She smiled. "Have a wonderful evening."

"Okay?" I walked toward the elevator and got in, and to my surprise the elevator actually had buttons for every floor so I clicked 11. The doors shut and within seconds opened again. I hopped out to see a door with 1120 on it, and to the left of it was 1118. I turned left down the hallway until 1114 was in my face. There was no lock, but a light pink dot radiated on top of the handle. I put my thumb on top and held it there. A lock inside the door clicked, and I pushed it open. I was starting to learn that thumbs were of the utmost importance in this society. I laughed to myself. Everything about this was just so ridiculous. The extreme need for simplicity that the future seemed to strive for teetered on the absurd. Although I don't know why this aspect got me. Evolutionarily speaking, thumbs had always been the most important appendage, so it was certainly a natural progression.

Inside, the apartment was a small but unexpectedly spacious room. A tablet was secured to the wall right next to the door. On one wall in the living room was a circular window. The room had a white couch and a small coffee table, also white. Everything was white, like always. This was going to drive me insane. I clicked a button next to a door in the living room, and it slid sideways to reveal a bedroom with a small closet. Inside the closet were six identical suits to my own, and a pair of slippers. I took my shoes off and slipped them on. While fashion seems to be dead, at least comfort wasn't. I lay down on the bed for a second and took a deep sigh.

CHAPTER 23

Violet's scream pierced the air.

I woke up with sweat pouring down my face, the small circular window in the bedroom showing nighttime. The bright white lights in the apartment were dimmed down. I walked over to the window. Across the street, the symbol of an aqua rod of Asclepius was placed on the building, identical to the spot where our 'Scout' symbol was. Several of the round windows there were lit up, but for the most part the building was completely dark. Orbs of light floated along the sidewalks, illuminating the ground. My chest rose and fell rapidly, still in a daze from the nightmare that had awoken me. That scream would never leave my mind— it was all too real. I caught my breath, turned, and headed out into the living room.

As I sat down on the couch, I placed my face in my hands and wept. Everything hit all at once. I wept for the past and the unsure future that awaited me. I knew that Violet was gone, but she was really gone. She would never be there waiting for me again after a rough day. When all I wanted was to feel her body wrapped around me in an embrace, it would never happen again. And I was never there for her again when I knew she needed me. We were always there for each other—we were best friends, the only friends we ever needed. Tear drops dripped down my hands and flowed down my forearm toward my elbow. I brought my knees up to my chest. *I'll always love you no matter what,* the words floated in my mind. "I'll always love you too," I responded aloud. "I'm sorry Vi, I just don't know how I can do this without you." My breath started to slow, and I took a deep breath and stood up.

"I'm so scared of forgetting what your face looks like," I said to the air. My knees were weak, so I grasped onto the wall. "I'm so scared, Vi." I had the sudden realization that I had a picture of her in my wallet. I reached down into my pockets, but there were none. My old clothes. "Fuck," I sighed, and looked up. Those goddamn white walls stared me back in my face. I brought my fist up, and my knuckle collided with the wall. Again and again, over and over, until blood stained the perfect surface. A small trickle slid down. I grasped at my mangled knuckles and walked back into the bedroom. With my left hand, I grabbed at the door handle next to the closet, and it slid open. A light buzzed on before I stepped in. I turned the sink on as I held my bloodied hand up to my chest. The water stung like hell. It felt good. The light red liquid swirled around the drain, and I looked up and caught my reflection.

The deep bags under my eyes highlighted my face. My neatly trimmed beard and short, unkempt hair looked foreign to me. The only thing I recognized was my eyes. Pink surrounded the golden-brown irises. I stood there and stared for a while. Eventually, I put my back to the wall and slid down. Just sitting there, a thousand thoughts racing through my mind. I was so tired of all of this already. It had been one day, and I knew that the real shit was coming soon. I took a deep breath, stood up, slapped my face a couple times, and walked out. The lights were still dimmed, but I had no will to try to search for a light switch, if there even were any. I held my thumb to the breast pocket of my suit and the clothes shed like a snake's skin. I hopped back into bed and held the pillow over my face and screamed myself to sleep.

CHAPTER 24

Iwoke up to a ringing resonating all throughout the apartment. The sunlight shone in through the window. My stomach clanged with hunger pains, but I had no idea how to get more food pills. I would have to find some soon before I left. So groggily, I got up, emotionally exhausted from the breakdown in the middle of the night. *Eep eep eep.* The sound rang every couple seconds, I walked into the living room to see the tablet by the door flashing, and pressed a green button on it. "Hello?"

"Louis?" the voice asked.

"Lydia?" I asked in disbelief. Her tongue couldn't have possibly healed quickly enough for her L's to be so clear.

"Yes," she replied. "Louis, I don't like it here. Everyone is so mean. Except Halia, she was so nice. She held my hand while they sutured my tongue back together. She's one of our faction leaders, and she is just so nice. The only nice person in this city I think. Besides you and August, of course. I sure hope he's alright." Lydia clearly had gotten her talkative nature back, but there wasn't a trace of the original peppiness. She sounded defeated. "Are you in the Medics too?" The inflection in her voice raised momentarily.

"No, I'm not—they placed me with the Scouts."

"Oh," she said solemnly.

"But I think you actually might be right across the street, if they put all the new recruits in the same area."

"Oh?" she said with a hint of her original peppiness.

"I believe so," I said, happily. Genuinely happy—it would be nice to have someone I knew close by in this outlandish city. Even just picturing her in there put my mind at ease a bit.

"Well then maybe..." she started, but was cut off, and paused for several moments. "I'm sorry Louis, I have to go—apparently we have to get ready for training. It was really nice to hear your voice though."

"Yeah, you too." The call ended and was immediately followed by another ring. "Hello?"

"Be down in the lobby in ten minutes," an unfamiliar voice said. "Not a minute later—your training is scheduled to commence." The phone clicked off again. Well damn, they could have given a little more notice. I hurried back into the bedroom and put back on my suit from the day before. This time, after I put it on, the symbol on the front was no longer red, but the same forest-green color found everywhere throughout the building. I used the bathroom and looked for a toothbrush, but couldn't find anything that resembled one. Nothing that resembled any type of hygienic product, for that matter. Well shit, no time. I rushed out the front door down to the elevator and pressed the button, and within seconds the door opened.

In the lobby, I was greeted by fifteen or so people waiting around—some talking, some looking as confused as I did. I scanned the crowd a couple of times to see what everyone looked like, and all of them looked exceptionally ordinary. Until I caught a glimpse of fire-red hair.

"Rose?" I asked. She turned around, saw me, and then turned back. Well, that wasn't the response I expected. I figured she would want to stick together since we came in together. Fuck her—if she didn't want anything to do with me, then I certainly didn't want anything to do with her.

"Hey man, your girl's pretty mad at you, eh?" a short guy with jet-black hair and bulging brown eyes, probably in his mid-twenties, asked me with a laugh. "Women, am I right?"

"Erm..." I didn't know how to respond. I hated people like this. Why was he the only one out of the bunch to talk to me? It would have been nice to know that douchebags were erased from this new world, but unfortunately they seemed to have been around for all of history and didn't appear to be going anywhere anytime soon. "No, we just came in on the train together, I don't even really know her."

"Oh well, that's a shame," he said smugly. "She'd already be having my baby if I were you. Here watch this." He strode over to Rose, grabbed her by the shoulders, and whispered in her ear. Rose turned around, looked him in the eyes, and smiled. The first time I saw anything on Rose's face besides indifference. He smiled back, grinning from ear to ear. She softly grabbed his face with her thumbs, caressing his cheeks, the rest of her fingers behind his head. He leaned in a little, and then an audible thud stopped everyone in the lobby from talking.

"You fucking *bitch!*" the guy screeched, and fell to his side holding his groin. I couldn't help but laugh—maybe Rose wasn't all bad.

"Nice to meet you too, Travis." Rose smiled and turned her back to him. He rolled up onto his knees, still slumped over. The front door slid open.

"Better count your days, bitch," he gasped.

"Alright, that's enough of whatever is happening here," Nikola said with an indifferent tone as he walked in—though I thought I saw him briefly flash a smile at Rose. Travis got to his feet, still slightly slumped over. "I'm in charge of training you all to make sure you don't get yourselves, or any of your faction members, killed. We've only lost three this month and I would very much like to keep it that way." He darted his eyes at Travis. Through clenched teeth, the man nodded. "Okay, good. Follow me." Nikola spun on his heels and walked back toward the front door. The panels slid open, and on the other side there was a ramp that led to a bus hovering slightly off the ground. One by one, we all loaded onto the vehicle and took our seats.

CHAPTER 25

The bus drove through the brilliantly terrible city until it arrived at a massive coliseum. A white exterior screened in hundreds of green vertical lines all around it loomed before us. Everyone shifted around, struggling to get up with the katanas plastered to all of our backs. Nikola laughed, "Don't worry, you'll all get used to carrying those things with you wherever you go." Once everyone managed to get to their feet, we all exited, following Nikola. Outside, the day was overcast, and light gray clouds covered the sun. We approached a massive arch with dozens of flags draped over it. Every other flag was of the Scout symbol, while in between them were flags of the symbol found all over Arcadia.

As we entered through the arch, part of the stadium resembled the grand room where I'd originally met Nikola. Trees, small rivers, and a couple waterfalls scattered the landscape. However, there was also a large body of water, a huge circular sand pit with a white line crossing through it, an impossible amount of targets, an obstacle course, and more toward the far side of the arena—I couldn't quite make out what the rest was. It appeared to be a number of bright white fence poles. Tens of thousands of seats stretched upward, surrounding the grounds. Nikola stopped on the grass and turned around to speak to the rest of us.

"This is the arena. These are our training grounds, and they will soon become a second home to you all. You'll learn to become extremely proficient with the tools that have been provided to you. By the end of the month, you will have proven to me whether or not you will be best utilized in this faction. In addition, those with the highest marks will be given retrieval duties, while the rest of you will be made to watch and guard different points of the wall. Both jobs are of utmost importance, so whichever duty you are given, take comfort in the fact that you are essential to the safety and growth of our city." He paused and scanned us all. "I know you have it all in you. Show me."

Nikola turned and walked toward the forest area, and we all followed. The sky above us became a darker gray, the sun almost impossible to make out through the clouds. No one said a word. I looked back and saw Travis smiling at Rose. She either didn't notice, or didn't care. We approached a massive willow tree with twenty or so bins underneath, and Nikola stopped again.

"Okay," he said. "Everyone put your weapons into a different bin, and remember which one they are in. We don't need this to get too messy right off the bat." He paused and waited for all of us to fuss around and remove the weapons on our bodies. Some other people were still fidgeting around, trying to remember how to get them off, while I stood there waiting for Nikola to speak again. "There are fourteen white flags hidden throughout this forest. As I'm sure you've noticed by now, there are fifteen of you. Don't be the one who doesn't get a flag. Once you have secured one, bring it back to the bin you placed your weapons in. You will then wait for the rest of your faction members to find and retrieve theirs." He paused for a moment and then resumed. "If you find one, try to be discreet when you return it. Violence is encouraged, and you are welcome to take a flag from a fellow member by any means necessary. We're weeding out the weak, and if you die in here, it would be a lot better for us than if you die out there and put your fellow scouts in jeopardy. That said, please don't try to kill each other—you're not quite as disposable as you once were." He looked at us all again. "Well, what are you waiting for?"

In an instant half of the group sprinted into the wooded forest, while the rest of us were still processing what was happening, me included. Then I took off running, realizing that the only thing I had eaten in hundreds of years was one little pill. I was half starving, and everyone else seemed exceptionally prepared. I half-expected to immediately approach a brawl between Rose and Travis, but they were nowhere to be seen. Branches, leaves, and nettles littered the ground, and all I could hear were the sounds of twigs snapping under other feet. Rain started to trickle down in between the clearings that weren't sheltered by the canopies of the trees. "Yes!" I heard a shout from the left, followed by a hard thud and a groan of pain. Half of me wanted to leave him there, because I certainly didn't want to find out what not getting a flag meant. But against any rational thought that I had, I just couldn't do that. I approached where the sound came from, and a kid in his late teens was sprawled out on the ground, clutching at his face. I reached down a hand to pick him up.

"Come on, we have to go—worry about your face later,"
I told him rapidly. He grabbed my hand and I pulled him up.
"Thank you," he said, and took off in another direction.

Where was I supposed to find a flag in all of this? I
quickly scanned the ground, tree tops, and everything else
I could see. There was nothing. I picked up my pace a little
and went into a light jog, darting my eyes back and forth,
looking for anything. Occasionally I would see a flash of
black as someone ran past in my peripheral vision. A voice
out of a loudspeaker announced that one of the flags had
been retrieved. Seconds later, the voice told us again that
a second had been. I started toward the river. The water
was rushing quickly away from a small waterfall. Atop it, I
saw a figure crouch down, then stand back up and shove
a white piece of cloth into the front of its jumpsuit. Then
the person looked at me and took off in the other direction.
Don't worry man, I have no intention of chasing you, I thought
to myself. I looked across the river, and another person
was climbing down from a tree with a flag in his hand. He
quickly took off toward the containers.

"Three flags retrieved," the voice announced. Starting to panic a little, I stepped into the river. The current
pushed at my knees, but I managed to maintain my balance.
With heavy steps, I trudged across. "Four flags retrieved.
Five flags retrieved," the voice announced in quick succession. Now the rain was falling heavily, and it was starting
to get hard to make out what was in the distance. I wiped
the drops from my face and stepped out of the river. A
boulder stood in between a circle of trees, and I ran over
to it. Circling around it, I found a box behind it. I opened
it, and inside was a flag. Thank god. I stuffed it in my suit
and started making my way back across the river. This time,
the current knocked me off balance and forced me to put

my right arm down into the water to steady myself. I stood up and slogged through to the other riverbank. I walked back quickly, still pretending to look for other flags along the way so as to not alert others. I was almost back when I saw someone on the ground getting the shit beat of them. On top of them, Travis was swinging his fists wildly. Shit, I couldn't just leave them here like this. I ran full speed and slammed my shoulder into Travis's side, knocking him off a girl with blood pouring from her mouth and nose.

"Well hey there, buddy," Travis laughed as he scrambled backward to his feet. "How did I know I'd run into you?" He put his fists up, and a huge, shit-eating grin filled his face.

"Look man, there's still plenty of flags for us to—" I started.

"Where's the fun in that?" He cut me off and ran toward me, colliding his shoulder into my stomach this time and pinning me to the ground. The girl on the ground got to her feet and tried to come over to kick him. He grabbed her foot and ripped her to the ground next to us. Kicking sideways, he made contact with her face with a sickening crunch. She screamed out and rolled onto her knees. I squirmed to get out from underneath him. It didn't work—I had no energy to fight this little weasel fuck. The voice announced that a sixth flag had been retrieved. A fist connected with the side of my face. Then another, and another. The girl got to her feet and started limping away. "Where the fuck do you think you're going?" Travis hopped up and grabbed the girl by the front of her jumpsuit, reached down the front of it, and retrieved a white flag. He immediately buried a knee into her stomach and she doubled over. "Now was that so hard?"

"I'm sorry," she cried over to me, and limped off into the distance as quickly as she could. I sighed. At least he got what he wanted. I rolled over to my stomach and pushed myself up to my knees.

"Oh, you think I'm done with you?" he laughed. In a moment, a kick connected with my chin. That sent me back down to the ground. I felt blood warmly filling up my mouth, and spit out a pool of red. A dull ringing in my ear began to get louder and louder with each connection from his fists. I held my hands over my face, but it was useless. At this point, I just had to hope that his intention wasn't to kill me. Suddenly, he reached for a stone, grasping it firmly in his hand. Rain poured down over his head and dripped down onto my blood-drenched face. The stone came down in an instant. Then black.

CHAPTER 26

I awoke to the rain pouring on my face and the announce-ment that twelve flags had been retrieved. My hands met my face with a painful sting. I pulled them away, and there was only a little bit of blood from where it was still com-ing out of my nose. I rolled over to my side and coughed. Spurts of red fell out of my mouth with each cough. I didn't remember being punched anywhere but the face, so maybe I was lucky and that psychopath left me with no internal bleeding. When I got to my knees, a splitting headache sent me onto all fours. With all my strength, I pushed myself onto one knee, with my other foot planted firmly on the ground. I clutched at my chest—the flag was still there. I was surprised that asshole didn't want two of them. Or he just didn't notice while he was busy smashing my face in.

Head pounding and ears ringing, I started heading back to where I thought the containers were. Although I wasn't completely sure, my mind was so fuzzy. Someone ran past me, looked my way, and gave a sympathetic look of pity and continued on. Moments later, the voice sounded, saying a thirteenth had been retrieved. I could see the group standing around, looking into the forest, and from behind me in the distance I heard running coming toward me. I picked up my pace and fell down in front of my box. A man about my age came running out of the trees toward me. As quickly as I could, I reached into my suit and dropped it into the box. The lid slid shut on its own and locked. The man fell to his knees, defeated.

"I'm sorry, 100982. You've reached the end of the line already with the Scouts," Nikola said apologetically. The lid on the man's box snapped shut, enclosing his weapons with it. "There will be a car waiting for you outside the arch we came in at. I hope your future in another faction is more promising. The rest of you, follow me for your rations." The man got up from his knees and walked solemnly back toward the arch. We followed closely behind Nikola, rain still pouring over our heads. Most of the group appeared unscathed, besides the girl I helped and me. A couple other people had minor scrapes and bruises.

"Thank you," the girl said to me, so quietly I didn't know how Nikola heard her.

"No talking yet, please," he said without turning his head. I nodded at the girl with reassurance that I had accepted her thanks. The nod shot me into an unbearable ache. I grabbed at the side of my head and caught Travis grinning at me. I turned away and kept walking.

We all gathered underneath a canopy to block out the rain. Nikola walked over to a box and kept pulling out bottles of water and throwing them to each faction member until we all had one. He then pulled out a handful of pills and gave one to each of us. "We'll take a ten-minute break while you guys have lunch." A couple people looked at the pills in their hands and then at one another, while others, Rose included, popped them immediately and washed them down with a sip of water. I popped mine in my mouth and swallowed. To my unpleasant surprise, it tasted strongly like fish, but almost immediately my hunger disappeared. I hadn't eaten a thing, or I guess swallowed a pill since the one that August had given me, so I'd take what I could get.

A few people started nervously talking to each other, glancing over at Nikola to see if it was okay. He looked annoyed, but didn't say anything this time. I sat down next to Rose and again tried to strike up a conversation. "So where did you end up finding your flag at?"

"Look Louis, nothing against you, but I'm not here to talk."

"But I figured..."

"You don't know what to figure. Go check on that girl." Her eyes flashed over at the girl I'd tried to protect from Travis.

"Okay," I said, and got up and walked over to the girl.

"Thank you again," she said. "I was afraid he was going to kill me over that stupid fucking flag. I'm really sorry I couldn't do anything to help."

"It's fine, I know you tried. We just have to keep our eyes on him from now on. I'm thinking it's only going to get worse from here on out."

"Damn right," she replied, and took a sip from her water. "Are you sure you're okay? You look really rough."

"You're not looking too hot yourself," I laughed.

"Oh, I'm sure," she laughed back. "I'm Hera, by the way." She stuck her hand out to shake mine.

"Louis." I shook back.

"You look particularly lost out here," Hera said. "You must have come from the train."

"Yeah, you didn't?" I asked.

"No." She paused, and then laughed. "I've been preparing for this moment my whole life. I guess I didn't know exactly what we were in for. I wish my parents had been around to prepare me for this, but it probably wouldn't have mattered. I guess they change up the training regimen pretty often."

"This seems like such a strange test to throw is into."

"Yeah, from what I've gathered, every faction is put into tests with little to no prior explanation. They say it's good to show the true character and nature of each candidate. I call bullshit. Probably a couple of the upper class laughing around a table doing Snuss just to get their kicks out of watching us struggle."

Inferring that Snuss was probably another drug, I asked the more important question. "Who are the upper class?" With every new thing I learned, it seemed that the world just got more confusing. But before I got a solid answer, Nikola cleared his throat.

"Alright, break time's over," Nikola announced, cutting our conversation abruptly short. "The second half of the day will consist of an agility test. Don't worry, no one else will be cut today; this is just a marker to look back and check the progress and growth of each of you throughout the next month."

Everybody stood up and waited at attention for more instructions. The ringing in my ears was hard to ignore, and the splitting headache was pounding at the back of my skull. "Does everyone see that wall in the distance?" A fifteen-foot-or-so wall was obscured by the heavy rain. Everyone nodded. "The goal is to ascend to the top of that, and once over, you will be greeted by more obstacles. Make your way through it until you get to the green button at the end. Is that clear?" Everyone nodded again. "Good. When I say 'begin,' run to your weapon containers, put them on, and begin your ascent on the wall." He looked down at his watch momentarily. "Begin."

Everyone broke out into a sprint back toward the boxes. When I approached mine, the top snapped open again, and I surprisingly swiftly holstered my weapons to my body. My body was extremely sore, like I had just run a marathon already, or at least what I imagined the feeling after running one would have been. But it felt like the soreness only came from not being able to move my muscles for hundreds of years, combined with a good measure of the ass-kicking I'd just received. At the moment, none of the symptoms that had plagued me before the freezing were present. My balance was there, and I didn't feel like the world was constantly shifting. The headache was in full tilt, but again likely due to circumstances from the new world.

Only one person was ahead of me on the way to the wall. Rose had about twenty feet on me. Lightning cracked across the sky and lit up the arena momentarily. A man in a dead sprint passed me up on my left, and I tried to pick up my pace a little more. Then Travis passed on my right. "Try to keep up—you're falling behind," he panted.

I arrived at the wall, and Rose was already halfway up while everyone else was figuring out how to mount it. Lines were carved about four inches deep into the slick metal, randomly and at all different angles. I found a couple holds and pulled myself up, and immediately slipped down.

I tried again, pressing my body completely to the wall, and held my palms pushed tight. The fingerholds were relatively dry, but the outside of the whole wall was extremely slick. I forced my hand in another higher hold and didn't fall this time. I kept up the routine until I was almost to the top and had to stop and take a deep breath. To my right, a woman's foot slipped, and she slid down a little bit and completely fell. She let out a sharp groan and limped back toward the wall. I continued my ascent and reached the top, where a rope down awaited. Looking down, I saw several people at the bottom, already starting the next challenge. Grabbing onto the rope and wrapping my feet around it, I started to let myself down slowly. Then I lost my tight grip and slid faster, the parts of the rope that weren't completely soaked burning into my hands.

My feet hit the ground, and a field of electricity formed a net pattern a couple feet off the ground. I dropped to my stomach and started an army crawl underneath it, like the people before me had done. The electricity buzzed above me. Another crack of lightning pierced the sky. I made it to the end of the crawl and stood up a little too quickly. One of the electrical currents made contact with the back of my calf, and it shocked me back down to the ground. *So that's what being tased feels like. Fun.* The pain in my face and head took priority, and the initial shock dissipated quickly. I stood up and got to the next obstacle.

A beam about half a foot wide increased in elevation until it reached a platform at the top. I stepped on and steadied myself, then put one foot in front of another. About halfway up, my foot slipped off to the side, but I was able to regain my balance. At the top of the beam was a couple-foot gap to the platform. I jumped but slipped a little; one of my feet planted firmly, while the shin on my other leg slammed into the edge of the platform. Pain shot through my whole body and I fell forward. Pushing myself up, I shook out my leg, trying to ignore the pain. In front of me were five more floating platforms spaced about four feet apart. Underneath the last platform was a pool, violently rippled by the raindrops. I limped forward and planted on my good leg and jumped. My foot contacted the platform and sent another shock of pain. I continued the same process until I was standing on the last one.

I took a breath and plunged into the pool. Swimming during a lightning storm clearly didn't seem like a good idea, but somehow I knew that not swimming would be even more dangerous. Sinking deep into the water, I kicked with my good leg and flopped my other. I broke the surface and started kicking and stroking my arms as best I could. The end of the pool had a ladder, and I pulled myself up. Looking back, I saw Hera jumping in.

In front of me were weighted gates that you had to pull up in order to go under. I got to the first one and gripped the handles. Trying to pull it up shot pain through all my extremities. The door budged a couple inches and fell back down. "Need help?" Hera asked as she emerged from the pool.

"I wouldn't say no," I replied. She came up on my right and reached down and gripped a portion of the handle. "One, two, three," I counted as we both jerked up, and the door slid all the way up. I held it while she went under, then slid my way after her. The door banged shut. We worked our way through the next four doors the same way. Lightning was constantly cutting the sky now. "Thank you—I couldn't have done this without you."

"I know you couldn't have," she laughed, and smiled at me. A flash of lightning illuminated her swollen and bruised face. In the light, her eyes looked a light purple, and behind all the bruises were beautiful features. "Let's get this shit over with." She spun and headed to the next obstacle.

A few ropes hung over the ground, but the ground was rapidly moving back our way like a giant treadmill. "You first," she told me. I hopped up to grab the first rope, then swung to the second, grabbing with my right hand and wrapping my leg around it. The momentum carried me to the third. I grabbed, swung, and jumped off, the impact sending me back down to my knees. Turning back, I saw Hera easily clear the ropes. A bang sounded, and another faction member appeared on the other side of the last weighted wall and approached the ropes.

In front of us stood four different tiers of five-foot walls, all stacked up and set back on top of each other, like stairs for a giant. I grabbed the top of the first wall and with all my strength pulled myself to the first tier. Hera got up next to me, and we scaled the following wall. The third wall was absolute hell, and my arms shook uncontrollably as I lifted myself. I sat dangling my feet over, catching my breath while Hera pulled herself to the top. The other man behind us mounted the ledge and stood next to me. "Come on man, you got this." He reached his hand down to grab mine. With one pull, I was back on my feet. "Let me help you." He interwove his fingers in both of his hands together and leaned over.

"Thank you," I panted, and put one foot into his hands while he pushed up. I rolled onto the last ledge. He pulled himself up easily, and I stood up to stand with him and look over the wall.

"What now?" Hera said. The other side of the wall was a twenty-foot drop to solid ground. Past it was the green button shining brightly in the gloomy, dark gray day.

"I guess we take a leap of faith," the man said, his shoulder-length brown hair drenched from the downpour.

"Bold," Hera replied. "From all the things wrong with this fucked-up world, I don't have faith in much of anything anymore. I guess just try to tuck and roll."

"All at once?" the man asked.

"All at once," Hera agreed.

We all jumped. My stomach dropped, and I prepared for the excruciating pain. But there was none—the ground sunk down with all of our weight and bubbled back up. We quickly realized that our legs below the knees were still submerged under the ground. I flopped over on my stomach, trying to push down with my arm to pull my legs out, and my hand sunk in a little. "Of course," Hera laughed. She dropped onto her stomach and flopped around, trying to kick her legs loose. The other man did the same. We all lay there, flopping like fish, trying to free our extremities. I would have laughed at how absolutely absurd we looked if I wasn't so exhausted. Once our arms and legs were free, we slid along until finally the ground felt solid.

"Ladies first," the man said, and gestured forward for Hera to hit the green button.

"Fuck off," Hera laughed. She hit the button, then the man, then me. Nikola stood waiting with a couple other people, including Travis and Rose. We waited there for the rest of the recruits to finish up. About ten minutes later, the last person showed up and slammed the button. It was the girl who had fallen off the wall next to me. She limped over to the rest of us.

"Not bad," Nikola said, looking down at his watch. "Obviously, there is room for a lot of improvement. However, we're going to have an easy day and cut training short. You've all shown great promise, and I look forward to watching each and every one of you succeed." He turned and walked back toward the arch while we all followed. The bus was still waiting, and we climbed on board. This time Hera sat down next to me.

"So what's it like?" she asked.

"What's what like?" I asked in return.

"The past. You did come from the trains, right?"

"A hell of a lot different than this. Everything is so sterile here. My world was filled with different colors, different people, different everything." I paused for a second and grabbed at the nape of my neck, trying to force the pounding headache to subside a little. "I don't really know what else there is to see here—maybe some of the same stuff still exists. I just don't know though."

"Try to paint me a picture with your words, and I'll let you know if we have any of that here still." She smiled.

I thought about it. "Well, for starters, most of us had the freedom to do whatever we'd like, for the most part. We weren't told when or where to be all the time."

Hera cut me off. "That sounds beautiful."

"Yeah, it was beautiful for the most part." I paused as my mind drifted back to Violet. The times that we had laughed together, and cried together. The latter highlighted by our last month or so. But it was beautiful. Through all the pain and heartache it caused, the years that we were together made life worth living. Her presence painted the world with vibrant colors that just didn't seem to exist anymore. I couldn't tell if the new world was as bad as it really appeared to be, or just the fact that she wasn't in it anymore. "It was beautiful, but it was still filled with bullshit." I lingered over the thought of how the people you are surrounded by affect how the world looks.

"I'm sure it's hard," she said, sensing my discomfort. "This new world you're in. But, we do what we can to get by. I doubt the Aristocracy, even with all their fancy things, are truly happy with how things are either."

"The Aristocracy?" I asked.

"Some people here were born luckier than others. If you're born into the Aristocracy, then you're able to indulge yourself. They live free. Free to do whatever they like. I'm sure you saw many of them on the way to our building. They all live off our labor."

"All those people in the shops, parks, and the like were Aristocracy?"

"Every single one of them. Our kind isn't allowed down there."

"What do you mean?"

"I mean eventually, some of us are lucky enough to work our way out of this, but nine times out of ten we'll be dead long before that." She looked out the window at the few people walking around on the sidewalks with their umbrellas. "Those fucking assholes don't even realize everything we sacrifice for them. I can't hate them, though—they don't know any better. But I doubt that we're even a second thought to them."

"You clearly weren't from the train. How did you end up here?"

"Most of us didn't come from any trains. There are trains bringing people in from the past almost daily, or some people who were lucky enough to survive beyond the wall. However, most of us were born into it." She paused and sighed. "When I was born, I was taken from my parents; I don't even know which faction they belonged to. Every child born in a faction is taken into protection of the West Empire and raised to the age of eighteen, at which point we go through the same interview process and are placed where we fit best."

"So you're meaning to tell me that we are essentially slaves?"

"Indentured servants," she corrected me, but I could see in her eyes that slaves, in fact, was exactly what we were. "Keep your voice down, too—we're not allowed to use that word. The state wouldn't take too kindly to pushing that around into other people's heads. Which is complete bullshit. We all know exactly what we are. We're put up in nice apartments, given food and water, but that's exactly what we are."

"Shit," I said, alarmed but somehow not surprised.

"Shit, indeed." The bus whirred to a halt, and the doors opened. "Best not to talk about this with anyone else—you never know who you can trust." She stood up to exit the bus. The huge Scout symbol on our building contrasted the dark afternoon perfectly. Once inside, no one really talked. Half of us entered the elevator and got off on different floors. Rose got off on the eleventh floor with me and entered 1112, the door next to mine. Guess I didn't have to worry about getting to know my neighbors.

Once inside the apartment, the new familiarity of it actually felt kind of comforting. It was a lot nicer than getting my ass kicked in the arena, at least. I decided to inspect the space further, hoping to find at the very least a light switch. Everything was so barren. No artwork on the walls, no decorations of any kind, and worst of all, no light switches. Looked like I was going to have to permanently live with the lights on. Not the worst thing in the world, but the brightness killed my head. I could feel the blood pulsing through it, making it feel like it was going to explode.

I looked back toward the door and saw the tablet on the wall, and decided to check that out since it was about the only thing in the apartment that might be beneficial. Turned out I had no idea. On the screen was a plethora of different applications. Food, water, hygiene, medicine, lights, temperature, colors, and miscellaneous, all stared back at me as little squares on the screen. I pressed lights immediately, and a few different options popped up—luminosity, color, and control. Clicking luminosity, I was able to dim the lights down to a point where Dracula would be comfortable.

Then, fidgeting around with medicine, I found a pain relief option and clicked. A few seconds later, an invisible compartment opened on the wall to the left of the tablet, revealing a pill on a small tray. I grabbed the pill and swallowed it immediately, not really caring what the side effects could be. In an instant, my head felt clear and I couldn't really feel any of my body. Everything still functioned properly, but it was as if I were floating. This was a dangerous feeling.

I hit the water button, and without any more options popping up, a bottle of water came out of the wall where the pill had. The water tasted purer than any water I had ever had in my life. Like what I would imagine drinking from the purest mountain spring would be. With the bottle in one hand, I pressed a couple more buttons. The hygiene button let me retrieve a toothbrush, toothpaste, deodorant, shampoo, conditioner, and body soap from the wall, all popping out one after another as if from nowhere. I set everything on the floor and went to the color option. A gradient scale of every color imaginable showed up in a large circle. I clicked a shade of blue, and all of a sudden all the walls changed to the same color. No more white—fuck yes. I slid my finger around the circle, and the wall rapidly changed colors like a futuristic funhouse. Standing there fidgeting with the circle for much longer than a normal person should have, I ended up on a light beige color. The same color Violet and I had painted the walls when we first moved into our house. It's amazing how a color can be so comforting.

I took a deep sigh of relief and decided that was enough fucking around with the tablet for one day.

Gathering up all the goods I had accrued from the wall, I took them all to the bathroom. I looked in the mirror, where I could see the full extent of how bad my injuries were. Bruises splattered my face, and a large cut on my left cheek where the rock struck me had freshly scabbed over. Luckily the rain had washed away most of the blood or I would have looked straight out of an '80s slasher film. Some dried blood still clung to my beard, eyebrows, and hair. I flipped on the water in the shower, let it get to a reasonable temperature, and hopped in. The feeling of washing away the blood, sweat, and grime was indescribable. Almost like losing my virginity. It was a transcendent experience.

Getting out of the shower, I realized that I had forgotten to order a towel off of the hygiene menu. I grabbed one of the sheets off my bed and tied it around myself, then walked over to the tablet again. The towel appeared out of the little compartment, and I held it to my face for a long moment. Even though I couldn't feel the towel on my face, I know it felt great. Pulling it back, I could see that the wound on my face had reopened, because there was a large crescent shape blood stain. All at once, I decided that the day was over for me, even though it couldn't have been any later than 6 p.m. I clicked the food button to grab a bite to eat. Or a pill to swallow, I guess. A massive menu of different types of food appeared. I clicked 'hamburger,' and a pill lay waiting on the tray in the wall. Of course. The pill surprisingly actually tasted like a perfectly cooked hamburger on the way down. Not half bad. I walked back to the bed and fell face-first with the towel wrapped around me.

CHAPTER 27

I was walking next to Violet as we crossed over a stone bridge. Mother nature must have been pleased with my plan, because the day could not have been more perfect. The sun shone brightly on a beautiful 70-degree spring afternoon. Sounds of children laughing broke through the air from the park on the other side of the bridge. Grass lay a perfect green after the harsh winter, while the trees all had begun to blossom within the last couple weeks.

"I love this bridge." Violet smiled as she looked down over a lazily drifting river.

"I know, you never shut up about it." I smiled back and braced for impact.

"Oh shut up," she said, punching me in the shoulder. "You know you love it too." I did love that bridge—it was always so peaceful. It was the first bridge we crossed over as a couple. Anytime I saw it, it reminded me of just how lucky I was. We nicknamed it Butter Bridge. I don't remember why, some stupid inside joke that we came up with on the spot as we nervously got to know each other. Or at least, I was nervous. Nervous as hell. If I'd learned anything from my past relationships, this one was a once-in-a-lifetime opportunity.

But here we were, two years after that first date. Outside of the music festival, of course, if that could have even been considered a date. I had just moved outside Lincoln, Nebraska for a teaching job. Fate intervened, and it just so happened that she lived a half-hour out. There we were, two lost souls trying to make sense of the world. Quickly, I realized that she was the only thing that made the world make sense at all. After countless dates, we ended up moving into an apartment together a year later. Through the ups and downs, here we were again, walking across the same bridge where I can confidently say I first fell in love with her.

The ring was burning a hole in my pocket as I stood there, smiling at her. Inside, my stomach was turning over and my knees were completely weak. Descriptions that I thought only happened in cheesy love movies, but it turned out that they were somewhat based in reality.

"Who would have thought after our little meet-and-greet at Bonnaroo that we would be standing here together today?" she said pondering the idea in her head.

"No idea," I replied. "But I would give anything to be in this position."

"Well luckily, you don't have to give anything," she said. "We're already here."

"Violet," I said. "You have no idea what you mean to me." I choked up a little.

"I think I do, if it's half as much as you mean to me." She smiled and grabbed my hand. This was as good a time as any. My hands were sweating profusely, and I dug around in my pocket, the ring slipping a couple times. I finally got a hold of it, and with my hand still in her hand, I got down to one knee. Her hand covered her mouth, and small tears began pooling at the corners of her eyes.

"Will you..." I started to ask, but was immediately interrupted. She dropped down to her knees and embraced me.

"Of course," she cried. I tried slipping the ring onto her finger, but both of our hands were shaking so badly it fell and rolled off the bridge into the little stream below.

"Shit!" I yelled, which in turn sent us into a violent storm of laughter and crying.

"I'd marry you if all you had was a ring pop. Never mind—you wouldn't even need the ring pop. I love you so much, Louis," she cried into my shoulder.

"I love you more," I gave my rebuttal.

"That's fucking impossible." She looked up and smiled. "I suppose we should probably go look for the ring, huh?"

"I suppose we should," I replied. "Sounds like a fun first adventure as your fiancé."

"Fiancé." She turned the word over in her head, and I had never seen her smile so large. We both looked over into the water, and it began to swirl, mud obscuring the clarity, and then all of a sudden it stopped. A white flag floated up from the bottom.

CHAPTER 28

I woke up and leaned over to nestle up next to Violet. But there was no one there. My eyes shot up—outside the circular window, the sun had just risen. My heart dropped. I sighed and stood up, the towel still wrapped around me. At least now I could have part of a normal routine. I went in the bathroom to brush my teeth, and looked in the mirror again. My reflection of bruises and cuts stared back. I really had to stop looking into that mirror. Afterward, I got into the shower, grabbed a pancake pill, and washed it down. The clock on the tablet read 7:52. I went in and rushed into another suit, secured my weapons, and headed downstairs. Everyone was already in the lobby, but this time we were all silent. Clearly, I wasn't the only one who had a rough day yesterday.

The same routine followed of Nikola coming to pick us up and getting into the arena through the arch. Today was a stark contrast to the previous day. The sun shone brightly, eerily similar to the early spring day when I had proposed to Violet. Unlike most dreams that dissipate throughout the day, the one I had last night was of a memory that I would never forget. In all honesty, it would probably be the last I thought of before I died. Moments come and go, but the big ones stay forever, good or bad—there's no forgetting them.

"Today, we will be doing the alternate day routine. Each day we will alternate between different forms of training. Yesterday was recovery and agility. Today we will be focusing on weapons training and sparring. After today, we will begin each day with running laps, push-ups, crunches, and all that other good shit. But we've been instructed to treat the first two days as introductory courses," Nikola addressed us all. He gestured over to the sand pit with the white line intersecting it. "We'll begin in the sparring pit. I shouldn't have to tell you that no weapons are allowed, but I'm saying it anyway. Same routine—put your weapons in the containers outside the pit." As Nikola walked us to the pit, we all situated our weapons into the boxes. "Okay, good. Now, we're not going to be learning anything today in the pit, this is just to get a feel for everybody's individual skill levels. I've matched everyone according to their placement in yesterday's retrieval test. So last place 101023 will be facing first place 101022. Second place will be facing thirteenth place, and so on—you guys understand."

"Damn," I whispered to myself, knowing that meant I would be going against Rose. I looked over to her; she didn't look any happier than I did, and gave me a knowing look. Did she actually look sympathetic? "So how long do we go for?" I spoke up.

"Until it's over," Nikola said. "Until one person calls for mercy, is knocked out, or ends up dead." He paused for a moment to look at my face and gave a short-lived look of pity. "I obviously hope it isn't the latter, so please don't try to play hero. If you knock someone out, it's over—there will be no needless deaths. Obviously wanton murder of another faction member will reflect badly on your scores and may even result in some good old-fashioned capital punishment. But know that there is a chance that one good blow to the wrong spot might put you out of commission. So keep your guards up. Like I said, this is just a preliminary test of skill. When the horn goes off, you may begin. 101022, since you were higher ranked, you choose your side first." We walked over toward the circle, and Rose confusingly chose the side with the sun shining into her eyes.

"Just go down easy," she whispered to me as we separated and walked toward the opposite sides of the circle. I barely had a moment to think before the horn sounded and she came rushing at me. I put my hands up in a defensive stance and she immediately swiped at my legs with hers, sending me to the ground. A couple in the crowd of faction members snickered.

"You puss—" A distinct yell from Travis was cut off by Nikola smacking him in the back of the head. I scrambled back up to my feet, and this time as Rose came back at me, I swung out and my fist made contact with the side of Rose's ribcage.

"Good," she whispered before hitting me square in the chin with an uppercut. My head shot backward, and the previous day's headache came rocketing back like a bad memory. Another blow hit me in the stomach; this time it was from her knee. I grabbed at her thigh and ripped upward, sending her stumbling back a couple feet. It didn't really matter, as she was back at me, blow after blow. My arms were able to block a lot of them, but the others stung into different points on my body. Then one came square into the middle of face—my nose made a nauseating pop, and blood began pouring down into my mouth. I swung out madly, trying to make contact again. Here and there, a couple would land, but I was clearly in a losing battle from the start. All of a sudden, Rose wrapped her arm around my neck and pivoted. The momentum flung me into a sort of front flip, where I landed flat on my back. I gasped for air as the wind left my lungs. She was on top of me, with her hands around my neck. "Please, tap out," Rose said with genuine despair on her face.

"Uungh?" I managed to ask her through a choked breath. As if it would have made any sense. My face started feeling hot, and I could feel the air in my lungs losing the battle. With horror, I realized that she would actually kill me or at the very least choke me out if I didn't tap out. My arm shot out the side and slapped at the ground.

She released my throat and hopped up to her feet. I grabbed at my throat and gasped for air. Slowly, oxygen filled the empty spaces in my lungs. Rose held down her hand to help me up, and I grabbed it.

"Thank you," she said. "I really don't want to hurt you, Louis." Well, that was reassuring after she just made it clear that she would have killed me had I not tapped out. We walked back toward the rest of the group.

"Good," Nikola said, "very good." He called out the other groupings of numbers. One after another, pairs fought, one emerging the victor, while the other lay sprawled out in the sand like I had. Hera ended up winning her fight against a scrawny-looking kid about her age. Her kick to his temple sent him to the ground, knocked out cold. The last fight, between Travis and another man, ended with Travis's signature move—hopping on top of someone and beating their face bloody. It ended when the man slammed at the sand,

and Travis got one last punch into the side of his face. He hopped up and held both his fists in the air in a victory pose, kicking some sand toward the fallen faction member who was still getting up, blood staining the surface of the sand.

Nikola said nothing, but shook his head adamantly, disappointed, and typed into a tablet that he was holding. After he finished typing, he looked back up at us all. Travis observed the reaction from Nikola, and his victory pose soon turned meek and seemingly a little embarrassed.

"Everyone grab your weapons. I hope you all have steady hands," Nikola finally said, and started walking toward the targets. We all quickly grabbed our weapons from the containers. In front of the targets were twenty lanes, all marked with different roman numerals. Nikola gestured for everyone to choose a different lane. I stood on VII and waited for further instructions. "Okay, everybody unholster your pistols." I pulled mine off my hip and held it in my hands.

"Oh shit!" a man a couple lanes down yelled as a *tsst* quietly rang out next to me. An orange hole burned into the ground next to his feet. Nikola quickly walked over to him and ripped the gun out of his hand.

"Come on," he said impatiently. "Have some sense." He held the barrel of the gun, then handed it back grip first. "Keep your finger off the fucking trigger." The man took it back with his hands shaking, taking deep breaths. "Now, when I tell you to pull the trigger, I hope you will all be aiming down toward the targets." He paused and ran his fingers through his hair. "You'll have twenty shots. If I see anyone take any more than that, we'll have a problem. Is that clear?" Everyone nodded. He gestured his hand toward the targets, signaling for everyone to start shooting.

There were twenty targets in front of each of us, staggered at different distances and to the left and right. I shot the one closest to me, and the *tsst* sound quietly left the barrel. To my surprise, there was absolutely no recoil. The bullet left an orange glow toward the bottom left of the first target. I moved on to the next and hit it a little closer to the center. However, no marksman would tell me they were proud of that shot either. I kept alternating the targets to the left and right, hitting every one until the thirteenth, where I missed completely and the bullet went flying into the white walls at the edge of the arena. I moved on to the fourteenth target and hit it. The rest I hit as well. I'd always loved shooting guns back in the old world. Never had to use one, and never would have gone hunting. But the power behind a gun was just so appealing. Violet always protested when I went to the range, but after she came with me one time, she wouldn't let me go without her.

I stopped and waited for the rest of the faction members to finish up their shots. Most had missed at least half of the targets in the distance. Except Rose—all her shots were damn near perfect. A couple strayed off center, but it was clear she was no stranger to a gun, or she had some hell of beginner's luck. "Good," Nikola said as the last person finished his final shot. "Looks like most of you are going to need some extra training around these parts." He let out a little laugh. "Now try again." He swiped at his tablet, and all the orange glow from the shots fizzled and disappeared, leaving spotless targets in front of us. Even the shot I had missed that was embedded in the arena wall fizzled and then vanished.

Again, everyone unloaded their pistols into all the targets. This time, I was ready for the non-existent recoil, and my shots hit with much greater accuracy. The orange from the marks the pistols made was mesmerizing. They glowed like the sun on a fall evening. Beautiful, but haunting. I didn't even want to imagine what they would look like going into a living thing. The image of the kid who died in the waiting room was burned into my head and I wondered for a moment if that was what they looked like. So precise and so sterile. I quickly shook the image from my mind, and a shudder went up my spine. My thoughts were then broken up by Nikola's voice. "Okay, I've seen what I need to see, let's move on to the next test." He swiped on his tablet again.

A door rose from an area on the wall, and from it emerged fourteen different people, all dressed in perfect white. To my horror, I realized that those white posts that I saw in the distance yesterday were really these people. Every one of them was impossibly skinny. They looked just like any person you would see walking down the street, but as if they hadn't eaten in week, or months even. Each held a small white shield.

"Now these here are robots," Nikola sighed. "Your job is to disable them. They are made to be as similar to the human body is as possible, so don't be surprised when you see blood." He stared solemnly at the robots in front of him. "We will only be doing this test a couple times throughout your training, because bots are in scare supply these days." Nikola's voice droned off as I racked over in my head why in the hell we would be doing this exercise in the first place if these robots were in scarce demand. It seemed awfully wasteful, especially if they were used for any other purpose. Maybe this was all they were good for? If the robots were running low, did that mean that there were other resources running low in this society?

My train of thought was interrupted by Nikola's voice again. "So make this fight count. On the other days, I will be showing you different forms of swordsmanship, but for today, we want to see what your skills are right off the bat."

We lined up when the first robot took a step forward, and in his eyes I could see fear. Damn, they really made these robots realistic.

"This test isn't only a test of skill, but a test of your ability to separate yourself from your humanity for the benefit of the Empire. Therefore, they will scream, they will plead, and they will sound angry. Do your best." He gestured 100967 forward to be the first contender. Nikola stretched his hand out and waited until she placed her pistol in it. Then she reached for the hilt of her sword and swung it out.

The robot approached with its shield up, and she rushed out to meet it with a slash of her blade. It clinked off the shield, and the robot bashed her in the stomach. She planted her sword in the ground and doubled over, but quickly got back to her feet. The next slash slid off too, but she quickly came back from the other direction and caught the robot in its side. A terrible scream left the robot's mouth, and when she removed the sword, blood began gushing from its leg. It fell to one knee and held the shield over its head as a slash from her sword came downward, again clinking off the shield. The robot tried to stand back up but stumbled backward a little and lost its footing. Its shield went slamming from its hand as it hit the ground, and the woman stabbed downward, hitting the robot in the stomach.

With a cry of anguish, it brought its hands to its stomach, where blood violently began to pool while the sword was being removed. "Please, just kill me," it pleaded. The woman brought the sword up again and drove it into the robot's heart. A gasp left its mouth, and then it lay there, bleeding and lifeless. All at once, the woman bent over and vomited on the ground next to the lifeless robot.

She came back to the group trembling. "It all felt so real." She began to cry a little.

"That's what it's meant to feel like. That's your humanity—that's why it is so important to separate from yourself when the time comes when you may be faced to kill an actual person." Nikola put a reassuring hand on her shoulder.

One by one, each trainee went out to fight their opponent. Most came back visibly shaking, besides Travis, who bent down to wipe his blade on the robot's white suit. But even he looked a little disturbed as he returned to the group. After him, Rose went, and I heard her apologize to the robot before slicing its head off. Blood spurted into the air, and it fell sideways to the ground. By the time I was up, the field was riddled with dead bodies. The whole scene was completely horrific, even if these were just artificial beings.

I went forward to meet my contender, expecting a hard-fought fight. Immediately when I got up to it, the shield dropped from its hands. "Just do it," it said. Slowly, I brought the blade up and swung it at the neck of the robot. It got lodged halfway through, and when I brought it out an impossible amount of blood sprayed and dripped from the wound. I saw a shiny metal bar where the spinal cord should have been. It was bent to the side, with a few wires fraying out. It was the most revolting sight I think anyone could witness. The robot let out a gurgling noise, and its head tilted off to the opposite direction.

"Finish it!" Nikola screamed out to me. With another blow, I took the rest of its head clean off, and it slumped forward into me, smearing a long, wide line of blood from the hole in its neck down half the front of my suit before I jumped back. The sharp metal rod cut through part of my jumpsuit and slid shallowly through my skin, its blood covering most of my face. I wiped at my eyes.

Fuck, if it was this hard to kill a robot, I didn't think I could ever willingly take an actual person's life. That was the most horrifying experience I'd ever had—it was so re-alistic. I walked back to the group, doing everything in my power not to end up throwing up. But when I got back, I doubled over and vomited water all over the ground. I sat down and waited for the rest of the recruits to finish off their robots, but looked off in the direction of the forest instead of watching. But the disembodied sounds that came out of the dying robots might have been worse. All I knew was that I wanted to get the hell out of there. Eventually, the last body dropped.

"Okay, I think that's quite enough for today," Nikola told us, and we all headed back onto the bus to the apartment building. The rest of the day, I just sat on the couch, trying to get the image of the half-headed robot out of my mind. It was no use. It seemed this was one of those images that would never leave my mind. I tried to replace it with an image of Violet, but that morphed into her being half-decapitated, and I threw up again onto the table in front of the couch. Afterward, I got into the shower to wash off all the blood I could. It seemed like no matter how hard I scrubbed, the blood wouldn't come off. It's easy washing away your own blood; washing away someone else's is a different story entirely. Getting out of the shower, I still felt filthy. Hoping this feeling would eventually go away, I got a pill for dinner and some water. Luckily, the pill stayed down and I went to bed, caught in a nightmare of replaying the moment over and over again.

CHAPTER 29

The next couple weeks consisted of the same routine. Wake up, pop a pill, head to the arena, participate in a variation of the tests, run laps, work out, head home, shower, pop a pill, go to sleep. Almost every night, my dreams varied from either a memory I had of Violet, or me haphazardly hacking off someone's head. It wasn't always the robot's. Sometimes it was someone I knew from either the new or the old world, but normally it was some complete stranger. I wondered how many more of these dreams it would take to drive me completely insane.

A couple times throughout the weeks I would try to leave the building to go for a walk to clear my head. Each time, I was stopped by the receptionist telling me that we were not allowed to leave yet. Periodically, Lydia would call and we would talk on the phone for a while, exchanging pleasantries and talking about what our training entailed and how we were feeling. She would always tell me about how bad she felt for me when she was reminded of some of the tests I went through. For the most part, hers had completely involved helping people. Learning how to stitch, give CPR, cauterize a wound, use a tourniquet, and a variety of other medical skills that I didn't understand. Like auxiliary genetics, which she didn't seem to have a full grasp on either, but from what she explained it sounded like entirely replacing faulty genes. She went on in her longwinded way that it was extremely complicated and reserved for the higher-ups in her faction, but that she was there to assist them when need be.

At first I felt bad for what she went through with her tongue, but the roles quickly reversed when we both realized how much more mentally and physically taxing my duties were. We'd always make promises to one another that once we were allowed to leave, we would meet up in person. As of yet, that hadn't happened, and I didn't know how far into the future we would actually be able to do that, if at all. She would always tell me how happy she was that I was in her life, and would eventually end our conversations in an upbeat 'love ya.' Not in a romantic type of way, but in a familial sense. It took me a while to say it back without it being awkward and forced, but after all of our talks, I really did come to see her as a little sister.

For the most part, none of the faction members really talked to each other. There were of course a couple people who paired up into friend groups, but even they wouldn't talk much while we were all together. I still hadn't heard anything from Harold or his wife, even though the receptionist assured me that they were in good hands. I couldn't help but run through my head why

I couldn't talk to them, while they let me talk to Lydia so freely. For weeks, nothing remarkable happened. It was the same thing, day in and day out, over and over again. Until I got a knock on the door.

PART 2:

CHAPTER 30

A nother knock tapped at the door. I cautiously got up and walked toward it. Almost before I'd unlatched the door, the person pushed their way in. Standing in front of me was Rose, a piece of paper in her hand. Scrawled on it was *act normal*. What the hell was normal about this? Rose had probably said a combined twenty words to me since I first met her, and here she was, standing in the middle of my apartment. Her face was calm, but clearly determined.

"Hi Rose," I said, unsure of where to begin talking to her.

"Hi Louis, it's good to see you." She scrawled on another page of the notepad—this time it read, *they're listening.*

I had so many questions immediately, but decided it would probably be a good idea to go along with Rose's little charade. "Good to see you too," I replied. "What brings you here?"

"I just wanted to see how you're holding up. This training regimen is pretty brutal."

"It is," I agreed, while she scribbled a longer note on her pad, "but I'm getting used to it." The bruises and scrapes on my face had completely disappeared by this point. Besides minor cuts and bruises on the rest of my body, I was in relatively good shape.

"Yeah, me too. It was really rough at first. I'm glad that you've made it this far; I was really scared not knowing what we were going to have to do." This time she turned around the paper to show me a long note written on it. *I need you to beat out Travis for one of the last two spots for retrieval duty. He can't be trusted. I need people that I can trust.*

At this point, it was apparent that Rose was clearly the frontrunner in our group, while Hera, Travis, another member named Aeneas, and I were all contenders for the second and third spot. The rest of the contenders all periodically rose and fell in the rankings, but we all stood relatively consistent in the top five.

"Same here—my body seems to never recover still." I let out a forced laugh.

"Absolutely." Rose let out the fakest laugh I'd ever heard before scribbling down some more. *I need to know I can trust you.* I mulled the idea over in my head, knowing that clearly she was doing something that the government couldn't find out about. I held my hand out to take the pad and pen, then flipped to a new page and scribbled down, *whatever you need, I'm here. This place is the worst.*

For the first time since I met Rose, she smiled at me and nodded. "So how are you liking life in Arcadia?" she said aloud, and took back the pad and pen.

"I love it so far. Besides the intense training, everything is so beautiful and clean here," I said with my best attempt at false amusement. *Good, we're going to need you,* she wrote down. That sentence was the most confusing of all. Who were 'we'? What was I needed for? What did I just agree to? I asked for the pad and pen back so that I could ask some more questions, but this time Rose shook her head no.

"Yeah, me too," she replied. "I never thought the future would look like this, but I was pleasantly surprised." She tucked the pad and pen back down into the top of her suit. I mouthed 'what the fuck is going on' to her. But she just shook her head again and mouthed 'later.'

"Thank you for stopping by to check on me, I appreciate it," I told her with confusion in my eyes. She sympathetically smiled, and I suddenly questioned why I even told her that she could trust me. I certainly didn't trust her, but was too blindsided to question her motives at that point. Besides, this place really was fucking terrible—there was nothing to do but train and wait around for training to begin the next day. I hoped that she was planning to make an escape and we could try our luck on the other side of the wall.

"Oh, I almost forgot—I brought you a razor to shave with. You've been looking a little scruffy lately, and I didn't know if you figured out how to order one yet." She laughed a little and held out her empty hand.

"Thank you," I replied, and pretended to grab the non-existent razor. She was actual right about that one—my beard had grown longer than I'd normally prefer. I did have a razor though, I was just too tired after training to care about my appearance.

"Good to talk to you. I'll see you in the arena tomorrow," she said, and opened the door to leave.

"See you then," I replied, and went back down to sit on the couch. What the fuck was that about? I sat and thought about the million different outcomes that our chat could lead to. All of them seemed crazy, and most of them ended with both of us winding up dead. But honestly, death would be preferable if the monotony of it all continued. Coming back to do nothing but wait for that uniformity to commence all over again. Maybe after training was over, the tedium would change. But I didn't have high hopes, and figured because of the austerity of this society that it would be similar for the rest of my life. I contented myself to hope that what she was implying was an escape from this prison of a city.

I hadn't even really seen any of the city, and already the poison of it was slowly killing me. I'd rather die a quick death trying to do something than continue wasting away in this gilded penitentiary. I walked over to the window and saw people strolling outside on the sidewalk, wondering if once my training was done if I would be able to be one of them. Rain started to trickle, an occasional drop slipping down the window.

Eventually, I decided to act on what Rose had said. I went to the bathroom to shave off my overgrown beard. Baby steps, I thought to myself, and laughed. Laughed at my unsure future, which seemed to be becoming more unsure by the day. I thought that once the routine kicked in, I would be able to come to peace with my situation in the new world. I had too much of the old world in me, though. This was never going to work. I didn't know how I'd convinced myself that it would, if I ever had.

I was going to make that second spot in the retrieval unit, I decided. I had to.

CHAPTER 31

A few days passed with the same training regimen in place. I was exhausted getting ready to board the bus on our way back to the scout building one afternoon when Nikola stopped me. He placed a hand on my shoulder as I was stepping on and gently pulled me back off without saying a word. I caught a glimpse of a confused look on Travis's face as I wheeled around and back onto the pavement. "Walk with me," Nikola suggested.

"Sure," I said, confused, with a slight worry in the back of my mind that I had done something wrong.

"Don't worry, you're not in trouble." He gave a reassuring smile as the bus started to pull away. "Just wanted to talk to you about a few things." I felt a weight lift, but the feeling was short-lived as another weight of what he could possibly want to talk to me about replaced it. The bus was soon out of sight as he led me toward where the massive parking lot met a large field, where far off in the distance a portion of the wall broke the horizon. The sun was hovering over the edge of it like a halo in an old renaissance painting. Suddenly, my mind flashed back to the conversation with Rose, and I had an eerie feeling that he had found out about her plan and was going to get me to divulge the information she had told me. I shifted uncomfortably as we sat down on one of the many benches on the threshold of the parking lot and the field. He must have sensed my discomfort as he placed a hand on my shoulder. "It's going to be okay. I just need you to tell me what Rose came to talk to you about the other day."

My stomach dropped as the feeling of his hand on my shoulder started to feel like a weight pinning me down to the bench. I shifted again, uncomfortably. I really wasn't a good liar, but I gave it my best shot. "I don't know what you mean."

"Oh come now, I know you know that lying right now isn't in your best interest," he said calmly, with the tone of a parent telling you that they weren't mad, they were just disappointed.

I swallowed hard, but it felt like there was a cotton ball shoved down my throat. "Seriously, I haven't talked to her about anything in particular, besides training and how we're both taking it." My hands started to sweat as I wiped them on my pants. He took notice and gave me a meek smile, then with his hand on my shoulder gently turned me to look at him and put it down in his lap.

"I need you to be honest with me." He smiled. "I promise that you won't get in any trouble for any information that she has given you. As long as you come clean now, there won't be any repercussions for you. In fact, it might secure your spot as a top contender for the Scouts. We need honest, reliable people."

A thousand thoughts went through my head at once, and I took a longer pause than I probably should have while Nikola kept politely staring at me. I cleared my throat and chose my next words very carefully, knowing that saying the wrong thing could lead to some very serious implications. "I..." I cleared my throat. "She didn't say anything else." That lie came out much clearer than I had expected. Probably because it wasn't technically a lie. She wrote those things, but never said anything else.

"We caught her on camera walking in with some contraband, entering your room. A pen and paper. Contraband that has been outlawed for faction members to have since the last rebellion. I highly doubt she was there to draw you pictures." He smiled gently. "Now what did she write?"

The ridiculous idea that pen and paper were considered contraband almost made me laugh. But then the severity of the situation forced another chokehold around my throat. All that came out was a weak *hhhh*. Like I was trying to fog up some glass the way I used to when I was a kid. In all honesty, I hadn't felt this way since I was a kid, when I got caught marking up the walls with crayon and thought the interrogation from my parents was going to end in a death sentence. Only this time, that could very well be the outcome.

"I don't know," I said firmly. "She never showed me that she had either of those." I decided to stick to my story of naiveté, knowing now that it was probably too late to turn back. It was probably too late to turn back right from the beginning. Suddenly, an anger started boiling inside me. I was being set up. And I was being set up by one of the few people in the whole fucking city that I thought I could trust.

"Last chance," he said, but this time his face wasn't friendly. More like a lion who had just surrounded his prey and knew there was no escape.

"I can't tell you what I don't know. I'm sorry." My words came out clear, but even I could hear the anger in my voice.

He took a long pause, stood up, and looked out in the distance at the wall. Then he turned back at me, his inquisitive face now replaced by two cheery brown eyes. "Very good." He grinned. "Although you're certainly going to have to work on your lying skills. But I knew you wouldn't give her away."

"What?" I asked, genuinely confused now.

"We just needed to know that you wouldn't easily give away any of our plot. Although next time, if it isn't one of us, they're likely going to start doing some things that could get really painful." He grimaced a little, but then shook my shoulders and smiled again. "It's good to know we have people like you on our side."

Still not knowing whether this was a trick or not, I remained silent.

He laughed knowingly. "I know exactly what she wrote to you, but you still need to keep up the good work. For a little while, we thought that Travis could be a good addition to the team, because there is no doubt in his skill. But after seeing his continued disregard for the other faction members' safety and complete self-absorption, our focus quickly shifted to you. It appears that focus may pay dividends for us."

There was no way that he would have known that was exactly what Rose was writing to me without being a part of it, so I took a deep sigh. "You assholes," I said in relief.

He let out a hearty laugh. "We are, aren't we?" He gestured for me to get up, so I stood and started walking with him along the edge of the vast field. "But everyone's an asshole. At least we're the good ones. Relatively speaking, that is." He flipped around his tablet that he always had on him and then put it back away. My heart started back at a normal pace as I got over the fact that I was just in a situation that could have ended very differently. "We're not trying to haze you or anything. We just need to find out who we can rely on when push comes to shove. You'll have your place in the revolution. It may not be a pivotal role, but every supporting character is vital."

"I suppose so. God, you almost just gave me a heart attack." I didn't notice until then, but my hands were shaking vigorously. Sounds of the whirring city started to fill my ears again as I noticed that it had all been blocked out in my mind as I carefully chose my words.

"Yeah, sorry about that. I do really like you though, Louis. I see great potential in you, and I have from the first day of training—how you decided to help that kid up when you knew that finding a flag first was your task at hand."

"Anyone would have done the same," I thought aloud. "Except Travis, I suppose."

"No, not just anyone. A couple of people saw the kid sprawled out and didn't think twice before continuing on. Whether you like it or not, you have greater empathy than a lot of people are born with in this day and age." I thought about the statement for a second, disagreeing in my head. I was never more empathetic than anyone else. Sure, I cared about other people, but that's just human nature. But maybe some people had more humanity than others. The future seemed to have pretty low standards if I was the epitome of an empath just for helping a kid up. My train of thought was broken up by the whirring of a car stopping in front of us.

"Here," he said. "I'll give you a ride home."

"Thanks." I walked around to the other side of the car and waited for the doors to rise before I sat down. The interior exactly resembled the car that I had taken from the testing site. Every vehicle looked almost identical on the outside as well, ranging from the wide variety of colors, white to gray, with the occasional black car making sporadic appearances.

"So how are you faring?" he asked. My shock at the genuine question must have been apparent. "I know it's a hard world we live in. But we're going to change that." He turned to me to smile. "All of us together."

"I'm doing alright, I guess. There are plenty of times where I wish that I had never been found at all and would have just lived out the rest of my days in the cryogenic abyss. But knowing that we're working toward something actually feels nice." The astonishment of saying it out loud made me realize that when Rose had come, that was the first time I had felt hopeful about anything since I had reached the city. "I do miss my time though."

"I'm sure." He frowned sympathetically. "You had to leave some people behind, huh?"

"Yeah." I choked up a little as Violet crossed my mind again like a strike of lightning. It was like my mind in the new world was a violent storm, where sometimes she would leave momentarily, but it was only a moment before a hard crack illuminated the reality that she was gone again. And each bolt brought the pain back just as strong as ever. I wondered often if each crack would start to hurt less and less, or at the very least not strike so often. So far, they hadn't. "I left my whole world."

"Do you want to talk about them?" he asked. "We've got time."

I did. I wanted to talk about her to anyone who would listen. I wanted her to live on through my words, and maybe telling someone else would keep her alive longer. Or maybe I just needed someone to know how much worse off the world was without her. "I know it sounds stupid. But she was my other half. Hell, she was more than half of who I am.

You go on living your life and everything is fine until that one person comes along. That one person that, once they are there, you don't know how you got along without them up until that point. We were always there for each other, to push each other toward things that we didn't even know we were capable of. It just hurts more than anything knowing that I wasn't there for her in the end. It's hard to accept the fact that I'm still alive and living a life that should have been with her. We had our whole lives ahead of us together, and then we had our whole lives ahead of us without each other. It really doesn't make any sense to me. I feel fine now after that stupid syringe, and I keep having the feeling that I could wake up at any moment and be back in bed with her. Waking up to another perfectly imperfect day. But now she has already lived her whole life, and I have my life ahead of me. Time is such a fucked up construct." I forgot that I was talking to anyone—it just felt like things that I needed to say. "Wow, sorry, it's just... the world is a fucked up place."

He leaned over and gave me an awkward hug over the seats. "There's no need to be sorry." The embrace released something in me, or maybe it was just the word waterfall that I had let out. But my chest got tight and tears started rolling down my face. I was embarrassed, but it didn't make any difference. It still felt good to cry, and to be hugged. Genuinely hugged. I forgot how comforting a hug could truly be. "The world is a fucked up place," he agreed, "and I am sorry from the bottom of my heart that nothing can bring her back." I nodded and tried to pull back from the hug, but he held me in place. I conceded and stopped pulling away, understanding that this was exactly what I needed. With my forehead resting on his shoulder, I let the rest of the tears out, then sat back up and wiped at my eyes.

"Thank you," I said awkwardly. I had never cried in front of anyone else like that before. Not even Violet. There were many times I'd cried with Violet, but having her there was a comfort, knowing that no matter what we went through, she was there. But not having her there made the water-works come on tenfold. "…And I'm sorry. I'm not normally this emotional," I said sheepishly, with a small chuckle.

"Don't be sorry—you're going through something that very few people throughout all of history have gone through. Everyone experiences loss and death, but your situation is entirely different. You lost the chance to live a full life with the person that completes you, and you both had... have... to live full lives knowing that the other person was essentially dead. That's heavy. An extremely heavy burden to carry. But I am always here if you need someone to talk to, or a shoulder to lean on while you carry that burden. No matter how alone you may feel in this world, you have us. All of us."

"I appreciate it, Nikola. You have no idea what this means to me," I told him from the bottom of my heart. It was the first time in the new world that I truly didn't feel alone. Sure, I'd made connections and friendships, but I still felt isolated. His listening to me and just being there while I cried made all the difference. It made me realize that although the most important person in the world would never be there again, at least there were other important people who could be.

"Call me Nikki," he said, and smiled. "That's what friends are for."

"Thank you, Nikki," I told him as I got out of the car and onto the sidewalk filled with other faction members walking around.

He leaned over. "Keep your head in the game. The fin-ish line is within sight." Before I could say anything, the door closed and the car was moving.

"I will," I said quietly to myself. "I will."

CHAPTER 32

The next few weeks went by quicker than I would have liked. Even though the training was just as rigorous, the thought of what was to come after was even more frightening. I noticed that subtly, Rose would periodically do things that would help me out without gaining the attention of anyone else. When we would be searching for flags in the forest, she would pass in front of me and a flag would 'accidentally' slip out of her suit and land in front of me. Searching for the flags was easily the thing that I was the worst at, and she knew it.

After our chat in my apartment, I went from normally placing in the bottom third of the faction members in the forest to always one of the top five. Nikki took notice of my newfound retrieval success and even commented in front of the other recruits how much I had improved since the first day when I got my face smashed in. They wouldn't show us the ranks often, but at the end of each week we got to know our place—though no one else's. At the end of the first week after the Rose visit, I was in fourth place. I knew that I was basically a shoo-in for the spot, but that didn't stop me from trying harder and harder each time. I needed to prove my spot, for myself if no one else.

At the beginning of the next week, when Travis arrived, he had a limp which caused him to start falling behind in all of the agility aspects of training. He still excelled in the sandpit and forest, but ended up coming near last on the obstacle course multiple times in a row. It was pretty obvious to me that Rose had given him a 'talking' to by the glances of pure hatred he gave toward her. I would have been worried for what Travis was probably plotting against her if Rose were anyone else. But she could clearly handle her own, and always seemed ten steps ahead of the rest of us.

Hera also beat me out in almost every regard except for shooting. By this point, I was consistently hitting almost every target dead center—not even Rose matched my skill level in that regard. Although she always hit every target, it was clear my marksmanship was better. For a little while, she would glance over at my targets and nod, but after a week or so she didn't even pay attention anymore. At the end of the week, my ranking had risen to three. Good. Now I just needed to keep it that way going into the final week.

The final week began normally, but escalated immediately. It seemed everywhere you looked, someone was getting the tar kicked out of them by someone else trying to raise their rankings. Some of the faction members didn't partake in the brawl, probably because they were too far down in the rankings and were content with residing themselves to wall duty. Wall duty was probably safer anyway, albeit boring.

People would emerge from the forest regularly with battered bodies, trying to hide their limps from Nikki. It became a new normal for the first people up the wall to enthusiastically kick any other faction member in reach, sending them sprawling to the ground. At one point, Travis even kicked another member into the net of electricity causing them to get stuck and be violently electrocuted until another member pulled them back to safety while getting shocked themselves. Both members lay dazed on the ground for a minute until they both got up weakly and headed down under the net.

In the sandpit, every person I faced since Rose I had beaten, until Travis, who gladly went about trying to smash my face in again until he knocked me out for a second time. Toward the end of the week, I faced Rose again, who this time made a big spectacle of showing how evenly matched we were now. I knew that if she wanted it, I would be down on the ground gasping for air again in a matter of seconds. But her punches and kicks, although very convincing, landed much lighter on me. It ended with me getting a solid punch to the side of her face, and she took a dive.

The final day before getting our results, we did all the different forms of training, and ended with another wave of sickeningly realistic robots. It ended like any other day in the training grounds. There were no announcements, nothing. Just back to the apartment where most of us were nervously awaiting the news that would come tomorrow. Even with all the thoughts swirling through my head, the exhaustion from the last month took its toll and I fell asleep immediately.

CHAPTER 33

I awoke to the sound of a bird crashing into the window of my bedroom. A small trace of blood smeared the window, as if an ominous premonition of what was to come. Being uncertain of my placement in the faction was unsettling to say the least. My stomach felt as though I had gotten stuck on a tilt-a-whirl for years and finally gotten off only to find that the ground was sinking from underneath me. My mind was surprisingly clear, however. There were only two things I could think of: one option being that I would start my role in Rose and Nikki's plan, the other that I would be stuck indefinitely wasting away in this hellhole.

After getting ready and going downstairs, I found everyone talking more than I'd seen prior. Probably to avoid the uncertain future the day would hold for us all. The only person not speaking to anyone was Rose. Besides our chat in my apartment, she hadn't said a word to me since.

"You ready to watch that wall?" Travis said, and came up to pat me on the back. "I heard you might even get the chance to wash the bird shit off." He smirked at me, but behind his eyes I could see fear. He was uncertain of his placement too. He pulled me close and whispered in my ear, "Someone might have an accident out in the wastes too while I'm out there. I'd do my best to save her." He faked a cough. "I mean them. But I honestly don't know if I could. It's just so dangerous," he finished saying with an overwrought frown.

"Good luck with that," I said, laughing. "You've seen how many times she's handed your ass to you on a silver platter."

"Fists aren't the only part of my repertoire," he said, patting the pistol on his hip. His attempt at intimidation fell on deaf ears. Rose wouldn't let a little punk like him take her out. Plus, I'd seen his shooting—she would need to be pretty damn close for him to do any sort of damage. At that moment, the sliding glass door opened for the last time during our training period. We all hopped on the bus and waited nervously while it drove us back to the arena. My forefinger tapped at the side of my leg rapidly, like it would when my anxiety got the best of me. I focused on controlling my breathing and looked out the window to see the massive white buildings looming on either side of the bus. In my mind, they looked like they could tip over and crush us all at any second. Maybe that wouldn't be such a bad thing.

The bus whirred to a halt, and everyone exited promptly. We walked under the arch that we had dozens of times before. But this time it looked different. The flags were now all the same symbol of Arcadia. This time, there was a small crowd in the stands—about thirty people, all dressed in black, except one woman in red. The same one who had first met us upon our arrival into the city. On either side of her were Nero and Philomena, while Nikki walked us forward. All at once, a portion of the ground parted, and a stage rose up through the ground. On it were exactly fourteen seats, and a podium toward the front of it. Nikki gestured for us to follow.

We each took a seat behind the podium as Nikki addressed the crowd with his back to us. "Madam Chancellor and citizens of Arcadia," he eloquently addressed the crowd. "As you know, we are here to celebrate what is always a momentous occasion. The culmination of the hard work that each and every one of our initiates endured throughout the last month. These fine individuals have left their old lives behind to become the mortar which holds the framework of our society together. For that, Arcadia is eternally grateful." He paused to look back at us and smile. "As you all know, without the Scouts to protect our walls, to protect us from what lies beyond, and to protect our way of life as we know it, there would be no Arcadia. So can we have a round of applause for our 627th division of Scouts, and to the future of our city?"

The small crowd broke out into scattered applause, and I saw the woman in red give an assuring nod. She must have been the chancellor. As I wondered if she oversaw all the commencement ceremonies, Nikki began to speak again. "I won't keep you here long, because I know you all have important business to attend to. So without further ado, may I present the first-place Scout, who will join the brave men and women who risk their lives out in the wastes so that the men, women, and children of our fine city can sleep soundly at night."

He paused and turned around to gesture at Rose.

"Scout 101022 will you please rise?" She stood and got a small round of applause from the crowd. The chancellor leaned forward a little and squinted her eyes. Then she gave a small and elegant couple claps. After she leaned back, Nikki continued. My finger was still tapping the outside of my thigh, although now less rapidly, like I was trying to send a message in Morse code but couldn't remember any words. "The second seat is given to Scout 100973—will you please stand up?" Hera rose to her feet, her face looking astonished, and she glanced back at me. I gave her a waning smile. I was happy for her, she really deserved it, but now my heart started racing, waiting for who was going to be the third and final seat. I knew that it was supposed to be me, but if life had taught me anything, there were no assurances. Looking over at Travis, I could see that he was just as worried. The normal terrible grin that he wore was nowhere to be seen. His hands rubbed at his thighs.

I closed my eyes and wished that I were anywhere but here in this moment. I thought a thousand thoughts in what was only a few seconds, while the applause for Hera died down. I tried to picture Violet's face, but to my horror, it had already started to fade in my mind. I didn't think it could possibly happen that quick. Her eyes, however, would always be etched into me. Those impossibly beautiful eyes. Then, all at once, I opened my own eyes and everyone was staring at me. "101023? Hello? Will you please stand up?" I heard Nikki say with a soft chuckle.

The words sounded foreign to me, but I shakily stood up. "Congratulations," he said, beaming at me. More light applause from the crowd. "And that concludes the initiates to join the retrieval team." I looked over at Travis to see his reaction. He was staring at the ground, his right leg tapping away. "As for the rest of you, your duties are arguably more important—you are the last line of defense against whatever lies—" His speech was cut short with an almost inaudible *tsst*. Nikki slumped forward over the podium and slid, hitting his face on the way down. A red hue painted small lines down the back of the podium. Everyone sat dazed for a second until Rose got up and ran over to Nikki to flip him over to look at the sky. Someone in the crowd immediately pulled out a tablet, and soon after, Travis's arms snapped behind him and secured themselves to his back. The gun in his hand went flying off the stage from the momentum. Everyone in the stands stayed remarkably still. I couldn't process what was happening. It all happened so quickly, and then my brain, body, and heart took the shock at the same time. Like I had been the one shot, and the bullet had pierced my heart. But I stood motionless.

"Nikola?" Rose asked as she shook him, but immediately she knew it was too late. We all knew.

"Fucking prick," Travis spat at the body lying behind the podium. Rose gave him a hard kick, and he went sprawling off the side of the stage. With a loud exhale, Travis hit the ground on his stomach as he gasped for air and wriggled about. Two of the men in the stands casually walked down and picked Travis up off the ground. They dragged him back toward the arch as he screamed out profanities at no one. I went over to Rose; she had a tear falling down her face. Looking at Nikki's face, I took a couple steps back. There was a fading orange glow in the melted socket of his left eye. Blood pooled up and began running down the sides of his face into Rose's hands. She let go and backed up. I looked back up into the crowd and saw the chancellor—she stood still, but her eyes looked devastated. She whispered, then Philomena and Nero got up immediately and ran down to Nikki. Nero immediately wrapped himself over Nikki and held his head in an embrace. I could see now that he was crying heavily. Philomena stood over the both of them and crouched down to run her hands through Nikki's now blood-stained wiry orange hair. She kissed the top of his head, which left blood smeared around her lips like a gruesome shade of lipstick.

"Nikki," Nero sobbed into his chest. "What am I supposed to do without you?"

CHAPTER 34

She sobbed into my chest. We both knew that this had been a long time coming, but that didn't stop the hurt. I looked down over the body. It was always an unusual feeling looking at a body whose life had left it. They looked like they were sleeping, but at the same time, they looked nothing like that. It's one of the strangest feeling juxtapositions in the world seeing a body like that, where only minutes before they were talking to you. The sounds of the hospital faded out—all I could hear was her sobs that filled the room. Her mom died when she was a kid, and we were the only family that she had left in the world. Now I was her only family. The thought made me start to cry. She was the most loving person anyone could know, and the fucked up world loved tormenting her. Of course, everyone dies, that's inevitable. But life was completely unfair to her—it always was.

"I know he wouldn't want me to cry," she sniffled as she looked up at me with her beautiful, tear-stained, blue-green eyes.

"When did you ever do what he wanted you to?" I said lovingly. Violet had always had a rebellious streak. Sneaking into houses where the families were away to steal alcohol as a teenager. Smoking weed in school wherever she could find a place. Running from the police. Getting caught by the police. But no matter what she found herself getting into, her father was always there to try and set her on the right path. He never got mad; he would always just be there to pick her up at her lowest points. Even when she got picked up by the police for attempting to smuggle chickens out of a farm while high on acid. Even when she had to battle her way out of a heroin addiction. Though she struggled with the thoughts daily, she was proudly five years and counting clean. He always knew, or at least hoped, that she would find her way onto the right path. He was right.

She laughed through her tears and slapped me on the chest. "I really didn't. Did I?"

"No," I said firmly. We both laughed, and she wrapped her hands around me and pushed her cheek up to mine to look at him. "He was so proud of you," I told her.

"I know. I was so proud of him too." She stared at his face, his eyes closed and arms gently resting beside him. Then she reached out to grab one of his hands. "I'm going to miss you, Dad." She wiped at her tears with her other hand.

"He may be gone, but the love never will be," I said as I gently lay my hand on her cheek to wipe away some more of the tears.

"I know." She took a deep breath and sighed. We stayed there for well over an hour in silence as we both stared at him. Eventually, Violet stood up, squeezing his hands. "I don't know what I'm supposed to do without you."

CHAPTER 35

Nikki's body was covered with a sheet and carried off
on a stretcher toward a car awaiting his arrival under
the arch. The car hummed off and the crowd departed. We
were left by ourselves with Nero and Philomena. Nero was
seated at the edge of the platform with his hands over his
face and his elbows in his lap. For a long while, he didn't
say anything, Then he spoke, softly at first. "It's a tragedy.
Nikola was one of the best we had. He was my best friend,
my brother. Now you all will have to try and fill the massive
hole that Nikola's passing leaves in Arcadia." He turned to
look at us—we were all silently listening. A couple of the
other Scouts were crying softly. Even though he pushed us
hard, Nikki was never too hard on any of us. He was one
of the best people here. I had only known him a short time,
and it felt like losing a close friend. I could see why Nero
was so crushed by his passing.

Philomena walked over and laid a hand on Nero's shoulder. "He died proudly. He was proud of all of you. Whenever we spoke to him, he told us of how exceptional the group of you are. Please, for the sake of Nikki, continue to make this city proud." Nero shook his head gently. Philomena didn't notice, and continued. "Without him, we will need to fill his spot as one of the four faction leaders."

"This isn't the time to talk about this," Nero hissed back at Philomena.

"Yes Nero, it is. Nikola's passing is a tragedy, but that doesn't mean the cogs of the city stop turning. We will have to make a decision as soon as possible and clear it by the chancellor." She spoke directly at Nero as if none of us were even there.

"Fuck that. You're not even going to let his body get cold before you replace him? That's bullshit, you know it. The city will be fine," he shouted back.

"Perhaps." She turned his angry tirade over in her head. "Perhaps not. You know they will be expecting us to choose someone swiftly." Nero slapped away Philomena's hand, which was still gently resting on his shoulder. Without saying another word, he hopped off the stage and walked away. "I suppose we should get you all home," she addressed the rest of us. She walked down the stairs off the stage, and we followed her back toward the bus that was awaiting our arrival. Nero was walking down the street away from us. We passed him as we drove by, his head staring up toward the clouds.

Hera, sitting next to me, put her hand on mine. "You okay?" she asked.

"Yeah," I replied, feeling false as I said it. Although I was surprised at how okay I was with everything. It was true that Nikki was a genuinely great person, but somehow within the last month I had grown accustomed to the fact that people here were going to die. People I knew about, people I cared about. Hell, Hera could die tomorrow. Rose the next day. Lydia the following day. Me on the fourth. I was sure I would be heartbroken when reality sunk in, but if any of them died, I would be prepared. Sure, I was dejected at Nikki's murder, but it alarmed me that I was okay. "You okay?"

"Yeah," she replied. "I've grown up with this bullshit all my life. It's better not to get close to anyone." She pulled her hand off of mine.

"I'm sure. It's hard not making connections in such a lonely city. Make sure nothing happens to you. Okay?"

"I'll do my best." She laughed and smiled.

"So they were talking back there about choosing a new fourth. Who was it?"

"Augustus?" she asked.

"He's the fourth? Do you know what happened to him?" I asked, concerned.

"No. But he was one of the four people that I met at the weird forest room that I had to find my way out of. About a week before we started training."

"Yeah, he was taken away with a sack over his head when we got off the train." I paused. "They said something about how he didn't give us proper instructions because one of the people in my train group talked out of turn."

She held her hand to her mouth in shock. "They took him?" she asked, alarmed.

"Yeah, they did."

"Oh shit, and over not giving directions properly? That seems like an awfully small mistake to be taken for."

"I take it he isn't the first."

"Far from it. Most people, once taken, are never heard from again." She studied my face to see the immediate alarm.

"Nero said he was going to visit him shortly after it happened and that he was in Hedone's hands now? Was he talking about the Greek goddess?"

She actually laughed, but shortly after seemed to remember the situation and her face went grave again. "Yeah, the idiots out there practice under Hedonism. That's why we're all actually here, to fulfill their need to self-indulge. Why, what did people practice in your day?"

"All types of religions—Christianity, Judaism, Hinduism, Islam, and countless others."

She stopped me. "Maybe they're still practicing that out there." She pointed at the wall out in the distance. "But here, it's better not to talk about any of that stuff. Religion is dangerous. Especially when it's not a religion that our leaders agree with."

"Noted." I nodded my head. "Can we go back to what you were saying about being taken?"

"I can't. I'm sorry." She looked around. "All we know is that if you're taken, it's essentially a death sentence. Or at least no one knows exactly where they end up. Sometimes they're strung up, but more likely than not they just disappear."

"Shit," I replied as the bus pulled up to our building.

"Yeah," she said, and stood up to get off. I followed and took the elevator back up to my room.

CHAPTER 36

The next couple of days were surreal. It was so strange being able to completely accept the events that had transpired, especially to someone as kindhearted as Nikki was. Disgustingly, the only thought I had was that the real maddening thing was the fact that there was nothing to do in the apartment. I could only imagine that was what being in solitary confinement was like. The only respite I had was being able to talk to Lydia and Hera periodically. I would call Rose, but she never answered. Maybe she was fearful that I would say something that would jeopardize her plans, or maybe something had happened to her. There was no way of knowing. On occasion, I would leave the apartment and wander up and down the halls. Riding the elevator. Hanging out in the lobby. We still weren't allowed to leave. I would mess with the receptionist, talking her ear off and asking her questions. She didn't seem to mind. There was absolutely nothing else to do. It was completely vexing.

It seemed like it had been weeks when finally the phone rang on day four. "Come downstairs," the familiar voice said. I let out a deep sigh of relief that maybe I would be going somewhere finally. Quickly, I got everything I needed and shot out the door. Down in the lobby, Hera and Rose were waiting. After a moment, I realized that August was there too. In a strange way, I wanted to run up and hug him. After only knowing him for a short period of time, it was still so good to see him. Good to see that he was alive and well. I guess well wouldn't have been the right way to describe it—both of his pinkies were now gone. He had no bruises or anything, but that could have been expected after the amount of time he had been gone. A large scar followed his temple down to the base of his chin on the right side of his face.

"What? Did you miss me?" He smiled at me and shook my hand.

"What happened to you?" I asked, astonished both that he was standing in front of me and that he still had his cheery, sarcastic disposition.

"I accidentally walked into a door," he laughed, and said nothing more about it. "Now, are you guys ready to get into the real shit?" He waited for us all to nod and then spun around and walked out. We all followed. Even though I had nodded, I was in fact not ready to get into the real shit. But at least we were leaving the apartment. So I guess, in a way, I was ready to get into anything at all as long as it meant getting out. "We're tracking down a group of six deserters that are rumored to have been seen by a search drone somewhere about ninety miles west of here. Our job is to get them back. In one piece, if possible."

"Wait, so we're basically bounty hunters?" Hera asked.

"Part of the job description, I suppose. You didn't read the handbook?" He laughed again. It was good to have him back. Some people might not like sarcasm, but August's was a welcome respite from the lack of personality most people seemed to have around here. Outside of the apartment, there was a car waiting for us. I got into the backseat with Hera while August and Rose rode up front. The car sped off, and we were on our way to the unknown. Everything outside looked like business as usual—suddenly, I had a real hatred for these people. Their freedom. I hated it. Or I loved it, I couldn't tell. I had always taken my freedom for granted, and I think most people did in my time. Everyone always complained about the littlest things. I certainly always did. But in the grand scheme of things, nothing seemed to matter but freedom. Tears began welling in my eyes at the thought of all the people throughout history who didn't have their freedom. Even in my time, there were millions of people living under oppression. I had only been here a fucking month; I couldn't even imagine how difficult it was for all those people. The people that were born into bondage. Was it worse to know freedom and lose it, or to never have it at all?

"You okay there, Louis?" Hera asked. Her words snapped me out of the hole of despair my mind was slipping down into.

"Yeah," I lied. I looked away from the window and back toward Hera. "Just thinking about the lives those people lead."

"Best not to think about that," she said. "They all work very hard, too." She looked me in the eyes, shook her head, and pointed at the roof of the car. Either she was trying to tell me that someone was listening, or that the roof was a more interesting thing to be thinking about. Obviously it was the former, so I shut my mouth. "Besides," she said. "We are doing a great service to the West Empire and the city of Arcadia with the work that we do."

"That's true," I replied, and looked back out the window, observing the faces of the people that we passed by. They all wore the same jumpsuits but let what little they were able to show of their personalities shine through in terms of haircuts. People had wildly different styled hair and colors. Some people walked with dogs or cats next to them. As I watched one cat stray a little too close to the street, a man with a bright green almost-buzzcut patted the symbol on his jacket and the cat jumped in surprise and quickly made its way back to its master's side. Small children walked hand in hand with their parents, which filled me with a mixture of emotions. On one hand, I thought of the life that could have been with Violet, but on the other it filled me with an unexplainable sadness. Perhaps it was just the thought of raising a kid in this kind of society. That led me into another pit of consciousness, thinking about the cruelty of the old world and how for many kids it wouldn't have been much better, if not much worse. I shook my head, trying to get the thoughts to stop and just focus on the here and now.

The car sped down the streets until, through the front window, I saw the train station where we had come in. Instead of the large train that we had arrived on, there was a small one with two cars. The front car had circular windows, while the back one was windowless. It was painted with the signature Arcadia white, and *West Empire Recovery* was stamped on the side in perfect black letters. As we got out and moved closer, it became apparent that the train had no wheels and was hovering over the track. I wondered if that was how the first train had been and I just hadn't even noticed it with everything going on. I never saw the wheels, but why would have I really been looking at them? The train was hovering so low off the tracks that it was almost impossible to see that they were missing them anyways. It seemed like years since I had been here.

"Alright, here we go, into the great beyond. Speak now or forever hold your peace, because once we get rolling, there's no turning back," August told us.

"We're right behind you," Hera said.

"I'm already starting to like you," August said with a smile.

"Likewise," she said. "I've heard only great things about you."

"Sounds like you've been talking to a bunch of liars," he laughed, and swiped on his tablet causing the door to whir down, letting us enter the cabin of the front car. Inside, this cabin looked kind of like the one we came in on. It had the same benches, which I assumed turned into those cozy little coffins. But there were also a couple tables with large, cushioned, half-egg-shaped chairs. A tablet was mounted on the wall between windows.

"Take your seats children, we're going for a ride."

CHAPTER 37

As the train shot through the tunnel, darkness engulfed the outside. Then daylight streamed in again, and the view was extraordinary to say the least. From the outside, as the train turned to the left, I got my first view of the enormity of city. The wall, at least a hundred feet tall, spanned for as far as the eye could see. The enormous buildings littered the skyline, but the wall surrounded a great deal of smaller buildings, and as we got farther down the tracks there were either no buildings, or ones that just couldn't be seen from this side of the wall. It seemed like we were just circling the city until eventually the wall kept getting farther and farther away. I looked back at Arcadia as long as I could to judge just how vast it was, and came to the conclusion that I had no idea. The only thing I did come to realize was that it looked like it had to be an almost-perfect circle. We had to have been at least a dozen miles out and the city was still visible when the train took another sharp left turn.

"Like the view?" August finally said, as I realized we all had been completely silent for the last ten or so minutes. "It really is amazing what they managed to build out of the scorched earth that used to be here." I realized I had only been looking at the city and didn't even see everything else. The grass was a beautiful green that stretched out for miles. Flowers bloomed all over, and there were animals frolicking about. Deer were about the only ones that I could see at the speed we were traveling, but there were plenty of them out there. The only thing that marred the scenery was the occasional highway that we would pass over, always cracked and falling apart with greenery growing up through the gaps. Towns, for the most part, were shelled to the ground besides a couple brick buildings that stood as monuments to what once was. There were a few wooden houses along the way that still half stood, but appeared to be in the last stages of returning to the earth.

"So, where exactly are we?" I finally asked. It still looked pretty Midwestern around me.

"We never went far from where I first picked you up, I guess. Arcadia was built on what would have been northwestern Nebraska, pretty close to the border with Wyoming," August told me.

"Why here?" I laughed. "There is absolutely nothing in Nebraska."

"That's exactly why," he laughed. "I guess it's as good a time as any for a little history lesson, if you're down to listen to me ramble."

"Absolutely," I said.

"Well, when the nukes first fell in 2065, they fell so quickly that I don't think the world had time to realize what was happening. The first one fell on New York, which set the entire world into a mad arms race to get their nukes off first.

Within three days, every U.S. city with 500,000 or more people had been nuked, it seemed. Some multiple times over. It was the same with the rest of the world. It seemed like countries didn't really care where they were aiming anymore. Even neutral countries took massive hits from the blowbacks or from nukes that didn't quite hit their targets. By the end of the first week, Europe was basically completely gone. Those who didn't die from the initial blast would either go on to die from radiation or be completely abandoned by the rest of the world. There was no saving them."

"Holy shit," I said with widened eyes.

"Yeah and that was just the beginning," he said solemnly. "World War 3 was over in a matter of weeks. Nobody knows quite how many people died, but it is estimated that around 2.5 billion died from the initial impact or from the secondhand causes of radiation. Immediately, the remaining world superpowers converged to hold a ceasefire. It was signed right then and there, and the war was over. The main clause being a worldwide nuclear disarmament. Every country obliged, and just like that, nuclear power was only used in powering the remaining cities instead of destroying them. However, the survivors from major cities had to begin relocating to smaller cities, which caused a great deal of problems in itself. Famine, water shortage, and governments scrambling to try to regain stability topped the list. Nothing was ever the same following the war."

"How do you know all of this?"

"From books I've smuggled back into the city, and from people I've met outside."

"There's people outside the city?" I asked in stupid confusion.

"Of course there are—people found their way back to living off the land who didn't want to come and join the

West Empire. Technically, we're supposed to bring them back to the city if we can, but when you find a large group of people, they are normally quite happy with the communes that they have set up. Make sure not to mention any of this back in the city, though; there could be some serious repercussions for me, and I'm just recovering from the last slip-up." He laughed again.

"Of course not, so we're not being..." I pointed around the train car.

"Listened to? No. Outside the city, the leaders of Arcadia don't really care about any talk. The real danger lies within the city, of people trying to start a revolution from the inside. They can easily handle anything coming from the outside."

"Makes sense, I guess," I replied.

"Yeah, so anyway," he continued, "the ceasefire didn't last long because of the severe scarcity of resources. Nations decided it was time to take what they could with what they had left. Which leads us into 2071, which was the beginning of World War 4, or informally called World War 3 part two. For the next twenty-seven years, countries were constantly invading or being invaded by other nations. It seemed by this point there were alliances merging and falling apart daily. Allies would turn to enemies and vice-versa, depending on the state of affairs. Eventually, that caused the world to form into four superpowers. The West Empire formed from Canada, the United States, Mexico, Greenland, and most of the South and Central American countries that could still send resources and people north. For the most part, it seemed like the nations in closest proximity banded together simply because of geographical location. Russia, China, North Korea, India, and most Asian countries formed together to become the East Empire.

Countries that allied with the United States, like South Korea and Japan, surrendered immediately after being almost completely wiped out by the force of the East Empire. Australia, New Zealand, and other oceanic countries became the Oceanic Empire. They were peaceful and were left almost completely alone. They have a flimsy alliance with the East Empire today, where they send over resources periodically in exchange for protection. But by this point, it's rumored that their cities make Arcadia look like an ash heap and their power is probably to the point of exceeding the East Empire. So it could only be a matter of time before they stop making payments to the East Empire and things fall apart all over again."

"Oh shit. You have to think that both would want to avoid a war after everything that has happened?" I asked.

"You would think, but you never know. At least Arcadia and the West Empire are small potatoes in comparison, so we live in relative safety over here. Then finally, the African Alliance formed in the relatively untouched countries of South Central Africa. That's where most of the survivors from Europe immigrated to. I've heard they have the highest numbers of people and resources, but they want nothing to do with the fighting and put all of their resources toward their own people and their defenses. It was mainly the East Empire vs. the West Empire in World War 4, and when it became clear that we were going to lose, the presidents met and ended the war. In all honesty, we could have been completely wiped out easily, but everyone was so sick of the fighting that the ceasefire came with no terms but to end the constant bombardments on each other. After the ceasefire, people began forming communes that turned to towns that turned to cities that turned to megacities. With all the old-world resources, the brightest minds were able to pick up where the world left off before the wars and continue advancing. However, the drastic need for work caused those same people to become the Aristocracy and offer shelter to those who needed it. Eventually, those who took shelter became faction members, while the ancestors of those who originally innovated solutions became the Aristocracy."

"Huh." I really didn't know what else to say—it was so much information to take in at once. I looked over at Rose and Hera; Rose was staring out the window while Hera seemed mildly interested in listening to August's account of the events.

"And the rest, as they say, is history."

"So Arcadia is all that is left of the West Empire?" I asked.

"No, there are smaller cities scattered throughout what used to be the United States and one in what was formerly Canada. But Arcadia is the capital city, and without it, the rest of the empire would likely fall to ruins. We should get prepared—we're almost there." August got up and walked toward the back of the train car. As he got next to it, a door slid open, revealing the next compartment. Inside were a couple of cages and another hovering car, as well as some drones attached to the wall. He grabbed a drone off the wall and began pressing buttons on it until it started hovering above the car. Moments later, the train started slowing to a stop. "Alright, everyone hop in—we have business to take care of."

CHAPTER 38

The back door of the train dropped down to the ground, and we shot out of the back like a bullet. I looked back out the window to see the drone tailing us closely. We were now in the ruins of an old small town. There were rolling hills around us, and as we entered the town there was a crumbling sign that said *Chadron State College, Est. 1911.* All of a sudden, the drone darted out in front of us and the car hurriedly followed it. This car, unlike all the ones in the city had a steering wheel, which August gently rested one hand. The car zipped down different streets until it approached one with an old rusted *Main St.* sign. On the street, there were brick buildings, still almost all remarkably intact. Besides masonry crumbling from most of them, it was still easy to imagine what the town once looked like—a small town like many others you would see scattered throughout the Midwest.

CRYO

As the car slowed to a halt, the drone hovered over one of the brick buildings. The windows were all smashed out, and whatever sign had been on the front was long gone. The old tan brick building was wedged in between two red ones. The building on the right had half its surface peeled off, exposing the interior with bricks scattered around it. The drone decreased its altitude until it was directly in front of the far right window on the building. All at once, objects started flying out the window. Chairs, books, bricks, and whatever else was inside. The drone easily floated around them as they came flying at it.

August stepped out of the car. "We can let this end peacefully," he called out.

"The hell we can!" a low voice grumbled from inside. "You know damn well it isn't going to go that way." This time a chair came flying toward August, but it landed well short, splintering into pieces. We all stepped out of the car now and stood behind August.

"The last thing I want is for any of us to get hurt. I know you have other people in there depending on you. Please, do the right thing," August called out again calmly.

"The right thing is letting us go, and letting that fucking city burn to the ground," he replied, and I caught a glimpse. An unkempt beard defined his round face and his eyes were hollowed. He turned around and whispered something I couldn't make out. There was a lot of rustling around, and then a rusty pistol poked its barrel out of the corner of the window. "Just go away—we don't want to hurt you. We know that you're just doing what you have to. But if you come any closer, we won't hesitate to blow your fucking brains out."

August sighed. "You may have more people but you are well aware that if that happens, we are more than equipped to take you all out in a matter of seconds." The man turned around and whispered again, which brought about more loud rustling.

"Just tell them you found us and we were all dead by the time you found us. Please, I'm begging you."

"You know I can't do that," August said sadly, and pointed at the drone.

"Fuck!" he yelled out, and pushed the barrel farther out the window. August ducked a little behind the car, although he never unholstered his pistol. "I guess this is the way it has to be then." We had all ducked behind the car at this point. I saw the man take aim at the drone and fire a first shot. The result was horrifying. With a bang, the gun exploded in his hand, sending the barrel back into his face. He sprawled backward into the darkness of the upper level of the building.

"Shit," August said, unholstering his pistol and running inside.

"Thalia, get out of here!" the man screamed to an unseen person.

"I'm not leaving you," a woman's voice said, remarkably calm.

"Please Thalia, I love you, you know what they'll do to you."

"I know. There is no way I'm leaving you." I didn't hear any more of their conversation as we all followed August inside and up the stairs. The inside of the building's stairwell was completely dark, until we reached a door at the top of the stairs and August kicked it in. Inside the room was a woman holding a bowie knife and the man next to her lying on the ground, propped up against a wall, with blood pouring down his face from where the barrel hit him. Both were wearing polyester clothes that they must have found in town.

"Just please kill me and let her go. They won't question you as long as you come back with one of us." The drone outside was still focused directly on the two fugitives in the room.

"Where are the others?" August asked as he gestured his head toward the drone.

"We got split up when a group of wolves attacked. I have no idea where they are now." The man clearly was lying—the rustling inside the building couldn't have been from just these two. August backed up a little until he was completely out of view from the drone. The room was silent for a second besides the whirring of the drone outside the window.

"Come at me," August said to the man in an almost inaudible whisper. A confused expression formed on the man's face. "Please," he whispered. August, with his back to the wall, shuffled around the room until the man was between him and the window. The man stood up slowly and balled up his fists. At once, he rushed at August, and in the blink of an eye August fired his pistol. The *tsst* from the bullet hissed through the air. There was a crash outside—I walked over to the window to see the drone with an orange, glowing hole smashed on the cracked sidewalk. "Now we can talk freely," August told the man, who was standing there with an even more confused look on his face.

"What do you mean? You're not taking us in?" he asked.

"You know I can't come back empty handed," he told the man sadly.

The man sighed. "Yeah, I figured as much. Just please let Thalia go. I'll go without any more struggle."

"I already told you, I'm not going anywhere without you," Thalia told him.

"Please," he said. "I'll tell them that I forced you to come with me, and then maybe they won't keep coming after you."

"You know that's not going to happen," she replied.

The man nervously looked over at August, and then sighed a deep breath. "You know you'll be safe with the others," he said. "All you have to do is reach the coast. They only need at least one of us. If this man is doing what I think he is doing..." He gestured at August. "He is trying to save you all." August nodded.

"I don't care. There is no living without you." She started to cry and went over to hug the man tightly, his blood dripping onto her shoulder. She backed up again. "If they're taking you..." She raised the bowie knife in her hand quickly to her own throat.

"No!" he yelled.

"I love you—this is the only way," she said, and in a moment her throat was split wide open. Before the man could have another thought, August put a bullet through the middle of his eyes. He stumbled back into the wall and slid down, the hole in the back of his head leaving a neat streak of blood down the dimly lit wall. On the floor, the woman lay gurgling in her own blood for a couple moments until the room was completely silent again. I wanted to ask August why he ended up killing the man, but from the look in his eyes, I could see that it was out of sympathy. A tear formed in his eye as he wiped it away.

"Perks of the job," he said in a choked voice. The whole situation had gone down within a matter of minutes, everything happening so quickly it was hard to process the situation that had just unfolded. The two bodies lay next to each other on the floor as their blood began pooling together. "They both knew that anyone who returns is strung up and made an example of. This was probably for the best, no matter how horrific it looks. At least they got to die together. That's a lot more than can be said about most people."

He sighed and leaned down to examine the bodies closer. "I didn't know these people, but that never makes it any easier." My mind was still trying to wrap around what the hell we were doing, coming to the sinister conclusion that we were bringing people back to their deaths. I said nothing. "Please, you can go now," August said to no one. All of a sudden, a couple wardrobes at the back of the room popped open. A man, two kids, and a pregnant woman came running out and shot down the stairs out the front door. "Good luck," he whispered when they were long gone.

"Help me with them," he told us. He grabbed the man's arms, and Hera took his legs and they dragged him down the stairs back down to the car, while I took the woman's legs and Rose took her arms. There was no emotion on Rose's face as we hauled the body down the stairs. For a small woman, she was remarkably heavy. The thought made my stomach turn, and I felt extremely lightheaded.

Outside, Hera and Rose were loading the man into the back seat. We placed the woman on the other side of the back seat and slammed the door shut. The car took off without any of us inside and headed back toward where we came from. We all stood there silently, watching as the group of four vanished off into the distance down the street.

"How did you know there were more people?" I finally asked.

"There almost always are," he sighed. "I hope they can make it far enough." The street was now silent as we all stood, looking off into nothing but a ghost town. "I suppose I should let the two of you know what the plan is now."

The two of us?

CHAPTER 39

"What is this?" I asked, holding up the small baggie, knowing fully well what it was. Violet was in tears, her legs clutched to her chest on our couch. My heart felt like it was going to fall out of my body entirely. I sat down next to her and put my arm around her, tears gently falling from my eyes as well.

"I haven't used any," she said, staring at the little bag of light brown powder. Since her dad's death, she had gone into a deep depression, her old habits constantly trying to resurface, but her strength up to this point had held out. I was always there for her; I was the only person who could comfort her. But sometimes, even that wasn't enough. It was completely understandable—depression was a monster of unimaginable dynamism, and that monster could take you to places that you never wanted to visit. It was an unexplainably terrible feeling knowing that you couldn't help the one person you loved the most in this world.

Knowing that every word that you said could either help or drive them further away. But I knew from the hurt in Violet's eyes that the feeling was nothing compared to what she was going through.

"We'll get through this," I said. "You'll get through this."

"You have no idea what it's like." Her words cut into me, her harsh tone causing me to pull back for a second. But I put my arm back on her shoulder.

"I know. I don't," I conceded. I'd lost many people in my life, but it was clear she wasn't talking about that. Everyone deals with situations in completely different ways, that can't be helped. Just knowing that I had no idea was probably the most important thing. People can be sympathetic and pretend to know what a person is going through, but unless they struggle with depression themselves, they have no fucking clue. That much I knew.

"I'm sorry, I know you're trying to help." She was crying harder now. I didn't say anything, I just kept my hand on her shoulder, letting her know that I was there. By this point, I realized that just being there was probably the best thing that I could do. I waited, and looked out the window. Snow had just laid a fresh blanket on the ground. The small cherry blossom tree that we had just planted cowered under the falling torrent. At once, she got up and grabbed the bag off the table, then walked quickly down the hallway. I followed until we reached the bathroom. She stared at the toilet a moment, and then back at the bag in her hand. In one motion, she kicked the toilet seat up and feverishly threw the bag into the toilet. We both watched as it swirled its way out of view. She turned around and put her face into my chest and hugged me. I wrapped my arms around her. Then she muffled into my chest, "We'll get through this."

CHAPTER 40

"We'll get through this as long as you both can be trusted," August said. "It's about fucking time this empire of slavery, murder, and deceit falls." My eyes widened. Was this what Rose was talking about when she came to visit? Bringing down the whole fucking empire. I thought at the very most she was talking about escaping the city, not tearing the whole thing down.

"Wait, what?" I said stupidly. My heart was pounding a thousand miles a minute. I looked over at Rose and Hera. Rose was still completely stone-faced, while Hera had the biggest grin.

August laughed. "You told Rose you were all in? Well, this is what all in looks like. I'm going to be honest with you all—there is a distinct possibility that we will all be killed before this is all over. Hell, there is a pretty high probability of it. But I think in each of your hearts, you know this is what needs to be done."

"What about all the people in the city?" I asked. "What is going to happen to them."

August's face got more serious. "Many will die. But as in any successful revolution, that is the price that has to be paid."

"So you mean to tell me that the four of us are supposed to be able to bring down an entire government?" I asked astonished.

"God no." August laughed heartily this time. "We have some people in every faction working together. Up to this point, no one has grown the wiser. However, we are instrumental in finding the necessary components to light the fire. Until now, every past revolution has failed because of one weak link who doesn't have the heart to face the consequences. Every time that link breaks, the repercussions get more and more severe."

Rose carried on, "At first, they would kill off those who wanted to revolt, but the idea of revolution kept on coming. Soon, they started killing off entire families of those who got it into their heads that a change of pace was necessary. Which eventually led us to the last revolt. They had entire faction buildings destroyed through controlled demolitions with explosives. The revolutionaries, along with all the unknowing faction members, all perished alike."

"What? And the rest of the Aristocracy didn't care?" I asked. "They can't all be that evil."

"The leaders used the guise that it was an internal attack of domestic terrorism." Rose shook her head.

"And the people bought that?" I asked.

"Everyone is so brainwashed into thinking that the government is incapable of doing that amount of evil. So yes, they bought it immediately. The government uses their propaganda to convince them of exactly what they want them to believe. So unfortunately, when this all goes down, it seems like there will be an unfortunate number of innocent casualties on both sides." All of a sudden, I started to wonder why Rose knew all of this.

"How the hell did you learn all of this in the month since we've been here? Who trusted you enough that quickly to tell you all this? Cause I'm going to be honest, I got a real lone-wolf vibe from you from the beginning."

Rose laughed a sincere laugh. "I'm sorry, Louis—I couldn't be honest with any of you from the very beginning. It was much safer that way."

"What do you mean?"

"I'm not who I say I am," she said.

"Well that's not as shocking as the rest of what you just said. Maybe you should have led with that," I said in a smartasstone.

She laughed again. "August is my brother. Our mother was forced to flee the city when she became pregnant with me. The strict two-children-per-couple rule is enforced on both sides of the board. If either a faction member or member of the Aristocracy has another child, that child has to be put to death. Or alternatively, one of the parents can give up their own life."

"Which ended up happening anyway," August said solemnly. "Once our mother left with Rose, they tracked her down and had her executed and harvested to be made example of. To show that no one was allowed to disobey orders, no matter who they were."

"Hold up. Harvested? What the fuck does that mean?" The thought made my stomach turn over, and I had to keep from throwing up.

"She was given over to the donor faction, but instead of given the lavish life they are given until harvesting day, they killed her immediately." I thought of Harold and his wife, and this time couldn't keep the vomit down. I doubled over and threw up water and fragments of that morning's breakfast pill.

I stood up and wiped my mouth. "So you're telling me the donor faction is about harvesting the organs of people?" I asked with shock.

"I'm surprised you didn't find out sooner," August said. "For the most part, they live the best lives of anyone in the city up until the day they are requested. I guess that's how the empire justifies what they are doing. When a member of the Aristocracy needs anything; a heart, kidney, liver, eyes, etc., they take them from a matching donor. Normally the ones that have been there the longest."

"So you brought in Harold and his wife fully knowing that they would end up being harvested?" I asked with intense anger.

"Yes," August said sadly. "Unfortunately, donors make up a huge portion of the people we pull from cryogenic chambers. If I came back without any, that would have raised some major red flags. I didn't want to separate them either, so that they could live out the rest of their lives together. The business that we are in isn't black and white. It's full of shades of gray and red. Many people have died, and many more will. That's why it is imperative that this time the revolution doesn't fail." I was shaking with anger, but everything that he said made sense. But, it still didn't make up for the fact that he'd put the stamp on their death sentence.

"So they're probably dead by now?"

"Not necessarily. But unfortunately, probably. One of them at least," August affirmed.

"It's the way the world is these days," Hera chimed in. "Things might have been better in your time, but this is the life we were all born into. I'm just as surprised as you are about some of what is going on, but we need you to be all in, Louis."

It only took me a matter of seconds to come to the conclusion that I was all in. "You can count on me," I said. If there was any chance of making the new world anything like the old one, or hopefully better, I was ready.

"Alright, we'll talk later, but time is of the essence," August said quietly as the car whirred its way back up the street toward us. The bodies that had been previously in the back seat were now gone. All that was left was the immense amount of blood splattering the back half of the interior. It looked like the inside of a slaughterhouse more than anything.

"I think I'm going to walk," I said, turning away from all the blood.

"Unfortunately Louis, you have no choice. Get in," August said sympathetically.

I squeezed myself in toward the edge of the back seat, trying to avoid the majority of the blood. As I sat down, the blood underneath me made a gut-wrenching squelching sound, and I decided to kind of hover over the seat instead of fully planting myself. When the car took a sharp turn, my hand on the front seat headrest slipped off, causing me to fall sideways into the pool of warm liquid. The warmth was the worst part of it all. The blood covered the entire left side of my suit and my hand slipped along the slick seat.

"This is fucked," I said, shaking my hand out and deciding now that it would be better to just sit in the pool of blood. I didn't know if I was talking about the situation at hand or everything that I had just learned in general. Even with the windows open, the metallic smell was overwhelming. I leaned my head out to try and get some fresh air. I left it hanging out the window until we arrived back at the train. Inside the back compartment, the two bodies lay on either side of where the car parked itself. So Hera and I had to step over the corpses to exit. "Are we going to do anything with them?" I asked.

"Not yet," August replied. "They're fine where they are." That somehow made me extremely angry.

"Do we not have any decency anymore?" I hissed. "We're just going to let these poor people rest in a pool of their own blood?"

"And what would you have us do?" asked Rose.

"I don't know? Fucking anything but this. It seems so degrading."

"Unfortunately, we don't have anything to cover them up with, so I don't know what more we can do," she said.

"Fuck it," I said, and hoisted the woman up from under her arms and leaned her against the wall. Then I went around and grabbed the man and dragged him around the car while the others watched. When I got him around, I propped him up next to the woman so that they were leaning up against each other. In all honesty, I didn't know what the hell I was doing, because the scene then looked like some twisted ventriloquist show. Maybe it would have been better to leave them, but I didn't know what else to do. I had already seen people die in Arcadia, of course, but this was the closest thing to me being involved in one of the deaths that I had encountered.

"That's nice," Hera said, and leaned down to place her hand on my shoulder. "I'm sure they would have appreciated the gesture." She stroked my hair and stood back up.

"This is why we need you, Louis," August said. "You're a good person in an evil world. We need all the good people we can get."

The entire train ride home, I was silent. So was everybody else. I had so many questions burning into me, but at that point, I had learned and seen so much that I didn't have it in me. There would be more time for questions later. We departed the train, leaving the bodies on board. When I arrived back at the Scout apartment building, I was surprised to hear from the receptionist as I walked by.

"How was your first outing?" she asked, clearly not expecting an answer. "I'm pleased to tell you that you are now allowed to leave the building at your leisure. Just make sure you do not go out of the designated zones." She had a friendly smile on her face. I said nothing, getting into the elevator and heading to my room. When I got into the bathroom, my reflection shocked me. I knew that I had a lot of blood on me. But this was Carrie-on-prom-night level. The blood had already dried to my skin, but was still wet on my suit. I took a shower for what must have been at least an hour; this time I actually felt clean when I got out. I sat and washed all the blood out of the suit and hung it over a bar in the bathroom.

Then I lay down in bed without taking my dinner pill, expecting to be up for hours thinking of all the things I had just learned and witnessed. Instead, I was out like a light in a matter of seconds.

CHAPTER 41

Violet turned to look at me, the veil covering her face. It was the happiest moment of our lives. I looked out at the crowd of people gathered to see our wedding. Everyone was there. Even her dad. Her dad? I pulled the veil back, and two bloody sockets stared back at me where her beautiful blue-green eyes used to be. Suddenly, her skin began peeling off her face. She opened her mouth, saying, "I love you, Louis," as worms wriggled their way out and through the holes in her cheek.

CHAPTER 42

I shot up out of bed. A cold sweat covered my forehead. Slowly, the world I was in began to become clear again. The tablet at the door was ringing, and I got up and walked over to it.

"Louis!" Lydia's voice came through the speaker when I answered.

"Lydia," I said, still dazed from sleep. "How are you?"

"Great!" she said excitedly. "Did they tell you that you could leave now also? I went to the hospital and helped perform my first surgery yesterday, and when I got back they said I was free to leave." She paused. "At least as long as I stay within the boundaries."

"Yeah, same," I replied. "Do you want to go explore what we can?"

"Umm, yes! Of course," she replied.

"Okay, give me a couple minutes and I'll meet you outside my building?"

"Sounds like a date," she said happily, and hung up.

After getting dressed and doing my morning routine of showering, finding a pill to swallow, brushing my teeth, and getting dressed, I went down to the lobby. Through the glass door, I saw Lydia already there, excitedly waving through the window. As soon as I left the building I was welcomed with a hug, which was more like a tackle. Who knew a girl as small as she was could hit like a linebacker? Outside it was a beautiful spring day. There wasn't a cloud in the sky. The gorgeous crisp air smelled like a sort of freedom. After not being able to leave the building except for work purposes, it was hard to describe how enjoyable this was.

"This is so exciting, isn't it?" she asked as she linked her arm around mine and squeezed. It was nice to see that most of her original peppiness had come back. What was once an annoying trait was now a breath of fresh air, although her linking her arm around mine was slightly uncomfortable. But whatever, any form of empathy should be welcomed at every chance in this new world. "Well, where should we go?" she asked.

"Wherever you want," I replied, and she squeaked with excitement. All of a sudden, she started running, dragging me along with her. Somehow, the impossibly large city seemed even bigger on foot. We passed a few people on the sidewalks, until we arrived at a park a couple blocks down. Cars hovered down the streets as they passed us. "Watch out," I cautioned as Lydia tried to drag us across the street with cars hovering toward us. In an instant, both cars stopped and we ran across.

"I don't think it's possible for them to hit us," she said.

"Maybe we should play in traffic then," I laughed.

"Oooh that could be fun," she said, clearly not taking the joke. The park looked extremely similar to Central Park in New York. At least the size of it. But this one was more like a forest. At the beginning of the path, there was a giant sculpture that appeared to be of Athena. I honestly had no idea, though; my knowledge on Greek mythology was severely lacking. Whoever it was had a shield and spear in their hand, standing beautifully like it was protecting whatever was in the forest park. Perfectly white paths led off in three different directions. On both sides of every path there were little lights sprinkling each trail. The faint white lights were hard to make out in the perfect sunlight. "This way?" Lydia asked as she started walking down the middle path.

"Sure, looks about as good as any," I replied. A little sign hovered at the edge of the trail, reading *Lakeview Trail.* We walked about fifty feet in, and all of a sudden it became extremely difficult to believe that we were still in a city. The lush forest surrounded us in every direction. I looked back and saw the white of the city peeking through the end of the trail. It was nice seeing it disappear, even for a moment. The sounds of the forest flooded my ears. Birds chirping in every direction, water rushing in the distance, and other sounds that I wasn't completely familiar with. Periodically, the beautiful noises were interrupted by the sound of a drone zooming overhead.

"This is incredible," she said breaking the silence. "I know there are a lot of bad things about this city, but when you see things like this, it is hard to think of anything else besides how beautiful it all is." *You don't know half of the terrible things going on here,* I thought to myself. Suddenly, I wanted to tell her all of the things that I had learned yesterday. But knowing Lydia and her mouth, I decided that was one of the worst ideas I've had since I got here.

"It really is," I decided to say, staring up at the impossibly tall trees. The sun twinkled through the rustling leaves.

A couple people walked past, avoiding eye contact. Lydia looked back at them and watched them leave, and then all of a sudden grabbed my arm.

"Louis, I have to talk to you about something," she said seriously. "It's something Halia told me, and it's very important." She looked around nervously to make sure no one was watching or listening. "She told me to come here to talk to you, because it's one of the only places where they aren't listening." Holy shit, did she already know? I really liked Lydia, but I honestly could say I would never trust her with any important information. "Halia told me she was part of a..."

"I think I already know," I interrupted her. Her eyes widened.

"How many people do you think are in on this? I hate this place so much." She looked down. "I tried to like it, I really did. But when they started bringing in the donors for us to work on, I just couldn't take anymore. It's so crazy—this place doesn't seem real, does it? Like we're in some kind of sick joke."

"It is a weird world we're living in," I agreed.

"Exactly, like how did this happen? We're..." she lowered her voice even further, "... slaves. And we're forced to do whatever they say, or—" She started to cry now. "It's just so unfair." She stomped her foot, not unlike a child who didn't get what they wanted for their birthday.

"I know. It will all be different soon if what they are planning actually pans out. We just can't talk about this with anyone else."

"Of course," she said. "Halia just told me to talk to you, because she knew you were the only other person I knew and that you were going to find out if you didn't already."

"Lydia, can I ask you something?"

"Absolutely."

"You said you were working on donors. Did you see Harold or his wife?"

"Oh my god!" she gasped. "I didn't even think about that. That poor couple." She put her face in her hands. "No I didn't see them yet, though I hope that we can do all of this before anything bad happens to them."

"Agreed." The wind rustling through the tree tops caused us both to pause and look up. My heart skipped a beat, thinking it was a drone that had been listening in on our conversation the entire time. Instead, a lemur was staring back down at us with its beady little eyes, a small, blinking collar around its neck. It paused for a second and then continued swinging along in the canopy. Seeing the monkey swinging in a park in the middle of a city would have normally given me pause, but nothing seemed to be out of the ordinary anymore. "I think we better continue this conversation at a later date," I said, watching the monkey disappear into the distance. My heart was still racing from the idea that we could be discovered at any moment.

"Agreed," she said, and wrapped her arm back around mine. We continued walking through the park, making small talk here and there, talking about what life was like for each of us before all of this happened. She told me about how when she was a kid, she loved playing doctor with all of her dolls, and how even though we were in such an undesirable place she actually got to live out her dream of becoming a doctor of sorts. How her parents had both died when she was a child in a car crash and that she had become an orphan at the age of eleven. How terrible the adjustment was in her preteen years to that, and how the only way to survive was to be falsely optimistic about the future. That false optimism had quickly shifted how she looked at the world and actually became real optimism. She had never had a boyfriend, but kissed a boy at a party once.

Some of the things she told me made my heart break. She was just a kid still, that same optimistic one that froze herself all those years ago. Now she would never get the chance to do all the normal things a kid does. But I guess that was how it was for most people these days. Born to serve the Empire. We were the mortar in the foundation. Hopefully, soon, that mortar would shift, causing the walls to come down.

"That's so sad," Lydia said as I told her about Violet. "I'm so sorry." I told her just about everything that I could remember of her. I don't know if I was telling her to let her know about her, or to remind myself of all the beautiful things about Violet so I wouldn't forget anything. Besides Nikki, Lydia was the only other person in the last couple hundred of years to hear her name. They say that you only truly die when the last person you know stops saying your name. I guess in that regard, Violet had lived a lot longer than most people did. Her being gone hurt every time I thought of her, which was constantly. But maybe it was better that she would never have to see a world like this. I suddenly realized that she might have lived to see the breakout of World War 3. Maybe she got lucky and died before the world went to shit.

Seeing the hurt in my eyes now, Lydia squeezed my hand. "Violet seemed like a wonderful person—I wish I could have met her."

"She really was," I conceded. "I'm sure she would have liked you too." We arrived at the end of the trail, which was surrounded by a half-circle-shaped waterfall that was running into a crystal-clear lake. Trees surrounded the embankment.

"Here," Lydia said as she pulled out a knife with a glowing tip, identical to the one that cut her tongue on the first day. She walked away from me and stood next to a giant oak tree. The bark on the tree smoldered as she carved into it. Backing away and smiling, I saw that she'd carved *L+V* into it. I smiled as she handed me the knife. "I think you need to finish it."

"Thanks," I said, and retrieved the knife. The bark smoldered again as a I encircled the letters with a heart.

"Now she'll be here with you forever." She gave me a winsome smile. A drone flew overhead, breaking up the moment. "I suppose we should head back then, huh?"

"Yeah, let's get out of here." We turned to head back out into the city. A few people passed us on the way back, giving friendly nods and continuing on with their conversations. When we got out, the city looked so terrible in contrast to the beauty of the forest we were just in. The rest of the day we spent walking around, exploring the part of the city we were allowed to. We walked past all of the other faction buildings, excluding the donor one, which was nowhere to be found. There were restaurants, coffee shops, more parks, barber shops, and even a museum that we decided to not go into. But that was it—none of the other types of buildings or shops that I had seen driving through the other district we were allowed to go into.

"Please stop right there," a man told us as we got to close to entering at one point.

"Why can't we go over there?" Lydia asked sweetly. In an instant, he pulled out a pistol off of his hip and pointed it at her chest. He never said another word as we turned around and headed back the way we came. "Well, that guy didn't wake up on the right side of the bed this morning," Lydia laughed.

"I guess he really didn't," I laughed back.

"Aren't you just dying to see what all the fuss is about over there? I know I am."

"Eh, I feel like it would make me more mad about being stuck over here. So probably not."

"Yeah, I suppose that's true. Maybe someday? Someday soon." She smiled a little knowing smile.

We finished off the day by going into one of the coffee shops. A lady behind the counter with what I had come to know as the Administrators' signature white symbol on her black suit greeted us. "Hello, you two." She smiled. "What can I get for you?"

"Can I get a coffee with two sugars?" I asked.

"Certainly." She began pouring the coffee. "And how about you, sweetheart?"

"How about a large, iced, sugar-free vanilla latte with soy milk?" Lydia smiled. The order was met with a small chuckle.

"I see it's your first time here," she smiled. "I'll get you a latte with ice."

"Okay, that's fine," Lydia said sadly. When her order was done, she took the cup politely, but was clearly disappointed. I tried to stifle my laughter. "Yeah, I know it was ridiculous, but I can hope right?" She turned to me.

"That's all we can do is hope," I told her. "Maybe someday we'll be able to get you the latte you actually want." She smiled at the thought.

"I'm sure they can get coffee a million different ways in the other district. But I'm just happy they have something different here. I was tired of ordering black coffee at the apartment."

"I wonder how they even get coffee beans here. Everything else is just water and pills."

"One of my friends told me that the Assembly has farms that produce things like that. They even produce fruits, vegetables, and meat for the other district. That could be a rumor, though—I just don't know what to believe anymore."

"True," I agreed as we sat down at a pristine white table next to the window. The inside of the coffee shop was more dimly lit than any of the other buildings I'd been in so far. It was a nice change of pace. There were a few other people at another table talking to each other, but besides that, the place was empty. Outside, clouds started to form, casting periodic shadows when they passed over the sun. We sat in silence, looking out the window while we sipped at our coffees. We were just getting ready to go when five people in black suits with the red insignia on their chest busted through the door. The three people next to us tried to stand up quickly.

"Don't fucking move," one of the men said, but the three coffee shop customers tried to fight their way out. The woman behind the counter stood stone-faced waiting for it all to be over. One of the men slammed one of the customers' heads into the table and shoved a black bag over his head. There was a woman wildly flailing, trying to get past the men standing at the door, but it was no use. She was abruptly taken to the ground and had a bag thrown over her head as well. The third dropped to his knees and raised his hands. Within thirty seconds, it was all over, and we were left silently staring at each other, while the woman behind the counter went back to wiping it down..

"I wonder what they did," Lydia said wide-eyed.

"I have no idea," I told her, but was afraid that our cause just lost three people before the fighting had even started. "I think we'd better go home though."

"Yeah, for sure—let's get out of here," she agreed.

"Sorry about that," the woman behind the counter called out to us as we left. "It was likely some unsavory factionists getting big ideas again. Have a wonderful day." She smiled. I raised my hand and waved without turning around. It was at that point I realized it wasn't going to be an us versus them situation with the aristocracy. When we got back to the apartments, Lydia and I exchanged a long embrace, knowing what would be coming soon.

CHAPTER 43

The next morning, I was awoken by a hard knock at the door. I groggily got up, threw some clothes on, and headed toward the front door. My mind immediately went to the people who had gotten taken yesterday. Had they already found out about us that quickly, or did the people who got taken overhear something that Lydia and I were talking about? Times like this, a peep hole in the door would really come in handy. Maybe that was the exact reason they didn't have peep holes installed in the first place.

"I hear you in there, Louis," Rose's voice came through the door. "Don't worry, it's just me."

I cracked open the door. "Yes, Rose?"

"We're scheduled to head back out today and look for some new recruits—apparently, they have been disappearing at an alarming rate."

"Oh yeah, I saw..."

"Just come downstairs with us now." I opened the door a little further to see Hera standing out in the hallway as well.

"Why didn't you just call me?"

"We tried—you must have been knocked out hard," she laughed.

"Oh shit, sorry." I pressed the button on the tablet to get a random breakfast pill and a water, then closed the door behind me. "Also, quick question, what the hell am I supposed to do with these bottles after I'm done with them? I have about a hundred piled up in the corner of my apartment." The pristine white apartment was starting to look awfully hoardy.

"You haven't found the return chute in the bathroom yet?" Hera laughed heartily. "Behind the mirror, you put everything you don't want in your apartment anymore. Towels, bottles, clothes that you need dry cleaned."

"No, I didn't find the random magical chute hidden behind a mirror," I laughed. "I've been hand washing and drying my clothes and towels this whole fucking time." This time they both laughed hard.

"Well at least you figured it out now, I guess. Why didn't you ask someone?" Rose said, still laughing. I just shrugged and wondered the same thing myself.

"And not a moment too soon," Hera replied while the doors on the elevator closed. In the lobby, August waited for us, the normal chipper look back on his face.

"Morning, sweetie—did you get enough beauty rest?" August asked me.

"Yeah, yeah, yeah, whatever," I replied. "Where are we going today?"

"Well on this bright and beautiful day, your hometown is on the agenda. We're going back to Lincoln to search some of the bombed-out cryogenic labs to see if anyone by some miracle managed to survive on the backup generators for all these years."

"Sounds like a pipe dream to me."

"Yeah, well, we have to do something to try and find some more recruits to replace the ones that keep disappearing. Philomena and Nero are already out with their crews in the old Wyoming and Colorado territories, so we'd better get a move on."

Everyone loaded back up into the car, and we were back heading toward the same train that had carried the bodies back from Chadron.

"We're not taking the train you brought us back on?" I asked August as we walked up to the small train.

"No, Nero has that one in Colorado right now. We're not expecting to bring back many people, so we got the mini train for now." We all hopped in and it bolted out of the tunnel again. This time, the train veered off to the right when we got out of the city. The view from this side of the city was pretty much identical to when we last left. A vast, sprawling metropolis, impossible to see the end of until we were miles out. August kept flipping through pages on a clipboard. Eventually, he ended up tearing out a page and giving it over to Rose and Hera. "Okay, so you and I are going to be searching through three bombed-out cryogenic labs, Louis. I'm going to be honest, there's probably not going to be anyone there anyway, but it's worth a shot. Plus, we need to come back with at least a few people, or it's going to be all of our asses."

"What about Hera and Rose?" I asked. "There can't possibly be that many cryogenic labs in Lincoln."

"Oh, you'd be surprised how many popped up in the weirdest of locations. But yeah, we're going to be searching for people, while those two have other matters to take care of." The tone in his voice made me not want to ask what other matters they were attending to, so I let it go for now.

"Sounds good to me," I said. "No more shooting people in the face this time?"

"God, I hope not," August said. "But you never know. Might just end up having to shoot you in the face if you keep up with the subtle jabs." He laughed. I didn't. The thought of the two bodies sprawled in the back compartment of this exact train only two days ago made my stomach churn. "I'm sorry Louis, a little dark humor goes a long way these days though."

"I understand," I agreed. "It just takes a lot of getting used to."

"Amen to that," Rose said. "Who would have thought the 'civilized' people were so much worse than anything that lies out in the wastes?"

"Not me," Hera replied. "We were always taught that the people in the wastes were bloodthirsty cannibals."

"Not all of us," Rose corrected. "But to be honest, that isn't all lies. My mom and I ran into a whole array of unsavory characters while we were out here trying to survive. None to the scale that Arcadia holds though."

"I'm sorry that I couldn't have been there for you," August said sadly.

Rose laughed. "What would you have done, protected us with your wit and made them laugh to death?"

"Oh shut up," August said, gently pushing at Rose. She grabbed his hand as he pushed and twisted it behind his back. "Ow, fuck, you ripped my finger clean off," he laughed, and held up his hand to show one of his missing pinkies.

"You're lucky a pinky is all you're missing." She smirked at him. "Could have easily taken off your whole hand." She shrugged and smiled, turning to look out the window.

"Well you can't have my pinkies, a couple toes, and this gorgeous beauty mark, but feel free to take whatever else," he muttered, and gently gestured toward the scar on his face, like a person in an infomercial showing off the newest shitty product they were trying to sell. I tuned out the rest of August and Rose's little back-and-forth, looking out the window to see if I would start recognizing any of central Nebraska. But like it always did, everything looked the exact same. Long, flat expanses that seemed to go on forever. All the farmhouses and little towns that once stood were now non-existent, and the vast expanse looked even more barren. Who would have thought it could have looked even more barren than it once did?

Violet and I had always talked about leaving, but it's so hard to get out of somewhere when it's all you know. Looking back on it and how things ended up now, it seemed like it would have been extremely easy. Who knows, maybe if we did end up moving, I would have never been in the position I was now in. I would have been completely fine with that.

After a while, the tedious scenery finally changed when the train took a sharp left. I saw out the window the ruins of what once was Lincoln. The capitol that once stood proudly over the city was nowhere to be seen. A couple of the larger buildings still stood, but were either bombed out or looked severely dilapidated. I never appreciated Lincoln, because it definitely wasn't known to be the most beautiful city in the world. But now it was just abysmal. I kind of wished I would have appreciated it more while it was still standing proudly.

"Looks a little different now that you're seeing it from the outside, huh?" August asked.

"Yeah, it really does. I always thought it was kind of a shithole, but now that I think about it, it really had some beautiful aspects to it. It used to be such a safe place. Looks like no places were really safe when the bombs started dropping, though."

"They certainly were not," August agreed. "So when we get into the city, we're going to go to Crimson Cryogenics first. It was sort of a ma-and-pop style lab that popped up in 2042. It's only a two story building, so I don't have too much hope that whoever was inside is going to be able to come out and swap war stories with us."

"Okay, I'll follow your lead." The train stopped, and we entered back into the train compartment with the car in it. I half-expected blood to be smeared everywhere, but it was completely sterile, like nothing had ever happened. I wondered how many people and corpses had been hauled back there since it first started running. The prospect was disturbing. August and Rose both had identical suitcases to the one August had when I first met him. They threw them both into the trunk, and we all hopped in. As the car shot out of the back of the train, I caught a glimpse of the fallen train station as we zoomed past it in the opposite direction of the lab I had awoken in. As we headed closer to downtown, I saw what had happened to the capitol. There were decrepit cars abandoned in the middle of the road, some still had their doors open and rusting off their hinges. A massive pile of brick and stone covered the street where the capitol must have fallen onto during one of the bombing raids. People must have panicked and left their cars when the building finally came down. The base of the capitol still stood, but the massive structure in the middle had been completely demolished. Grass and trees had sprouted all throughout the ravaged streets, which had been blasted apart.

We stopped at a corner of the building, and Hera and Rose got out, retrieving one of the suitcases from the trunk. "Good luck!" August called out.

"Yeah, luck has nothing to do with it," Rose laughed, scoffing and waving him off. She unzipped the suitcase and shook out its contents onto the ground. Then she bent down to search through the pile that had formed on the floor. I drove off with August, and soon we turned a corner and then they were out of sight. We kept driving until we stopped right outside a red brick building that was almost entirely caved in. Besides about seven feet high of brick still standing around the base of the building, this two-story lab was basically a no-story lab.

"Well, this doesn't look promising at all," August laughed.

"Unless there is a basement, I'm inclined to agree."

"I suppose we should still see if we can get in there," August said as his door hissed open and he stepped out. I followed, and immediately stumbled into a small crater that was just outside the car.

"Watch your step," he called back to me.

"Thanks for letting me know," I said as I regained my balance. We walked toward the front of the building and pulled a couple bricks back.

"Here, help me move this," he said as he started pushing on a fallen beam that was crossed over the threshold of the door.

"Don't you have drones for shit like this?" I asked as I struggled to push on the beam.

"Come on, Louis, I thought you needed a workout," he huffed out. "We gotta... get you... looking strong for the ladies." The beam pushed over into a pile of bricks with a crash, causing dust to float up into the air. More bricks started falling down in front of us. "Nope, fuck that," he said as he peered his head inside. "We're out." He walked back to the car. "If someone is in there, they're just going to have to wait for someone who is willing to die to get them out."

"Fair enough. It's not like time is of the essence for them anyway."

"Now, what if I would have said that about you when I came across you?" August asked with a smile.

"Fuck, I wish you would have." We both laughed.

"Fair enough. Now we're headed towards a place called Freeze Time."

"Oh my god, what kind of janky-ass lab is that?" I laughed. "Sounds like a frozen yogurt place."

"You'd be surprised at how many of these labs popped up, and how lazy some of the people were with naming them. Toward the start of the war, they were popping up quicker than you could name them. I've honestly heard worse."

"How could someone have a worse name than that?"

"I don't know. Would Uncle Al's Freezing Hole top your list?"

"That is not fucking real!" I laughed hysterically.

"I shit you not," he joined in laughing. "It had to have been some kind of joke, or Uncle Al really wasn't a maestro with words, but there were actually a couple people in there."

"Okay, well suddenly Freeze Time sounds like the Taj Mahal," I said, still laughing as we drove off. "So why did I not get this VIP treatment getting picked up in a car?"

"You were so close to the train station, and I figured we could both stretch our legs a little bit," he replied. "Didn't know you were going to be all fucked up in the head—most people just froze themselves to avoid the war."

"August?"

"Yeah?"

"I'm not the only one who was fucked up in the head." We both broke out into laughter again. It was good to be laughing again; it was probably the most normal thing that I had done in the new world. It was clear that under different circumstances, August and I would have been friends too. There were rain clouds now forming above us, but no rain yet. The car zoomed along for about a mile until we arrived at another building. The concrete face of the building was chipped in numerous spots, but for the most part the building was still intact. It looked like the roof had collapsed in, but it was impossible to tell from the ground. Just the center of the face of the building dipped down a little bit.

We entered the building and all the lights were off except dull red ones, which meant that there was some sort of backup power in the building. Maybe this one actually had people in it. Water was pooled up in different spots on the floor where it dipped down. "Careful not to step in the water—you never know if there is a live wire that fell down into it," August warned. I nodded. He held an orb in his hand, and as soon as the light from the entrance was too far back to see, he tapped the orb and it floated above his shoulder.

The light blinded me momentarily. "Do you think it could be brighter?" I asked.

"Oops, sorry. Still not used to having trainees tag along." He tapped the orb a couple times until it was a much more acceptable dimness. We rounded a corner and opened a door. Inside the next room, there was a reception area that was more lit up, with red lights lining the base of the wall. "I think it's here," he said as he approached a metal door with a wheel on it. He spun the wheel, pulled back, and the door unhitched. As it swung open, a rush of cold air flooded out. "Jackpot." Inside, there were six chambers. All had soft white lights coming out of a window at the top. "Careful—everyone's reactions to being abruptly awoken are different. Some don't have any reactions, because they fully died somewhere in the process too."

"The lucky ones, huh?"

"Come on Louis, cheer up would you? I think a little too much of me is rubbing off on you." We walked past the first chamber, and a nameplate in the center of it read *Riley R.* "Here goes nothing," he said as he pulled on the handle. It opened with a whoosh, and we were hit in the face with frigid air. "Oh shit, run back to the car and get the suitcase would you?"

"Seriously?"

"Serious as a heart attack. Which this kid is going to have if you don't get out there quick." Before saying another word, I sprinted out to the car and retrieved the suitcase from the trunk. I ran back inside, banging my shoulder on the wall while rounding the corner. The suitcase dropped, and I hurriedly scooped it back up and ran back into the lobby. I stumbled into the room and handed the suitcase over to August. "Now that's what I call service," he laughed, calmly getting down on his knee and rummaging through the suitcase.

"I take it you exaggerated the time constraint," I scoffed.

"Only by about an hour. Did you ever think about trying out for the Olympics in track back in your time? I think you would have had a real shot," he laughed while he looked through the suitcase.

"Oh fuck you." I bent over to catch my breath. After a minute, he pulled out a disgustingly long syringe and without warning jabbed it into the kid's heart. I never had a fear of syringes, but after seeing that one, I was starting to consider it. He pushed down on the plunger and slid it out. Moments later, the teenager's eyes shot open and he gasped for breath.

"Who are you?" he asked groggily. "Where am I?"

"I'm Saint Peter, and my associate here is Mickey Mouse."

"What?" he asked lazily.

"I said, I'm Augustus and this is Louis." He paused. "You've been frozen for a while now. Do you know if you have any ailments?"

"I mean, my head hurts and I'm pretty hungry," he said as he started gaining lucidity.

"Louis, get this man a burger will you?"

"That sounds great," he replied. "With ketchup too, please. And maybe a Coke if you have one?"

"Ooh, sorry kid, we're fresh out," August replied. "I do have this though." He rummaged around in his suitcase and pulled out a couple pills and handed them over. The kid popped them in his mouth and struggled to swallow, but managed to get them down. "We'll explain more later. Sorry, we have more people to unfreeze." The kid got out of the chamber and stood stupidly for a second before sitting down in the corner. We walked over to the next chamber, but it was empty, so we moved on to the next. The far back left one had an old man in it with the nameplate *Christopher H.* We repeated the same process, opening the door and plunging the needle into his heart. This time, I looked away while he did it. "You want to do the next one?" August laughed.

"No, I think I'm alright—you look like you have this handled."

"Yeah makes sense. After a while you get used to it, but the needles used to scare the shit out of me too."

"What's in them?"

"A blend of epinephrine and who knows what else. I just pick them up, I don't make them in a little lab in my apartment." The man gasped for air, and reached out toward us. He had to have been at least eighty. "You okay, old-timer?" August asked.

"I think so," he gasped again. "Where am I?" His white, stringy hair stuck combed over to the top of his head. The sockets in his eyes were deep set, and the wrinkles on his face and hands truly showed his age.

"Do you think you can walk? Or do you need a cane or wheelchair?" There was a wheelchair next to his chamber, so it seemed like a pretty stupid question.

"Wheelchair please." I rolled the chair out in front of the chamber while August gently let him down into it. "What year is it?"

"2231," August told him.

"Wow," he coughed, and laughed. "That was quite the sleep I just had."

"Certainly was," August replied. I looked over at the kid Riley in the corner. His eyes were wideset with shock, but he didn't say anything. "So Chris—may I call you that?"

"Of course," he coughed again.

"Do you have anything wrong with you?"

"Oh, I'm old." He paused for a second and wheezed in. "I'd say that's the extent of my conditions."

"You don't look a day over twenty-five," August said as he wheeled him toward the front door and left him over there.

"Damn right," the man said, and went into a coughing fit.

"I'm just going to leave you right here," August told him as he put the brakes on the wheelchair.

"That's alright, kid," he said. "Do what you have to do." This time he didn't say anything more, just taking some shallow breaths.

Two of the chambers on the right were also closed, but they had nameplates on them. It seemed like someone either already found them, or they never made it to their resting place in the first place. The last chamber had another man in it, probably around his late thirties. His jet-black hair was clouded by the frosty air on the inside.

August pulled the door open and repeated the process for a third time of jabbing him with a new syringe. This time there was no response.

"Shit," August said as he took out another syringe. "One more try." He stabbed into his heart for a second time. We waited for a couple more moments. Still nothing. August left the door open. "We'll give him a few minutes, but this happens from time to time. Some people just refuse to wake up." He went back to talk to Chris in the wheelchair. "How you feeling now?"

"Tip-top," he said as he coughed and clutched at his chest. "Better than that guy at least." His wheezing was the only sound that could be heard in the dimly lit room.

"Here, take this," August said as he pulled a pill from his suitcase. "It'll help with the coughing."

"I don't need any of your damned fancy pills," he said, and waved his hand forward to gesture for August to put them away.

"Suit yourself, you tough bastard," August said, which made the man chuckle and go into another coughing fit. "You sound like death though."

"Feel like it too," he replied. "Don't know why I got into that tube in the first place. Probably to get as far away from my bitch ex-wife Mackenzie as possible." He coughed again. "So what's the world like nowadays?"

"Not great," August told him. "But you'll see for yourself."

"Eh, it wasn't so great in my time either," he muttered. "The world's always been a shitty place, and it always will be."

"Ain't that the truth," August said. "Unfortunately, you will have to take this pill though, or your old ticker might shut down."

"Fine," he said, taking the pill and swallowing it. "But I'm not taking any of the other shit you're peddling."

"Not even this miracle tonic?" August held up his hands like a bottle was in it. "It'll make your hair grow twice as thick and make you virile as a bull."

"Oh piss off," Chris coughed.

"It looks like"—August paused to look down at the name plate on the chamber—"Mr. Daniel M. isn't going to be joining us today." He closed the door back on the chamber and locked it tightly. "Hopefully someone in the future will have better luck than we did. Let's get out of here." He grabbed the back of Chris's wheelchair and held the suitcase under one arm, while I leaned over to give Riley a hand up from the corner he was sitting in.

"Thanks," he muttered, and sullenly followed as August zipped through the door and around the corner. I looked back at Daniel, still frozen inside the chamber, and couldn't decide if he was lucky or unlucky that he never woke up. A bit of both, I decided, and followed the rest of the group outside. When I got out back into the sunlight, Chris was doubled over in his wheelchair, having a terrible coughing fit. This time, blood splattered the ground with each cough.

"On second thought, I'm not feeling too hot doc," he groaned.

"Here, let me get you something," August said with a little worry as he put his suitcase on the ground and began rummaging through it. Like lightning, Chris grabbed at his chest, and with one more cough slumped back into his wheelchair. "Fuck, not again," August said as he slammed the suitcase on the ground and flipped a switch, allowing the compartments to float up into the air like when I first saw it. He rapidly looked up and down a couple times until he found a compartment close to the ground and snatched another syringe. Quickly, he stabbed it into Chris's neck, and the man jolted up a little, batted his eyes, then slumped forward, his arms lightly grazing the ground. "One more time," August muttered, and stabbed another syringe into his neck like a gruesome game of pin the tail on the donkey. This time there was no jolt. August felt for a pulse in his neck and shook his head. "Damn, I really liked that guy."

"He's dead?" Riley said worriedly.

"Dead as a doornail," August said sadly, and propped Chris back up into a sitting position in the wheelchair. His eyes stared blankly off into nothingness. August slid his hands down over the lids to close them.

"That could have been me," Riley said even more worriedly. "Holy shit, that could have been me."

"Calm down," August said. "This normally only happens to the older ones, you're fine. It's the shock on their system that gets them. Get in the car, would you?" I opened the back door as Riley got in, shaking. Then the door whirred shut while August and I stood staring at Chris.

"What should we do with him?" I asked.

"The crotchety old man would probably be fine with being here. Like he said, this is pretty far away from Mackenzie. Plus, we have a tight schedule to keep." Without another word, we hopped into the front of the car and drove off. I looked out the rearview mirror as Chris's silhouette got smaller and smaller until it was unrecognizable. We made a stop back off at the train. "Wait here, Louis. You come with me." He pointed into the back seat without looking and hopped out. The two of them disappeared into the front train car, and then August reemerged.

"I've been meaning to ask you—" I turned to August as he got into the car. "Why was I the only one left in that lab when you found me?"

"I had a quota to fill. We can only bring back however many people need replacing in the factions. It's calculated by the administrators, and we are given how many people to recover. The city only allows a certain number of outsiders in depending on how well the continuous flow of faction babies is going. But I think it's just a pretentious attempt to show off the city to newcomers, and it seems the people who froze themselves had an innate will to survive, which right off the bat allows for a good mindset when forced into slave labor. Anyway, my previous trip I had just reached my quota, so I had to come back for you on the next round. Sorry for letting you sit in limbo for those extra couple weeks, buddy."

"Makes sense. Thanks for coming back for me, I guess."

"No problem." He smiled. "What are friends for?"

"Where to next?"

"It's just called Cryo. I think I drove past it before, and if I remember right, the place looked to be in pretty bad shape." The car zoomed off, leaving the kid all alone in the train. Poor guy must be scared shitless right now. Trickles of rain began falling from the sky and splattering the windshield. August fidgeted around with his watch for a moment, swiping at the screen a couple times and then putting his hands back down in his lap. The bright white interior of the car was an eerie contrast to the gray of the day outside. We passed old neighborhoods that were completely rotted away and leveled to the ground. Houses that once stood beautifully were nowhere to be seen. Every now and then, we would pass a brick or stucco house that was falling into disrepair, until finally we reached a building that was completely steel and glass. Somehow, most of the glass remained intact, but the steel frame of the building was warped and sunk down into the ground where there was a crater on the left side of it. Half of the building was sloped down at about a 30-degree angle.

When we got out of the car, we were pelted with heavy raindrops, so we quickly ran into the doorway, which was protected by a glass overhang. The building next door was completely blown away, with bricks spattered all around it and a mountain of them formed in the center. The glass door was shattered, and glass at least a couple inches thick sprawled out around the ground while other pieces still jaggedly clung to the frame. August carefully maneuvered his way through, and I followed behind. Dull, pulsating white lights flashed from the ceiling. "Maybe there's still hope for this place," August concluded while staring at the lights. Immediately to the right, there was another door ajar. Inside was a filthy white waiting area. There were eight doors in the room—three on the back wall, three on the wall to the right, and two on the one to the left, one of them being the one we entered through. "Better start checking them. I'll start on the right, you start on the left."

I walked over to the next door on the left and opened. August's orb wasn't needed in this building, because the lights illuminated the spaces enough to see my way around. The first room was a bathroom, covered in filth from the years of exposure. The sink was broken off the wall and the whole room slanted downward at an even steeper degree than the waiting room. I closed the door again. The next door on the back wall to the far left was sealed tight. I forced it open, and a cool breeze hit me in the face. Once my eyes adjusted, I saw a massive steel beam had fallen and collapsed on top of the chamber inside. The light pulsated, illuminating it lying on its side, and a skeleton that was mangled in. The temperature of the room clearly hadn't been enough to keep the body preserved. I looked over to the right and saw that the wall had crumbled under the weight of the beam also. It poked through about a third of the way up. The next room probably would be a pretty similar scene.

"First one's empty over here," August called out.

"Mine's not empty, but I don't think you're going to be able to bring this person back." I left the room and went back out to go open the middle door. Inside this room, the top of the cryogenic chamber was smashed downward like a soda can. The glass on the front of the chamber was completely splintered all the way down, and all that remained was a skeleton contorted down into an uncomfortable shape. The beam crossed over into the next room but was pretty close to the ceiling, so the next room might be better off. I left and closed the second room and grabbed the third door handle. This one was much harder to open—I pushed my foot up against the wall and heaved on it. Eventually it cracked up as the frost broke apart. The entire room was covered in frost. It was like walking straight out of Nebraska and into Siberia.

"Second room was empty too," August called out. "Hopefully third time's the charm."

"Got one in here," I replied. The light pulsated, illuminating the bright white frost that covered every square inch of the wall and seeped up through the broken portion of the wall to the left. On top of the chamber, the beam gently rested, leaving just a hairline fracture down the front of the chamber's window. I went over and scraped away at some of the frost. As I held my hand up to the glass, even colder air seeped out from inside. A woman in her late sixties faced me, with her eyes completely shut. Her gray hair fell down neatly to her shoulders. She looked so familiar.

CHAPTER 44

My heart dropped to the pit of my stomach as soon as I realized who it was. I could feel my heart thrashing in my chest as I reached down to wipe off the frost covering the name plate. The words stared at me as I stared back. In perfect black letters engraved on a golden plaque: *Violet King*. I crouched down and placed my elbows on my knees and my hands to my face. "August!" I called out. My voice shaking as well as all of my extremities.

"Yes?" August said as he came running in. I couldn't tell if my shaking was from fear or excitement. I didn't know what the next couple minutes could bring. "Who is that?" he asked. Quickly, I realized that August would have had no idea—I never told him about her.

"My whole life," I said. He placed his hand on my shoulder.

"Well, let's get her out of there then," he said quietly. I stood back up and took a deep breath. My hands trembled as I reached out for the handle. I twisted the handle down and pulled open. The door hissed as a gust of arctic wind filled the room. It must have been excruciatingly cold, because August was now shaking as well. I couldn't feel anything—my entire body went numb. She was still so beautiful, even if she was now old enough to be mother, maybe even my grandmother. I brought my hand to her face and gently caressed it. Each wrinkle was exaggerated by the extreme cold. Her blue lips were still the same one I remembered kissing a thousand times before.

"Please be gentle," I told him.

"Of course," he assured me as he slid the cap off the needle. It glistened in the pulsating white light. I reached out at his arm and delicately grabbed his wrist to wordlessly tell him to stop. He paused for a second, nodded, and then backed away. I felt every fiber of my being vibrate at a frequency that was foreign to me. I should get it over with and have him wake her, I told myself, but I couldn't let him do it yet.

I studied each wrinkle in her face. Like a roadmap of the life that she had lived after I had gone. Each was a road that she had to navigate through whatever curve the universe brought her to. Only a few wrinkles were there when I left her, and those were now deeply exaggerated. The whole concept of time washed over me with a numb realization. For me, it had only felt like a month had passed since I saw her last, through the unforgiving porthole in my chamber. But gazing deeply at her, I saw a lifetime had passed. It had been at least forty years for her since she drove me to the clinic for the last time. But here we both were, over a hundred years later, ready to see each other again. Or at least I was. There was no telling what her reaction would be to seeing me exactly how she left me all those years ago.

I took a deep breath and gestured for August to come back over with the syringe. Slowly and tenderly, he slid it into her chest and pushed down on the plunger. The foggy liquid inside of it exited the tip of the needle and entered her heart. I waited with bated breath for her to open her eyes again so I could see the beautiful blue-green that not even the most talented artist could have replicated.

CHAPTER 45

Her eyes were shut as her chest gently rose and fell. To-day was going to be the first day of the rest of our lives. I had never seen her look more beautiful than she did at this moment. No makeup on, and resting peacefully. She always looked absolutely breathtaking, but something about the day made her look even more astonishing. She opened her eyes and stared at me for a moment. The comforting blue-green that I had seen almost every morning, and was blessed to have in my life.

"Honey bear?" Violet said softly.

"Hi Vi." I smiled back at her. "Do you know what day it is?"

"Of course I do." She leaned up and stretched. "It's the day you finally make an honest woman of me." She laughed and leaned in to embrace me.

"No one could do that." I grinned back.

"Well if anyone could, it would be you." She laid her head on my chest as I looked out the window. The forecast called for rain, but it was a beautiful April day and the sun shone through the window, highlighting every beautiful curve of her face. "As much as I'd like to spend eternity right here, you're going to have to skedaddle so I can start getting ready. You know it's bad luck to see the bride on her wedding day."

"I thought that I just wasn't supposed to see you in your dress?"

"Well, who knows? It's all bullshit superstition anyway. I just need you out of here so I can focus." She laughed and kissed me on the forehead.

"Fine. I guess my heart might be able to stand half a day away from you." I jokingly sulked away.

"Just get out of here, you big sap." She smiled and shooed me off. As the day went on, the sun made a disappearing act and was replaced by soft gray clouds. By the time I entered the small white chapel out in the country that we had chosen, rain had started to fall. For anyone else's wedding, I would have felt bad, but Vi and I had always loved the rain. It seemed like perfect conditions, even though our outdoor reception would probably have to be moved into the barn. There weren't a lot of people anyway—it would be just fine. We didn't have a lot of money, but neither of us cared, because we had each other.

I stood nervously tapping at the side of my right thigh, where only the minister could see me and not the thirty friends and family we had gathered to celebrate with us. "It's alright to be nervous, son," the minister whispered to me. "Everyone always is." I nodded and kept staring at the door Violet would be coming through any second. All of a sudden, the instrumental for "Space Song" struck up, the song that had played when I first saw her, which we'd decided on instead of the cheesy "Here Comes the Bride." It might have been just as cheesy, honestly, but as soon as it started playing and I caught my first glimpse of her, I had to choke back tears. It was like seeing her for the first time all over again. Her white sheath dress draped over her gave her the appearance of something wholly otherworldly. Like an angel, as cliché as that sounds. From the moment she entered the room, our eyes never left each other's. The stunning pools of her eyes had started to water, which in turn opened the gates for mine to do the same. Her smile was as wide as the world while she reached up with her hand that wasn't linked around my dad's to wipe away a tear with the back of her wrist. Finally, she was standing right in front of me, and the rest of the world washed away. I didn't even listen to what the minister was saying for the most part as he addressed everyone, because all I could see was Violet. I'm sure she wasn't listening either from the smile she wore across her face.

"Ahem," the minister cleared his throat while some people in the crowd chuckled a little. "I said, I believe Violet has written her vows." He smiled softly at her.

She blushed a little and started speaking through tears, "Louis. I knew from the first second I saw you that we were meant to be together. Even though we started off miles apart, in my heart I knew that fate would bring us together. You're the best thing that has ever happened to me. And when we're apart physically, I know that our hearts are always intertwined. No matter what the future brings, our hearts will always be one. The best times and the worst times to come, we will face together. All that matters to me is you, and I promise that for the rest of our time on this earth, we will be together." She slid the ring onto my finger, and as soon as her hand left mine I brought it up to wipe away a tear.

"And you, Louis?" The minister gestured over to me.

"Violet, since the first day I met you, you have been a ray of sunshine in an otherwise cloudy world. On our first official date, we walked around for hours. The rain poured heavily around us while we each held umbrellas down at our sides. With you, I never even noticed, or cared to notice, that it was even raining. When I'm by your side, the rest of the world's problems melt away, and all that matters is you. I promise that I will be by your side as long as the universe allows it. You are the one and only thing that I truly cannot live without." I slid the ring on her finger. Tears were flowing freely from my eyes, but I think I said what I rehearsed a thousand times before in my head clearly enough. I might have missed a part or two, but when I continued looking into her eyes, I knew that it didn't matter what I said. We would always be there for each other.

"By the powers vested in me, I now pronounce you man and wife. You may kiss the bride." I grabbed her face softly with both hands, and we leaned in for a kiss while everyone clapped. We would always be there for each other. We had to be.

CHAPTER 46

She never woke up. I sat there and stared at the ring on her finger. The same one I'd given her all those years ago. August frantically tried everything that he could, rummaging and pulling every last item from his case. Time was moving in slow motion. It was as if the whole world stopped turning in that moment. I didn't feel anything. Nothing at all. Not sadness, not anger, nothing. My whole body was numb as I sat there staring at the pulsing light reflecting off the ring. Fading in and out. Lighting it up momentarily, and then leaving it in blackness. Her stiff hands frozen in time. I had no thoughts. I just sat there observing. Her pretty little yellow sundress stiffly cloaked her body. Black leggings clung to her legs, and on her feet were a pair of black dress shoes with a small heel on the back of them. She was just as beautiful as ever. Even in death.

"I'm so sorry, Louis." August crouched down beside me. "I did everything that I could." I didn't say anything;

I just kept staring at her. All at once, it felt like someone had shoved a knife through my heart, and I doubled over. The moment washed over me, and it was more painful than anything I had ever experienced. Each inhale was physically painful as my breathing slowly began to pick up pace. I just kept staring, until an inexplicable rage tore through my heart. The world was such a fucking evil place. I shouldn't have expected anything less than this moment right here. It couldn't have left well enough alone. Of course it had to bring me right fucking here, right fucking now.

I leaned forward, put my hand on her foot, and burst into tears. Tears that couldn't be described by any one emotion. Tears of anger. Tears of sadness. Tears of despair. Tears of a thousand different feelings at once. For a moment, tears of relief as well. Relieved to know that she at least got to live well into her sixties, maybe even her seventies. What I wouldn't have given to hear what she had gotten to do in her life, even though I knew I would have never known before. Seeing her brought up, for even a moment, the idea that I would get to hear her voice again. Get to see those mesmerizing eyes one more time. Get to hear her explain everything that had happened in her life. But she died. Died without me. At least when I was dying, she was there right by my side— the only thing that made it easier and harder to say goodbye at the same time. I hoped she was at least hopeful and happy about the future when she decided to put herself in here.

"Louis?" August asked. "I can't begin to explain how sorry I am. The world is such a cruel and fucked up place. But we have to go."

"I have to bury her," I said. My voice sounded ethereal. "I have to."

"I understand," he replied sympathetically. "Take the car and find a beautiful spot for her. I'll meet up with the others—we're not far, I can walk."

"Can you help me carr..." I started, but my voice broke and the tears came again in full force.

"Of course I can." He tenderly wrapped his arm around her back.

"Wait!" I cried out. "If we leave her in there, is there a chance that someone could unfreeze her later? Like with the guy at the last place?"

"No Louis," he said lightly. "When they're gone, they're gone. That was just something I said to keep the kid from freaking out. This is the best we got—if there was any type of brain activity, this always works."

"Okay," I conceded, but felt numbed by the words. Her mind was the most beautiful thing about her, and those words each felt like separate daggers being driven deeper into my chest. "Okay." He now softly pulled her out forward. She was stiff. Then he slowly lowered her head back toward me. I caressed the side of her face for a moment, then took a hold under both of her arms. My tears fell gently onto her cheek as I looked down at her. The tears left warm streaks down her otherwise pale face. When we got outside, the rain was a downpour, washing away all the frost that was on her. As we approached the car, August fidgeted a little and the back door opened up. We placed her lying sideways across the back seat. I wished there was something we could have put over her. Every glance I got at her, my heart ripped open into a million pieces all over again. August ran back inside and came out with a small key and umbrella from his suitcase. I stood with my forehead pressed against the glass. Then an umbrella opened over me, and August's hand reached out with a key.

"Try to make it back in the next hour or two. We have urgent matters. But the most urgent thing for you now is to find a place for her. Good luck, Louis," he said as he put a hand on my shoulder.

"Thank you," I choked out as I held up the key.

"Of course," he said again, and turned around to walk away with his umbrella and suitcase in hand.

I got into the front seat and searched for a slot for the key for a second. My hand shook uncontrollably. The raindrops hitting the windshield wicked away, leaving a clear windshield in the downpour. I eventually found a slot in between the two front seats and twisted. The car turned on with a soft whir, and next to the steering wheel there was a switch that read automatic or manual. I flipped down to manual and slammed on the gas pedal. In an instant, the car was going forty down the residential streets. I glanced into the rearview mirror and saw Violet's midsection, and my breathing got ragged. I slammed on the gas again until I was going way too fast for the conditions. But I knew exactly where I was going, and I couldn't waste any time. Plus, the speed was the only thing distracting me from my whole life behind me.

I took a sharp left and the car turned on a dime. Under different conditions, driving a car like this might have been exhilarating. Taking lefts and right, I followed the route I had taken hundreds of times before until I reached the highway. It was completely empty. The only thing to watch out for were the cracks in the surface, but the car floated right over them with ease. Eventually I got the car up to 120 as the rain splashed off the windshield and the world flashed around me. Lightning cracked sideways across the sky in front of me. I got to the exit impossibly fast, sliding over the gore point as I sped down the road toward our house. The speed kept me from looking into the review. That was good.

As I turned on to our street, I saw it was filled with houses that had completely collapsed. Ours was no different. Nothing stood but the chimney, like an ominous gravestone of our old house and old life. The house didn't matter though. What did was still standing proudly in our backyard. Pink petals lined the tree that was now fully grown. By some miracle, it was still there, standing defiantly beautiful in contrast to the bleak day that surrounded it. We both knew that it would only live a couple dozen years at best when we planted it, and wanted to see what our lives were like when its life ended. But here it was, mystically watching the physical end of one of our lives instead, and for all intents and purposes the emotional life of the other. I drove the car over the lawn right to the edge of the tree. My mind went back and forth over whether or not I should take her out of the car while I did what I had to do. To keep her from being exposed to the elements as much as possible, I decided to leave her while I searched for where our old wooden shed stood. A lawnmower, a tool chest, the blade of a rusted axe, and the blade of an old shovel lay off in the corner of what would have been our yard. The shaft of the shovel had long since decomposed, so the warped blade would have to do. I picked it up with one hand and walked over to the tree, keeping my eye on the car the entire time, half expecting Violet to lean up and ask me what I was doing.

I feverishly slammed the shovel into the ground. The mud slopped up easily as I scraped away at it. Immediately, the rusty blade dug into my hand, causing deep cuts. I ignored them as I slammed it into the ground repeatedly, digging a wider, longer, and deeper hole. The mud mixing with my blood and tears. I was covered from head to toe in a deep layer of grime. When the hole was big enough, I tossed the blood-covered shovel head to the side and looked at my hands for a second. The base of each finger had deep gashes, but the only pain I felt was in my heart as

I stood up and walked toward the back of the car. I slipped on my way back to the car and left a long, bloody handprint down the window. Once I regained my balance, I grabbed at the handle and the door slid open, revealing Violet resting peacefully in the back seat. I wish I could have given her a more proper burial, but this was all that I could do. It was better than leaving her suspended in time in that terrible death chamber.

Reaching in, I clumsily grabbed at her and snagged at a pocket on her dress. There was something inside. I grasped for it and pulled out a picture. I sat down next to her and looked at it. It was a picture that we had by our nightstand of us after our wedding. She had slipped in the mud on the way out of the chapel, and her dress was covered completely. We both were beaming from ear to ear. I wanted to leave the picture with her so she could keep it, but selfishly I couldn't. I slipped the picture into the side of my shoe, the only safe place I had. Leaning down, I kissed her gently on the forehead. "We'll be together again someday," I whispered into her ear as I pushed the hair from her face with the back of my hand, doing my best to not get any blood on her. I brought my arms down and hooked under her armpits with the inside of my elbows, and slowly slid her out, until we were both standing straight up, embraced in a morbid hug. I leaned my head onto her shoulder and cried into it for a moment. Then, taking a deep breath I walked her backward into the makeshift grave.

She lay there, getting drenched by the rain for a second. I leaned down and kissed her forehead for the last time. "I love you, Vi. I always have. I always will." Then, with my forearms, I started piling the mud and dirt mixture back on top of her. Once she was completely covered, I rolled onto my back and looked up into the sky. Rain pelted my face as it mixed with and washed away my tears. My heavy breathing slowed as I laid my hand on the mound of mud. After a couple minutes, I rolled back over and got up to my feet. I got back into the car without looking back. I couldn't look back. Not anymore.

When I arrived back at the capital, all three of them were standing there waiting for me. Their sympathetic looks made me want to cry all over again, but I was able to hold back the tears this time. I got out of the car and went to join them, and they surrounded me in an awkward group hug.

"I hope you found a beautiful place," August said.

"I did."

"I'm really sorry, Louis," Rose said.

"It's really not fair. I'm sure she was a wonderful person," Hera told me as she laid her head on my shoulder.

"Thank you guys. I really appreciate it." I paused to scan their faces. "So what now?"

August popped open the back of the trunk and gently placed both suitcases in. "Now the fun begins."

PART 3:

PART 3.

CHAPTER 47

The train sped back toward the city with all of us on board. Sleeping off to the side because of a heavy dose of sleeping pills that August had given him was the kid we picked up. Rain pelted the windows as lightning flashed through the dark of the afternoon. August pulled out a knife identical to the one that Lydia had, and handed it over to me.

"You might end up needing this tomorrow," he told me as he passed out the other two blades to Hera and Rose. "Keep them hidden—finding another factions' tools on us will result in some very uncool punishments." He wriggled his fingers along with his stump of a pinky. "Did you get Hera up to speed yet, Rose?"

"She did," Hera replied, and nodded.

"Good—looks like Louis is the last piece of our little puzzle then." I was exhausted by the events that had just transpired, but I leaned forward to listen in on what the plan was going to be.

"Tomorrow." He paused. "Tomorrow, we will either go down in history, or get lost in it. Either way, with the state of affairs and how our allies are being taken by the dozens, this has to happen now. It's only a matter of time before they start taking down our buildings next. We have to stop them before that happens." Lightning cracked across the sky, illuminating the dark world and its barren landscape. "At the games tomorrow, we're going to—"

I cut him off. "Sorry, the games?"

"The stupid gladiator-style fighting that the Aristocracy decided to bring back. They justify it by saying the quote unquote robots no longer feel any pain. But any reasonable person can see that can't possibly be true."

"What do you mean quote unquote?"

"Well, back at the beginning of the founding of the West Empire, the founders, as they call themselves, meddled with the idea of cloning and robots. But after some major fuck-ups, they decided to 86 the whole idea. Both the clones and robots became too sentient for their own good, which oddly enough led to a bunch of issues with morality. With the state of things now, it seems somewhere along the line morality got tossed out of the window completely. But I digress. The so-called robots we have today are defectors, criminals, and other people that the empire find to be unsavory or worthless in other regards. Their spinal cords all the way to the brain are replaced with hardwiring, where they then can be told what to think and do remotely from any handler."

It felt like the world was turning at an alarming speed and all of a sudden stopped. The people I was supposed to be helping, supposed to trust, neglected to let me know that they were forcing me to murder people against my knowledge. "Wait—so the robots we fought in the arena were actually people?" My stomach turned over, and the image of the person's half-severed head burned my mind.

"Yes. And no. They were once people, but anything that made them who they were is completely gone. Or at least, almost completely gone. There might be the smallest amount of themselves there, but I've never seen anything to prove that."

"What the fuck." I said, relatively calmly given the circumstances. But my heart felt like it was being clawed apart. "So Nikola knew that they were people and he still made us kill them?"

"Unfortunately yes. But he was just as upset about the situation. It's tragic that we lost him, because he was an instrumental part in founding this revolution in the first place. He was the best shooter we had. Which brings us to you."

"So I'm going to be your shooter?" I was still reliving the image of all the people we had killed in the training grounds. But I shook it out of my head, knowing that these people wouldn't have let it go on if it wasn't completely necessary to what was coming.

"If everything goes according to plan, you'll only have to fire two shots."

"And who are those shots intended for?"

"One for the emperor. The other for his counselor." He paused for a moment. "Please make sure to not shoot the chancellor—she is the only person on our side that high up in the government."

"The lady who's always dressed in red?"

"Yeah," he laughed. "Should be easy to spot and avoid shooting."

"I think I can manage that. How far are we talking?"

"Far. You're going to have to use your pistol as well, but don't wear it on your hip. Hide it down your suit. Once your shot is fired, avoid further confrontation and make your way outside of the arena as quickly as you possibly can. With the two highest powers taken out, it falls to third, being the chancellor. She has the power to reform this whole fucked-up society, and she is planning on doing so. She'll be fine as long as you make your shots. However, if something happens to her, we have a backup plan. It just requires a lot more needless death."

"Wouldn't there be backlash from every angle when the chancellor decides to turn the whole system on its head?"

"Certainly. But the government system here is completely flawed, where the emperor has complete control. We're fully anticipating an assassination attempt on her as well, but as long as we can get her out safely into protection, the plan should go off without a hitch. Once we have control of the city, it will give us the upper hand for the first time in history."

"So what's the backup plan?"

"Fight our way to the capitol, take the whole thing down, and prepare for an all-out war. As long as you're able to, or someone else another faction has recruited is able to kill both the emperor and the counselor without the chancellor being harmed, the whole thing should be over in a matter of minutes."

"There's other people trying to kill them too?"

"Of course, Louis," August laughed. "I trust you; I just don't trust anyone enough to let the success of an entire rebellion land on their shoulders. You are, however, the only person I trust enough to take a shot from that far without accidentally killing the wrong person."

"So where are you guys in all of this?"

"I'll be right there with you to help fight our way out of the arena." August smiled. "Hera and I will be in place with the EMP in case plan A doesn't unfold how we want it to."

"EMP?" I asked.

"Yeah, electromagnetic pulse."

"No, I know what an EMP is, but what are you going to use it for?"

Hera chimed in, "You'll see if we end up needing it. August will be right there to explain it to you on the go. It will involve getting to the emperor before he can hide in his ivory castle, so we might have to try interfering with the city's electronic defenses."

"I'm glad you guys at least have a backup plan for your revolt."

"Louis. It's our revolt. You may not have been here as long as August and me. But we all believe in this, and I know you do too," said Hera. I did believe in it—the world was so much worse off now even though it was far more advanced technologically. Honestly, I was ready to die for it. Maybe I was just ready to die in general. The fresh wounds from Violet's death seemed so far ripped open that they would never heal.

"You're right. I said I'm all in. So I'm all in."

"Good," August said as he leaned over and patted me on my knee. "We need you."

"So how will we know if plan A failed?" Hera asked as she turned toward August.

"I'll have a bomb placed in a car in the parking lot of the arena. If you hear the explosion, do what you have to do."

"Okay, good deal."

"Everyone try to get a good night's rest tonight. Or as good as you can. Tomorrow is going to be a long day. It could turn into the longest of our lives."

I didn't know about that—this day already had already felt like the longest of mine. I pulled the picture from my shoe to examine it again in the bright light of the train.

Blood was smeared over the top of it, but our faces were completely unobstructed.

"Is that her?" August asked.

"Yeah," I sighed. He reached his hand out. With some trepidation, I handed it over.

He looked at it for a moment and smiled. "You guys looked so happy."

"We were." He passed it over to Hera and Rose to examine.

"Aw, you two are so beautiful," Hera said.

"Do it for her," Rose said as she handed it back to me. "I know she would be proud of you trying to change the world."

I stared at the picture for a long while and then agreed. "I know she would have been."

"Okay does anyone have any questions?" August asked. We all shook our heads. "Perfect." He stood up and retrieved a water bottle that came up through the floor, and poured the whole thing on the kid's face while the train started coming to a halt.

"Hello?" Riley said as he woke up out of a deep sleep. He looked at all of us and then got to his feet.

"We're here," August told him. "They'll have your uniform inside when we get off."

"Uniform?"

August sighed. "Yes. There will be some people outside waiting for you, and they'll direct you where to go."

"Okay?" he said as he got up to his feet. The train came to a full stop, and the door opened. We all got off. Outside, there was a group of ten people waiting. No chancellor this time.

"That's it?" one of the guys said as he looked at our sole recruit.

"Yeah, I think the city is finally running out of all these Cryo Kids, and we didn't see any other survivors. We're going to have to start venturing further out like we thought."

"Well, that's disappointing," he said. "Let's go." The man gestured for Riley to follow, and the kid did. They led him toward the building that I had first gone into off the train. He disappeared inside, and we all got back in the car to head to our apartment. Immediately when I got back inside, I was so emotionally exhausted I fell onto the bed. The mud had mostly dried, but it still left streaks as I rolled onto my back to stare at the ceiling. I thought about calling Lydia to tell her what had happened and see if she was ready, but decided people could be listening in on the conversation. Staring at the ceiling, I tried to think of nothing. Until nothing finally came.

CHAPTER 48

Dirt filled my mouth as I tried to scream. I clawed above me as earth collapsed down all around. Something was crawling all over my body. I swatted down, trying to knock them off, but the dirt caving in around me made it impossible. Punching upward, my fist collided with a piece of wood. All of a sudden, a flash of light illuminated my surroundings. I was in a coffin? The walls were half degraded to a point where dirt and mud was coming in from both sides. I dug out sideways and saw a glimpse of light. Rolling onto my side I clawed desperately at the side. Revealing more daylight.

Someone was standing above me, throwing more dirt in as I cleared more space. But it was filling as quickly as I could remove it. *Wait, stop. Please,* I tried to call out, but the dirt in my mouth made it impossible. All of a sudden, a flame formed around my feet as I kicked at it, trying to put it out. The dirt stopped filling in, so I clawed more desperately, trying to reach my way out. I got a look at the person filling the hole. Violet had tears rolling down her cheeks. "I love you so much, Louis. I'm so sorry it had to end like this." She brought the spade up, and with great force brought it back down on me.

CHAPTER 49

I awoke to the sound of an explosion in the distance. Shooting up out of bed, I rushed to the window and looked out to see if I could see anything. There was nothing. Another explosion sounded, causing the whole building to shake. This one was even closer. Quickly, I threw on my suit and ran out the door. Everyone was up and running out into the hall. People scrambled to get into the elevator, but it never came. Others rushed to the door to the right of the elevator, forcing their way in and pushing others out of the way. I looked over the crowd to see if I could see Rose. No luck.

The staircase was flooded with people running and tripping over each other. Someone had fallen and was twisted into a gruesome position while the crowd trampled him. I rushed down, getting pushed and shoved at every turn. Finally, at the bottom, people were rushing out of the lobby. I followed. Outside, thousands were gathered in the street. Smoke smoldered up from the remains of one of the faction buildings down the block. A storm of dust and smoke rushed down the street. I covered my mouth with one hand as the storm hit my eyes.

Another explosion across the street sent me sprawling backward toward my building. Shit, Lydia! Hopefully she had time to make it out. I searched through the smoke and ash for her, trying to call out, but the smoke filled my lungs. The building cascaded perfectly into the ground as if it were swallowed whole by the earth. It was hard to see ten feet in front of me. People were being trampled everywhere I looked as everyone started rushing away from the buildings in danger of being demolished. I tried to get back to my feet, but an explosion sounded in my building. I rolled forward to avoid being hit by debris. Looking up toward the building now caving in, I saw the Scout sign break loose and fall my way. It was as if it were in slow motion. I tried to move, but my legs wouldn't listen to my mind. Covering my head, I braced for the impact.

CHAPTER 50

The sun shone brightly in through the window as I received a call. What the fuck. I slapped at my face to feel something. It stung both my hand and face. I ignored the call for a moment while I caught my breath. Both dreams were so vivid it took a while for me to realize where I was, and even longer to realize what was happening today. Once I realized, I shot up out of bed and ran to the phone.

"Hello?"

"Holy shit, did you just wake up?" August's voice came through the receiver.

"Yeah." I wiped the sleep out of my eyes. "What's up?"

"It's 10:30," he laughed. "When I said get a good night's sleep I didn't mean go into fucking hibernation."

"Sorry, I'll be down," I replied.

"You better be—got a big day today ahead of us, sunshine. The games start in half an hour. So hurry your ass up." The call ended and I was left with silence. No time for a shower. I ran over to the wall and grabbed two pills, pancake and bacon. Then I downed a bottle of water, got dressed, made sure that the picture was still in my shoe, and ran out the front door. As I got to the elevator, I realized that I was missing a very important part. I busted back through the door and slammed it shut. My gun was sitting on the nightstand next to the bed. I tucked it into my shirt. It stuck out obtrusively against my chest, so I shoved it down farther where it was a little more inconspicuous.

Down in the lobby, August was waiting for me. "Morning, sleepyhead," he laughed. I shuffled awkwardly toward him, trying to adjust the gun near my groin. He turned and walked outside, and I followed him. Once we were out, he turned to me. "You look particularly well-endowed today." He broke out laughing.

"Didn't know where to put it." I shifted my weight as the cold plastic and metal brushed up against my stomach.

"I mean, I wouldn't have noticed if I hadn't known. Plus, your little penguin walk you're doing looks a little awkward. At least pretend you have a limp or something. You look ridiculous." He was still laughing.

"Well why don't you carry it then?" I asked.

"I'm not in the habit of taking things that were previously in someone else's pants." He hopped into the front seat of a car that he had parked out front, and I hopped in the passenger seat. Once we were inside, he held a finger up to his lips. "Well are you excited to see your first gladiator games?"

"I guess so. I don't really know what to expect."

"A lot of blood. It should be a good fight today."

"Oh joy." We were silent the rest of the drive to the arena, and when we arrived, there were thousands of people scattered everywhere. Cars were parking themselves in the massive lot as people hopped out by different entrances.

The arch was blocked off today with a massive screen. On it were alternating visuals of the Arcadia sign and faces of people who would be fighting today. "So do they actually fight to the death?" I asked as we got out and our car drove off to look for a parking spot.

"They wouldn't be very good gladiator games if they didn't," he said sarcastically. "But yeah, for the most part they do. Unless the emperor intervenes." We entered through an entrance marked *III*. As we lined up for security, my heart was pounding in my chest. I knew August had planned this part out—he had to have. There was no way he would fumble over such an important detail. We waited in line until we got to the front, where a machine that looked like one of the scanners you go through at the airport was in front of me. I looked at August, and he smiled reassuringly; I saw him glance over at the person behind the machine. The man nodded, and I saw him subtly flip a switch. As I stepped into the machine there was a high-pitched buzzing, and then a green light appeared and I exited, my heart still pounding at the rate of Darude's "Sandstorm."

Inside the forum of the arena was a white hall lined with black and red flags. Ancient Greek-looking statues periodically lined the walls. There were unisex bathrooms that we passed as we walked around the different sections. Floating holograms told people where their sections were. There were no gate numbers, just different symbols for each faction.

"What are the black-and-white-striped arcadia symbols for?" I asked as I pointed at a couple holograms we passed.

"That's for the Aristocracy. This is one of the only places for the most part that we have similar opportunities." I looked up as I passed while people in jumpsuits with the symbols filed into them. "Let's go have a smoke," he said, pulling out a pack of the Wax like when I first met him.

"I'm good." I waved my hand.

"I assure you, it's no problem." He gestured a little more forcefully my way. I took one this time, and we stepped out into a smoking lounge. There were a couple other people puffing away off to the side. I brought it to my lips, and it sparked on. I took a short hit and exhaled. My heart started thumping in my chest again. With each subsequent hit, it felt like it was going faster and faster, until I was sure that this time I was going to have a heart attack. I looked over at August, and he was leisurely smoking his, looking out one of the massive windows in the room and staring at the city. I was almost all the way through the stick when all of a sudden, the feeling became cathartic again. I could clearly hear the people next to us quietly having their conversation about who they thought would win the games, and they were making friendly wagers. The entire white city in front of me sparkled and shone at a wholly too intense level. There was almost a white aura radiating off of the skyline. I took a deep breath and felt at my chest. It was probably going a hundred beats a minute, but part of that was the anxiety about what was to come. And not knowing when it would come.

"Ready to find our seats?" August asked.

"Yeah." After stopping to use the bathroom and readjust the pistol that I had hidden away, I stood and stared at the mirror for a second. My pupils were almost entirely dilated, and I saw my face in a light I never had before. Each feature was extremely exaggerated. I looked fairly well rested, but for a moment I swore I could see streaks on my face where the tears had fallen the day before. Soft indents in my skin. I swiped at them for a while, trying to get them to go away but they never left.

"Are you alright?" a girl next to me asked.

Startled for a moment, I replied, "Yeah, I'm fine, thanks."

"Okay? Well, enjoy the show." She wiped her hands on her jumpsuit and walked out. I followed and regrouped with August. We entered through one of the tunnels that had the Scout symbol hovering over it. When we got out into the seating section, the bright sun blinded me for a second. There were tens of thousands of people, entirely filling almost every section. Toward the front of one of the sections was Nero, and someone else I didn't recognize. They gestured at us and we came and took our seats next to them. I sat in between Nero and August.

"Hope you're ready," Nero said as he leaned over to me.

"I think I am," I said.

"Good," he nodded. "That's all we can hope for."

"This is Zeno," August said as he introduced me to him.

"Good to meet you," Zeno said as he leaned over to shake my hand. He had wild gray hair, but couldn't have been any older than thirty.

"Nice to meet you too," I said as I shook his hand. All of a sudden, the crowd erupted into a roar. Everyone was on their feet now, so we all stood up as well. An impossibly large screen rose up out of the ground, hovered about thirty feet in the air, and started to rotate. All of a sudden, a man appeared on the screen with a few people gathered around him. He stood, while the rest remained seated.

"There he is," August whispered over to me. Then he nodded his head toward a section of the crowd about a hundred feet away. Holy shit, they wanted me to make that shot? With a pistol, no less? I hoped that the other people employed in his death had better laid-out plans. "You obviously recognize the woman on his right, but the guy on his left, closer to us, is the counselor." I nodded.

"Welcome everyone," the emperor's voice boomed through the arena.

"Here we go again," August groaned. "Hopefully this will be the last time anyone hears this self-righteous speech."

"Thank you for coming to bask in the glory of Arcadia. Like the Ancient Romans and Ancient Greeks, we came together as smaller city-states after the annihilation of the old world. Now we are a glorious Empire again. It's thanks to each and every one of you that we are where we are today. For almost two hundred years, we have strived to make a better future for ourselves. For our children, and for our children's children. Without you acting as the mortar in a once-crumbling society, we would have fallen to the ashes. I thank you for it, and present you an honorable day of battle to depict our strength and vitality as we push forward toward an even greater future." He paused for a second to wait for people to clap. The scattered applause around us was half-hearted, but as a whole the stadium erupted. "Without further ado, here is our opening event. Let the games begin." People around the stadium pumped their fists, cheered, and screamed. The noise was deafening. Probably partially due to the Wax I had just smoked.

All of a sudden, the training ground we had spent so many days at began disappearing into the ground as great holes formed underneath. A labyrinth of hedges just taller than a person formed, with a good-sized circular arena in the middle containing a variety of hand-to-hand weapons. The screen that previously had the emperor on it now rotated with a top-down view of the sprawling maze. Walls began popping open around each entrance to the maze as the competitors emerged. Some flapped their arms upward to the roars of the crowd, while others sprinted directly into the maze.

"After this is over, there will be two people to fight to the death. When the emperor gives the thumbs down at the end is when I need you to take your shot. So just be prepared," August told me calmly.

"Fuck. Okay." I half-expected to start tapping my leg nervously, but my hands were steadier than they ever had been. The crowd groaned as one of the competitors rounded a corner and was met with a wall of spikes. The camera focused on his body convulsing as the spikes pierced him straight through in dozens of points. Blood dripped from each freshly moistened spike and pooled up underneath the person, who had one foot still on the ground while the rest of his body was fixed into place. At once, the body stopped convulsing, and a red X formed on the screen. The camera jumped back to a top-down view. Almost immediately after, the view jumped to a woman who was running down a narrow straight. As she ran over a discolored patch on the ground, all of a sudden the ground shot up impossibly fast, sending her knees up into her chin, and her whole body went flying about twenty feet into the air. The camera followed her the entire time until she came back down, her legs hitting the hedges. She landed directly on her head. It twisted off to one side as the body fell limp. Again, a red X formed on the screen before it returned to a top-down view. There were still six people running around, trying to find their way to the center first.

"People volunteer for this?" I asked, nauseated.

"Some do. It's one of the only ways to make it into the other district. However, most are forced into it," Nero said this time. "I hate it."

"I can see why." The crowd roared as the first contender made their way into the inner circle. He went to the weapon container and pulled out a battle axe, and then looked around. Everyone else was making their way inward still, so he grabbed a belt and fastened a knife to it, then spun around, scanning each possible entrance. Then his eyes fixed on one where we could see a man making his way out.

The man with the battle axe went over to the entrance and hid around the side. The camera shot to him, and I realized it was Travis. My stomach felt an uneasy queasiness as the thought crossed my mind that I was hoping for his death. But he was forced into this just like everyone else, and I felt some pity for him.

"Holy shit, that's Travis," I leaned over to Nero.

"Yeah, I'm hoping he gets what he deserves for what he did to Nikki. Kind of like a consolation prize if this whole revolution doesn't work out."

"You knew he would be here?"

"Yeah, criminals are a huge part of the games. I have a gut feeling that someone caught wind of what we're planning and used him as a pawn to try and take us out."

"Why wouldn't they just kill us all?"

"Maybe they weren't completely sure of it. Plus, outright murder without certainty wouldn't reflect too well on the higher-ups. Probably didn't want another revolution on top of our own."

As soon as Travis caught a glimpse of the person running out of the maze, he swung full-force into his mid-section. The blow nearly cut the person clean in half as the axe drove in. Falling forward from the momentum, they fell onto the blade, which completely severed them the rest of the way. Their entrails slid out as the killer quickly snatched the axe up again. A red X flashed momentarily when all of a sudden someone came running out from the other side toward the weapon compartment. Travis came rushing with the axe, but another woman shot out into the middle area. She waited momentarily while Travis rushed at the man fumbling for a weapon. The axe came down hard, and he cut the other man's arm clean off. Blood rushed out uncontrollably as he fell to the ground screaming.

The follow-through from the axe got it stuck into the ground, and the other woman silently ran up behind him and snuck the knife off his belt. I shifted uncomfortably in my seat. As Travis spun around, she shoved the knife up through his chin. It stuck in there as he tried to scream, and she quickly pulled it out with a splash of blood. Immediately after, she swung sideways and lodged the knife in his temple. He twitched for a second, then fell to his knees as another X appeared on the screen. Once he was lying sideways on the ground, she dislodged the knife again. Just like that, the person who had been so menacing for the entirety of our training was gone, his life fled from him. I felt like I should feel bad. But I really didn't, and that scared me.

The other man was still wailing on the ground as he tried to put up his one remaining arm, but the woman jabbed it in through his eye and another X flashed across the screen. She then quickly ran over to the weapon cabinet and retrieved a spear out of it. Spinning it around in the air momentarily, she shifted her eyes toward where she must have heard the other contender running out of. They didn't even get a chance to make it into the circle before she rushed in and jabbed the spear through their throat, then quickly pulled it out to turn and face the other openings. The man grabbed at his throat and stumbled back further into the maze as blood poured out through the openings in his fingers. He tried to gasp for breath a couple times before falling to the ground and frantically moving his hands in an attempt to close the hole. It was no use—within twenty seconds, another red X flashed, relaying to the crowd that his life had left his body.

Two more people came running out, one after another. The woman surveyed her opponents and went for the burly man rushing for the weapons. She threw the spear, which went clear through the man's thigh and lodged into the ground. He screamed and tried to pull the spear out, stumbling a little before he got it fully removed. She grabbed the hilt and spun around as the blade sliced clean out through the side of his thigh. He tried to limp away on his one good foot as she brought the point into the back of his head.

That was the last thing I watched—I brought my attention over to the emperor and counselor. They were both on their feet, clapping as the rest of the crowd cheered and jeered. All of a sudden, the crowd gasped. I looked at the screen momentarily; a man was sprawled on the ground as the woman held the tip of the spear to his throat. She looked back up at the emperor as I did the same. He held his thumb out sideways. I reached into my suit and pulled out the gun. August and Nero stood by my side, protecting me from the sight of others. I took aim as his thumb slowly started to point down. The chancellor ducked. I pulled the trigger and let out one shot toward the counselor, and millimeters to the left pulled the trigger again. The first shot burned a hole through the counselor's temple, and the second ripped clean through his forehead. Fuck. I tried to fire off another shot, but the emperor had dived down, and the chancellor was now in my way.

It took a second for everyone to realize what had happened. People looked back and forth at each other as if in question. But then the screen went black, and all at once people started trying to rush out. Bodies were fumbling over each other trying to be the first one out. The entire arena erupted into pandemonium.

Then a person with a knife came running toward the section with the emperor. The chancellor stumbled backward and spun around, a knife lodged in her chest as she fell down and out of sight. All of a sudden, beams of light shot up around the section, and whoever was unlucky enough to come in contact was split clean in half. Hands, arms, legs, all thumped to the ground, including the chancellor from her chest up. As the beams shot up into the sky, the entire section submerged into the ground and disappeared out of sight.

"Fuck," August said as he fumbled at his watch while we all exited with the rushing crowd. An explosion sounded outside, and he put his wrist back down. "Let's go." He picked up the pace. I followed him, Nero and Zeno close behind. We got out into the parking lot, where a faint buzz could be heard in the distance. All the cars that were driving by stopped immediately. Drones began falling out of the sky like dying birds.

"Good, at least something is going right."

CHAPTER 51

"We don't have much time," Nero said as he started up into a jog. "We have about three hours before the power to the city comes back on. Four hours max, if we're lucky. Without the help of the chancellor to take over and put an immediate stop to the opposition, we're going to have to take control ourselves. Which, needless to say, is going to be a hell of a lot harder, until we can track down the emperor and gain control of the defenses around the city." The area around the arena was filled with panic as people abandoned going for their cars and took off down the street. Not that the cars would work anymore anyway. The panic in the streets was a strange contrast to the beautiful blue sky above us. Drones were replaced by birds flapping by. The air felt cool on my skin as we sped down the streets with the rest of the people.

As we ran past the faction buildings, people were all rushing outside to see what was going on. It seemed like tens of thousands of people were all confused, walking around, trying to make sense of everything. That was when I heard the second explosion of the day. I heard it before I saw anything. One explosion, followed in quick succession by ten more. The first building to the left behind us fell neatly into the ground. The twenty or so stories vanished in an instant, replaced by dust and debris. A few people unlucky enough to be still exiting the building or too close vanished in an instant. More screams filled the streets, as people were no longer casually looking around. A stampede formed, but we pushed our way through. I had no idea where we were actually going.

"Holy shit," August panted. "They're actually doing it." Another explosion followed by the same subsequent ten, sounded off again, and this time a building in front of us to the right disappeared into the ground, taking everyone inside and around it with it. It was becoming increasingly hard to see as smoke and ash covered everything in sight. The sun and sky were no longer visible. Explosion after explosion came like ghastly fireworks. Only these fireworks couldn't be seen, just heard and felt deep in your chest. Buildings kept coming down, one after another, until the smoke and debris obscured everything that wasn't a couple feet in front of me. All I could see was August's back and several other people around us. Everyone was completely gray from head to toe. All of a sudden, it was getting extremely hard to breathe from the surrounding smoke. I pulled the corner of my jumpsuit up over my mouth and struggled to inhale through it. The gun by my midsection contorted uncomfortably. I reached in and brought it out to holster it next to my side. I had a feeling discretion wasn't on the table anymore. After about two minutes, all the explosions stopped and were replaced by screams of fear and agony. The sounds of the explosions were actually preferable.

Several blocks down, the smoke began to clear up a little, to the point where I could now see about ten feet ahead of me. The farther we got, the clearer the day became, until finally we were out of it completely. I looked back to try and see the extent of the damage, but the massive gray cloud we had just ran out of blocked the view entirely.

"Jesus," August panted again as he looked back. Out ahead of us, I heard the familiar *tsst* sound, accompanied by screams. People were falling down left and right as the bullets ripped through multiple at a time.

"This way!" Nero shouted as we rounded a corner to the right. This street still had hundreds on it, but not nearly as many as the main one we were running down. Most people behind us followed to avoid running into the death squad that faced them. Nero ran to a car parked on the side of the street, its windows obscured, and quickly opened it up. Inside, it was stacked to the ceiling with pistols. He grabbed one for himself and handed another to both August and Zeno.

"I got this," Zeno said.

"See you on the other side." Nero gave him a quick hug and took off running again. "We have to go."

August patted Zeno on the back, and I followed them, looking back. Zeno was handing out guns to absolutely every person that he could. We rounded another corner, and he was out of sight.

"Where are we heading?" I asked to neither of them in particular.

"The capitol," August replied. "We have to try to get there and cut him off from getting inside. He has a bunker that is well fortified. If we can stop him from getting into it, we can prevent more needless death." We picked up our pace a little until we were almost in a dead sprint. My chest hurt from the smoke as I wheezed, trying to keep up the speed. Finally we came to a gate that was guarded by five people. They stood no chance against the army behind us. They were firing upon the unarmed people in front of us when we and a group of about fifteen others unloaded. Riddled with holes, they all dropped instantly, and we rushed through into the other district that we were never allowed in before. People were running scared inside of businesses.

"Don't shoot them!" Nero called out to the people behind us. But in the noise and confusion, some of them started plastering everyone they saw with bullets. Bodies fell left and right, littering the streets. Some people even started shooting blindly into the buildings. It's amazingly terrible what hate mixed with a little confusion can do. Periodically, a lone guard would come out to try and pick off some of us. It was no use. By this point, we had a small army of about four hundred people rushing with us. People hid behind and under cars but were dragged out by the angry mob and summarily executed. It made me sick to my stomach, and for the first time I pondered if this was actually the right call. I understood the anger and animosity they harbored toward these people they were murdering in cold blood. But it made me rethink if this was just the beginning of something much worse. I shook the thought from my head, hoping that once we reached our destination and did what we came to do, the high anger and tension would dissipate in time. Thankfully, at the very least, it seemed like the mob wasn't intent on hurting children, as they ran and screamed and clung to their parents' lifeless bodies. There were going to be a lot of orphans after today. My stomach dropped further at the thought.

The pristine white buildings were now splattered with blood almost everywhere you looked. Some of the people behind us started running in front. As I looked around, I caught a glimpse of Lydia, pistol in hand, looking scared and disgusted.

"Lydia!" I called out exhausted, but it caught her attention.

"Louis!" she called back and ran over toward me. "I can't..." she huffed. "Believe this." We kept running; talking hurt too much. All of a sudden, a group of thirty or so guards met us in the middle of the street as we rounded another corner. People were getting shot all around us, screaming and falling to the ground, but they were replaced by more people firing toward the guards. Bullets hissed across the sky in every direction. I periodically ducked down as they flew around us. I knew why people always did that in the movies now. It didn't seem like ducking would actually help avoid the bullets, but instinctually it just felt like something that I should do.

I fired as many shots as I could toward the guards, hitting a couple in the chest and face. At least I think they were my bullets. They honestly could have come from anywhere. We never stopped running, and by the time we got to the line of guards, they were all sprawled out on the ground, some still writhing around in pain. Without a second thought we vaulted over the bodies. A significant number of our own fell with them, crawling around in pain behind us as I looked back, or lying completely motionless. But the sheer number of people we had with us overwhelmed all the smaller guard posts, and it seemed the rest of the population was too afraid to fight back.

In the confusion, people were still firing behind us, hitting some of our own as they continued to fall at an alarming rate. "Only another two blocks," August called back. Somehow, even though it was getting impossible to breathe, everyone got a burst of energy and sprinted until we were only a block out. Now the streets were completely desolate, with everyone already aware of the chaos and hiding inside. We stopped at the edge of a building and waited. Surprisingly, everyone else paused with us. There was now easily over a thousand people behind us. There was no way there were that many guns in that car. Someone else must have been distributing them as well, although it appeared that some of the people were only armed with knives and the katanas that we normally carried. Some didn't even have weapons.

Lydia turned to me. "I'm so happy you're still okay," she said with a strained smile. "This probably isn't a good time, but Harold and his wife are gone." The words barely meant anything to me at this point. I felt for them, I really did. But I had already written them off as dead, and given the circumstances, that was the last thing on my mind.

"Oh," is all I said.

"Yeah. It happened the other day. I would have done everything I could to stop it, but I couldn't risk blowing our cover. It was their turn to serve the donor faction. At least they went together. But I'll have to live with that the rest of my life." She let out a strained cough, choking back tears as we ran.

"Well, I'm just glad you're still here," I told her.

"Me too."

Once everyone caught their breath, Nero yelled out to the crowd. "This is it. Shoot absolutely everyone you see in here. We have no friends in there anymore. Every ally we have is out here, fighting tooth and nail with us." He pointed down the street, but the building on the corner obstructed the view of the capitol he must have been pointing at. In an instant, a barrage of bullets rained down on him before he could continue his speech. They were coming from above. He fell down to the ground, unrecognizable.

"Nero!" August called out, but he didn't run to meet him. In the anger, everyone lost their rational judgment and started out into a dead sprint around the corner toward the capitol. Lydia, August, and I ran with the middle of the crowd. Flashes came from windows all around on either side of the street, and people around us fell to the ground. It was like shooting fish in a barrel. Some of the people blindly fired back up at the windows, but it was unlikely that they ever hit any of them. Maybe one or two at most. At the end of the street, we rounded the corner and pushed up tight against the building. Those who weren't pressed tight had people firing straight down upon them. There were only a hundred or so of us left now, but down another street another group of people came sprinting in. And then one more down another street. Each had a group roughly the size of ours.

"We need to go quickly—the EMP will only stop their real defenses for so long." August paused for a short moment and then shouted, "Now!" as we made a dead sprint for the doors of the capitol. As we ran, people fired an excessive amount of bullets into the massive glass door until it finally shattered. The building was an enormous, ornate white monstrosity. It wasn't as tall as some of the other buildings, but the architecture would have been beautiful under other circumstances. It resembled a cathedral more than a capitol. Once inside. we were met with an unsettling silence. The only light came through the windows.

Our group continued on forward with one of the other groups, while the others took their places and watched out the front door, waiting for guard reinforcements. The inside of this place, as far as I could tell, wasn't white like the other buildings. It had all sorts of art and beautiful statues. A red carpet led the way down the middle of it. Ornate gold architecture decorated the walls. At the end of the carpet was a huge, gorgeously decorated door.

"Do you have it?" August called out to someone I'd never met before.

"Of course," the man smiled crazily. His rough face and wild black hair made him look like a madman. The bright yellow symbol on his suit shone in the dimly illuminated immense hall. He must have been part of the Assembly faction. He reached into his jumpsuit and pulled out what looked like C4. Quickly, he pasted it to the door and backed up slightly. He smiled as it lit up and started to fizzle in a blinding light. "Ah," he sighed with pleasure. "I love thermite."

Once the light was extinguished, he gave a kick to the door, and it swung open slightly. Then a couple other people pushed up against it, swinging it wide open. Inside was a council chamber. It looked like it came straight out of Ancient Greece. Marble was everywhere, shining from the light through the long, narrow windows. The round walls came together to form a perfect circle. All of a sudden, the lights flickered back on.

People were still entering the room when a huge gate closed down with a loud clang. A couple people let out screams as their bodies were pinned into the solid marble floor. "Shit, I thought we had more time—looks like the capitol's backup power's kicked in," the wild-haired Assembly member said. "Looks like the party is just getting started."

From the other side of the solid metal gate, screams could be heard for about thirty seconds. Then there was complete silence. The people under the door had died and there were only a few arms and legs that remained on our side as a gruesome reminder. I looked around frantically to see the numbers we had left. Forty max—even that was probably pushing it.

The room was even more awe-inspiring in the light, and a huge Arcadia symbol inlaid with gold spread across the middle of the floor. There were several levels of marble table and chairs, six on each level. At the front of the room by where we were standing, a huge, ornate throne gilded with all types of jewels and metals sat.

"What now?" one of the people asked.

"Now we go to the subterranean tunnels connecting the city. Find the panic vault, and deal with this once and for all." August pulled out a knife and jabbed it into the armrest of the throne and pried up. A compartment with a keypad underneath appeared. "These dumb, vain bastards should have accounted for this better." He pressed down on the numbers 11831491. "For future reference, if you're trying to come up with a secret code, don't use the name of the city in numeric form. It's kind of easy to remember," he smirked as the floor started to shift. All of a sudden, the symbol on the floor twisted and parted, revealing a spiral staircase down into a brightly lit cavern.

CHAPTER 52

All of us coiled down the stairs until we were met with an incredible view of what lay underneath the city. It was breathtaking. The ceiling mimicked a beautiful sunny day, and it was impossible to tell that we were really probably about fifty feet underground. Small shops and restaurants lined the walls, while trees grew out of their neatly placed cutouts. A light artificial breeze pumped in the purest and cleanest air I had ever felt in my lungs. The room expanded as far as the eye could see forward, and it was hard to tell just how wide it was. Walls to either side of us depicted a cityscape that was meant to give the feeling of grandiosity. A couple people walked down the alleys between the shops to touch the wall, just to make sure that the width of the room didn't in fact span for miles.

"This, friends," August spoke up, "is where the lucky elite souls were prepared to wait out another war if it came knocking back on our cities' doors, while we fought for our lives. But here we are, kicking down their fucking door. Bringing the war to them. You have to appreciate the irony in all of this." He let out a little laugh, which brought about more laughter around him and many nods. "Now, are we going to die in here, or are we going to make sure those fuckers get what's coming to them?" He paused to cheers. "No longer will we be used and disposed of at their leisure. No longer will we worry about what we say, and who we say it to. No longer will we toil all day every day while these hedonists live out the fantasy of their every whim. This is our city!"

This time he was met with enormous roars of approval.

"What do you say? Got a little more fight in ya, you skeevy bastards?" Everyone raised their weapons to the artificial sky and hollered. "Then what are we waiting for?" He turned around and started marching down the middle of the path in between the buildings. Everyone followed. Damn, August made a pretty great leader. I never would have thought that from when I first met him.

"This is absolutely insane," Lydia said to me as she looked around at everything that was down here. "It's like they could have lived down here forever. I wonder how big this place actually is."

"It really is," I agreed.

"Who would have thought our little Auggie had all this fight in him?" She giggled.

"Right?" I laughed. "That guy is full of mysteries." As we got further down into the subterranean bunker, the shops changed into beautiful little houses. Each had their own yard with lush green grass. The houses looked even stranger because they looked more like old-world buildings. Some of them were white, but most of them were uniquely designed and had names on them. One in particular light blue Cape Cod-style house with beautiful columns and a small front porch must have been nearly scraping the ceiling from its second-floor rounded turret with picturesque stained glass windows.

It seemed like every house was from a different decade of architecture. Colonial, Tudor, Modern, Cottage, Contemporary, Art Deco, and dozens of other styles lined the streets. Different family names were engraved on each door. Perhaps whenever they built it, the head of each elite family was allowed to choose from whatever design their hearts desired.

We came to a fork in the road, where two paths split off in either direction and the one we were on continued forward. Down either side, more houses lined the streets. Some had hedges, some had white picket fences, some had wrought iron, or fountains and other lavish decorations. Everything was mindboggling—the time and labor that must have gone into creating an entire city underground. As we continued on, the houses became fewer and far between and were replaced by gardens and farms with all types of fruits and vegetables growing in them. A couple people went over to grab some low-hanging apples off a small tree.

I ran up to August. "Who the hell is growing all this stuff?"

"Beats me." He shrugged his shoulder. "Why? Do you want to compliment them on their exceptional agricultural knowledge?" He laughed.

"If I do see them, I'll be sure to let them know." I laughed with him.

"We're really here, Louis. I can't believe it. This is even wilder than I could have ever imagined."

"You and me both."

"I couldn't have done it without you."

"Yeah right. I'm just here for the ride—I have no idea what the hell is going on."

"I mean you did kind of fuck up half of your job." He laughed again. "But I'll cut you some slack. You are new to this whole coup thing."

"That's what you get for trusting me." I shrugged my shoulders and grinned.

"Seriously though, the fact that you at least hit one of them made a world of difference. The three of them are instructed to split up in a case like this. But when there is only one person left, that makes it kind of hard to split up. Our numbers never would have been able to support two different sieges. Although there were other people scheduled to take them out, you were the only one to get the job done. Some dumb fuck couldn't listen to instructions either and ended up killing the chancellor instead. Looks like that big old professor brain of yours came in handy after all."

I laughed hard this time. "I hardly think it takes a professor to listen to like six words of instructions."

"Either way, we did it, buddy." He clapped me on the shoulder. "We're in the final stretch now."

CHAPTER 53

As we continued down the sprawling corridor, the scenery soon changed to the sterile white environment everyone was so used to.

"Oh my god, they have even better equipment down here," Lydia said to me as she peered in through the windows of some clinics we passed. "I wouldn't have even thought that was possible—we have so much at our disposal up there."

"I guess the people down here were just more important than the ordinary aristocracy. Higher class than the highest class."

"That's so unfair. But, like, what if they were to get sick up there?"

"I suppose there were probably other places that you never got a chance to see that they were taken to."

"Yeah, that's true. That definitely could have been the case. But why have the equipment for it if everybody can't use it? It would have been super easy to replicate these labs up there with all the resources they have."

"I stopped asking questions about what goes on here long ago." I shook my head.

"I suppose I should do the same. It just seems so unnecessary."

"Sure does." The ceiling was no longer depicting the sky, now white with fluorescent lights brightly illuminating the tunnel. The end of the tunnel was in sight. A steel door blocked the rest of the way through. The scene was very familiar. On either side of us, hundreds of cryogenic chambers lined the walls, four rows deep. All of a sudden, the door slid up a little, and a previously unseen door slammed down from the ceiling behind us, trapping us in the cryogenic room.

"Shit, get to cover," August yelled out, and slid behind one of the chambers. Most of us followed suit. Lydia and I hid behind a couple to the left. A couple unfortunate souls were too distracted talking and didn't have time. Two drones slid there way underneath and floated up to head level. In an instant, there were five *tsst* noises, and five bodies dropped to the floor. Clean orange glowing dots shone on the middle of their foreheads as their bodies thumped to the neat white flooring. Their blood didn't even get a chance to start pooling before the drones zoomed down the chamber, looking for their next victims. Some tried to shoot at them and were immediately left with glowing holes in their hands, and soon matching holes in their heads once the drones reached them. "Louis!" August called out from the other side of the tunnel. "As soon as I shoot, you're going to have to make your shot count. Everyone else, start shooting!"

In an instant, bullets were flying from all directions at the drones while they precisely spun around, hitting each person in the blink of an eye. August pulled out his gun and kept firing. Even as he was hit twice, he somehow managed to get another shot off. In the meantime, I shot once while it was distracted trying to take off August's hand and sent one bullet through its center. It smashed down into the ground. The other drone zoomed toward August, and as it got to the other side, he pushed the whole cryogenic chamber over, smacking into it and causing it to go off kilter. I jumped out to take my shot. Another *tsst* sounded right before I got my shot off sending it back into the ground.

"Fuck. That was a close one," August said as he examined his hand, which was now dangling with blood spurting out of it. Lydia quickly rushed over to him.

"Auggie!" she cried out as she took her knife and quickly cut off her own sleeve. When she got over to him, she delicately took his arm in her hands and examined it. "We have to take it off," she said horrified. His dangling hand was so mangled it would've been impossible to tell what it had once been if it weren't still been attached to his arm.

"Eh, I never really liked that hand anyways," he laughed, then winced. She tied her sleeve tightly around the middle of his forearm. Then she brought the knife up.

"I'm so sorry—this is really going to hurt."

"Will you hold my hand through it?" He laughed. But in his eyes was excruciating pain. His ability to conceal his extreme discomfort was astonishing. "Just do it, please."

Within an instant she sliced clean through the hand, and August let out a howl of pain. Then he hyperventilated for a moment before laughing again. "That wasn't so bad." She pressed the glowing tip to the stump on his arm multiple times, while he let out a couple more screams, until the blood stopped flowing almost completely. Just a few droplets here and there. Suddenly, I felt an excruciating pain in my abdomen. "Thanks doc, you did a fine job." He smiled up at Lydia. I felt a warm wetness running down my stomach now. I brought my hand down to where the pain was coming from and winced. When I brought it back up, blood was smeared down my palm. Shit—not good.

CHAPTER 54

I didn't say anything for a moment; I just stared at the blood on my hand. It felt so surreal, until the pain came back full force and I doubled over. Blood slowly dripped through the hole in the fabric on my suit and plinked onto the ground. It was starting to pool a little bit there, which was alarming to say the least. It was happening so quickly.

"Louis?" Lydia rushed over. "Louis, what happened?" She looked down at the floor underneath me and screamed in alarm. "We need to get you out of here now," she said in a half cry.

"No can do," I said. "We have a job to finish. And even so, there's no way out of here but forward."

"Yeah," she said, and let out a little teardrop. "Here, I'll try to help you." She cut off her other sleeve and split it down the middle. Without asking, she went over and did the same to August. They both came over to me this time.

"Come on, you can't die on us now man," August said to me, clearly upset. "We need you here."

"I'm not going anywhere yet," I told them, but the pain to my abdomen was almost unbearable. That could have been a complete lie—I had no idea. Lydia had tied them both together when she came over to wrap them around my stomach tightly.

"This is the best I can do for right now," she said sadly. "If the bleeding doesn't slow, we can try cauterizing the wound, but that could do more damage than good. Also, it's likely that it would just rip open again right away."

"It's okay, Lydia." I smiled up at her. "Thank you." I tried getting back to my feet, but it was too hard. Quickly, Lydia and August both grabbed me from under my arms and hoisted me up. Once on my feet, the pain grew even greater, and I inhaled sharply, letting my breath out slowly.

"I brought a couple of these just in case," August said as he reached down into his shoe and retrieved a couple pills. Their state was laughable; they were broken up, and appeared to have melted a little. I could have laughed if the pain wouldn't have sent me doubling over again.

"Thank you for the sweaty foot pills." I smiled.

"Anytime," he replied. "You don't even want to know where I stored the other ones." I laughed a little and bent over a little bit, forcing out a wince. "Sorry about that, I'll keep my comedic talents to myself from here on out."

"What talents?" I smiled as I popped the pills in my mouth. Immediately, the pain disappeared almost completely, replaced by a dull ache in the hole going through my body. I reminded myself to periodically check the bleeding, because there was no way in hell I was going to feel it if it did start gushing again.

"Yeah, yeah, everyone's a critic," he said as he went over to examine the small opening under the door where the drones had flown out. He winced, looked down at his missing hand, but only for a moment, then looked back. I followed his gaze to examine the rest of the group we had remaining. A couple of them were talking to each other, while the rest of their eyes followed August. All in all, there were fourteen people left, including us. "It looks like this is it." He got up with a huge smile on his face. "Everyone go through, one at a time. Louis, thanks for volunteering."

"Fuck that, you go first," I laughed.

"I'll go first," Lydia said as she dropped down and did a little elegant roll underneath. "Oh my god," she gasped as she got to the other side, then reached an arm through. "Here, I'll help you Louis." I got down slowly and lay on my back, then kind of did a little shimmy sideways as Lydia grabbed my arm and gently pulled. It was a really strange way to go through, but the thought of army crawling or rolling sounded like a surefire way to reopen my wound. Then August followed through, army crawling his way under, his new stump of an arm swaying back and forth with each movement. I turned around to see the place we were in.

Either I was starting to hallucinate, or I was getting up to look at a massive estate. The sky was now a beautiful sunny day again. A fountain sat in the center of a driveway that wrapped around it. Four pillars surrounded a fantastic wooden door. The house itself spanned about one hundred feet sideways. Huge, ornate windows looked out into the front yard. On either side of the driveway were perfectly landscaped gardens. Standing two stories tall, with chimneys protruding from its peak, it looked like a mansion you would find in a tacky movie about 1800s high society. The tan brick was in perfect condition, and the rest of the scene was immaculately taken care of. It was official—I did fall down the rabbit hole this time. It was the time to find where that white rabbit ran off to.

The gate behind us slammed shut before anyone else could come through, as soon as August was safely all the way inside. Out in the distance, someone was trimming hedges and didn't even take notice of us. We must have looked so out of place covered in dirt, dust, and blood with the perfect backdrop of the estate sprawled out in front of us. August smiled and shook his head as he took in the scenery, while Lydia and I just kept staring around. Beautiful classical music could be heard playing in the distance.

"Am I hallucinating, or is all of this real?" I turned to ask Lydia.

"Oh, it's real," she replied, her jaw still hanging open.

"Okay, cool, thought I was already dead." We started approaching the front huge wooden front doors. As soon as we got up the stairs, they swung inward, revealing a spectacular entryway. Two people stood dressed in handsome three-piece suits, silently holding the door open while they looked on, straight forward, never making eye contact with any of us. Two curved staircases led upstairs and a diamond chandelier hung majestically from the ceiling. In the center was a replica of the Venus de Milo. I honestly wouldn't have been surprised if it was the real thing at this point. The white marble floors echoed as we walked over them.

Claire de Lune was playing softly from somewhere inside the house. It took all of me to not burst out laughing from just how ridiculous the whole situation was. I really didn't want to accidentally rip off my tourniquet, so I stifled the laughter. I was exhausted—everything just seemed like a dream. Granted, part of that feeling could have been from the pills August had given me. Lydia was shaking her head in disbelief, while August actually broke out laughing again.

"Now, I really didn't think this is what his house would look like," Lydia said.

"It's crazy how modest the man is," August chuckled. "If someone were to just see his house, they would think he's just like everyone else."

"My house had more marble," I scoffed. "This is just a trash heap in comparison." August gripped at his wrist and rubbed his hand around it, recoiling a bit, but still managed to flash a half-grin my way.

"Right this way, sir." Another man in an identical black three-piece suit interrupted our gawking. He gestured his hand up the staircase, where a door at the top stood menacingly. We all began to ascend the stairs when the man spoke again. "Not you two." He pointed at Lydia and me.

"Piss on that," August said. "If the old coot wants to talk to me, he's talking to all of us."

"I'm sorry, I cannot allow that."

"Welp," August said as he began to turn around. Then he spun around on his heels and connected his one remaining fist into the side of the man's face, sending him sprawling to the ground. In a matter of seconds, the man was back on his feet, standing in front of the staircase. He gave no hint of emotion.

"I will speak to him," he said.

"Now that's the service I was looking for." August smiled politely. We waited for a few moments in relative silence while Clair de Lune continued playing. The door at the top of the stairs reopened.

"You may all enter," the man said in a monotonous tone from the landing. August tipped a fake hat at him and started to climb the stairs. I followed slowly, step by step, while Lydia helped me. The wet blood on my hands left marks on the handrail as we ascended. Once at the top, August kicked open the door and walked in. We followed behind him.

"You sure know how to make an entrance," the emperor said. His gray hair was perfectly coiffed and matched his neatly trimmed beard. He had striking blue eyes and was likely somewhere in his late sixties. His eyes pierced into August, but not just with anger—it looked like disappointment more than anything. I looked back at August, who was smiling wider than I'd ever seen him.

CHAPTER 55

"Hey dad," August said chipperly. "It's good to see you again." Lydia and I looked at each other in disbelief.

"Can't really say the same thing," Emperor Olysseus retorted.

"I came home so you could meet my friends." August gestured at us. "Louis, Lydia, meet the one, the only, the greatest of all time, Emperor Olysseus."

"A pleasure," Olysseus said, bored. "So you've finally come to do it. I always knew it would be you, Aug."

"Oh, don't be so melodramatic," August said mockingly. "Your time was always destined to come to an end this way. All great emperors die. The mediocre ones too."

This time Olysseus laughed. "I should have sent you out with your mother and sister when I had the chance. I gave you every opportunity in the world to become the greatest person you could be. You were in no way qualified to be leading anyone, even if it was just a handful of disposable assets. I thought the position would help you grow up a little. I see now how foolish I was to think that would have worked."

"Oh come on, I'm a big boy now." August smiled back. "Look how big and strong I got."

"I'm glad you were only the third person to come in, I couldn't have handled any more of those leeches coming in to suck the life out of this place. They've been handled, though." He let out a slight grin, folded his hands, and placed them on a desk in front of him. He was sitting in a lavish burgundy leather chair with gold inlaid on the mahogany armrests. The sun shone in through a window behind him, while the rest of the room was dimly lit. Chocolate wood bookcases lined the walls, and a fire burned off to one side. Red chairs with a side table between them rested in front of the fireplace. A decanter and two glasses sat on the table.

"Those leeches were the only thing that kept this city going in the first place."

"Order." He paused. "Order was the only thing keeping this place going. See, the thing you seemed to never understand, Aug, is that we're not evil—we're opportunists. When your great-great-great-grandfather helped found this city, it was nothing. People from all over came to seek safe haven. Those who developed the city, helped in its creation, and their ancestors are those who belong here. Not the leeches who came crawling out of every hole once they heard there was a new society being formed."

"And what about these two?" August gestured at us. "What about those that were born into it or kidnapped and now are forced to stay in the city under punishment of death?"

"What about them?" Olysseus asked, and leaned back in his chair as he put a little tobacco into a pipe that he retrieved from a drawer in the desk. "We feed them, we clothe them, we shelter them, we give them their lives, and we protect them. In exchange, all they have to do is keep the machine running."

August paused for a moment, his anger clearly building. "And that gives you permission to use them and dispose of them when you feel like it? To hold them captive until the day they die? Force them to do your work while you sit back and live off the spoils of our ancestors, who are long since dead? What gives you the right?" He was yelling now.

"You always had a weak heart," Olysseus said calmly as he sparked up the pipe. "You were never cut out for this. Your brother, on the other hand. He..."

"My brother was just as fucking sadistic as you were. I'm glad that he got himself killed all those years ago out searching in the wastes."

"I'm sure you are," he smiled. "You never would have gotten this job without it. He was one who could follow orders. You, on the other hand, couldn't even keep one of your recruits from speaking out of turn."

"Yeah, and you almost fucking killed me for it?"

"How else would you learn how important order is?" He smiled gently as he puffed on his pipe. "You think just because you're my son, that gives you leeway to do whatever you want."

August smiled at that. "You still never answered my questions. What gives you the right, you narcissistic piece of shit?"

"It's the way the world has always been. I'm sorry its unfair and that you can't wrap your head around that. The world is an unfair place—you should have just gotten over it like everyone else does."

August laughed again. "Get over it? You tell me to get over it. Tell that to the people who you've forced into slave labor to do your bidding. Tell them to get over the fact that their entire lives they will work, and then they will die. Tell them that is what their children will have to do. Tell them to get over it, while you sit here, watching, laughing, drinking, and waiting. I feel sorry for you."

"You feel sorry for me?" He laughed heartily this time. "And why is that?"

"You will never know what it's like to live a real life. One with hardship and heartbreak. You will sit here spoiling yourself to no end, and then you will die, never having lived a day in your fucking life."

"Well, I have to disagree." He pulled out a glass and bottle from under his desk and poured himself a drink. "I'd say I'm living a pretty good life from the looks of it." he took a sip and then gestured around the room with his glass.

"That's not life," August affirmed. "That's hiding in a glass room of your own vanity, looking out into a world that you know nothing about."

The emperor's smile faded. "And what do you know about the real world? Huh, Aug? You're so enlightened. Look at you, how noble you are. It's so admirable. You're willing to die for these plebeians."

"I'm not just willing to die for them. As you should know by now, I'm also willing to kill for them." He pointed his pistol at his father's forehead.

Olysseus laughed a hearty laugh. "You're willing to kill for the people who wouldn't even be here without us? We're the ones who built upon the least-irradiated parts of this scorched land. We're the ones who provide people with protection from the radiation and the outside world. We protect, while they serve. That's the way of life."

"It truly is amazing." August paused. "How somehow, you've convinced yourself that you are a part of the toils of our ancestors. You've done nothing. Absolutely nothing."

"I brought an ungrateful bastard into this world." He chuckled. "I did that, didn't I?" They both smiled and laughed softly. "I do wish I could have done things differently. We have never seen eye to eye, but you're still my son." August's gentle grip near the trigger loosened slightly. "So what exactly is your plan then? Kill me, free the slaves, and be a hero to everyone?" He laughed. "I wish I could see how that works out for you. It'll be a week before the whole system collapses."

"Once the people are free, they will stay to rebuild under a leadership that actually cares for them."

"Oh, the best-laid plans." He laughed again.

"Well, we'll see. Maybe the whole empire will collapse and people will start to form tribes again. And maybe those tribes will come together to form a new empire. If it's the end of this one, then I think it is long overdue. Or maybe the other strongholds might come looking for me, but I can be very diplomatic." He smiled. "In any case, what you've got hidden in here puts this whole city at our defense, and I'll take those odds any day."

"It really is a vicious cycle, isn't it?" Olysseus asked.

"It really is."

Olysseus got up from his chair, intertwined his fingers behind his back, and slowly walked over to the fireplace and stared into it. The room was completely silent besides the crackling of the fire. The music outside had either stopped or was completely sealed off by the closed doors. He was staring at the flames when he broke the silence. "Some say the world will end in fire, some say in ice. From what I've tasted of desire, I hold with those that favor fire." He quoted the Robert Frost poem distantly. He sighed deeply. "You're playing with fire, Aug. I hope you know that. Killing me won't be the end of any of this. If anything, it's simply a symbolic act. You desire change so much that I know in your heart you recognize that fire is the only option, and that fire will burn those that you aim to protect."

"Sometimes you need to do a controlled burn to keep the inevitable from spreading. We all recognize the risks," said August.

I nodded in agreement, realizing that it was the first time I moved an inch since the interaction between the two began. I'd completely forgot about the hole that was burned through me, and I looked down to make sure I wasn't pouring out blood. To my pleasant surprise, I wasn't.

"I always knew it would be you," Olysseus said as he turned away from the flames to look August in the eyes. I could see for the first time a hint of sadness in both of their eyes. August nodded wordlessly. "Can't say I don't wish things would have turned out differently," he said with a soft, despondent laugh. "But you're just like your mother." A small smile pursed his lips—he seemed miles away from the room, lost in thought.

"I miss her," August conceded. "She always kept you in check."

"That she did." The drink in his hand swirled around with his hand as he took another sip.

"So Eden sank to grief, so dawn goes to day, nothing gold can say." August quoted Frost this time.

"I see you've been reading the books I gave you."

"Every one of them."

"That was her favorite, you know? She had me read it to her while she was awaiting her execution. I really wish things could have ended differently, but there was no choice for me. I tried to protect her, I really did." August said nothing, but a single tear let loose from the corner of his eye. He wiped at it with the back of his hand, the gun still clutched in it. I half expected Olysseus to make a move to try and disarm him. But he just walked over and put an arm on his shoulder. "I guess that poem is pretty applicable here too, huh?"

"I wish there was another way," August said quietly.

"Mmm," Olysseus murmured. "There's always another way. But you've made your bed, and now it's time to lay in it." He pulled him in for a hug, and they both embraced for a long while before Olysseus pulled away and mussed up his hair like a father wordlessly telling his son that he loved him. "Can you do me one favor?"

"What is it?"

"Bury me next to your mother and brother." August nodded wholeheartedly as Olysseus sighed and walked back toward his chair. As he sat down, it was easy to see just how tired the man was. Far more than a man his age should have been. "Well, I suppose it's time then. Take care of Arcadia, Aug—it won't be easy."

"I will," August said as he pulled the trigger. Olysseus's head shot back in his chair, and it was all over in an instant.

Then August turned to look at us, clearly troubled by the events that had just transpired and shaking slightly. He took a deep breath and regained his composure. His father's body lay lifelessly slumped in his chair. The glass that had been in his hand fell to the ground and rolled a few feet. I was expecting the people outside to bust in at any second, but no one did.

"I'm so sorry," I told him after a moment's silence.

"Patricide shouldn't be easy." He gave a sad chuckle. "But the old man got what was coming to him." He walked over and brushed Olysseus's eyes shut, then kissed him on top of the head. Taking a long pause, he looked at the old emperor's lifeless body and shook his head. Then he turned around to face us "You're looking at the new emperor now. Why aren't you bowing?" He laughed, but it was easy to see the real hurt behind his eyes.

"All hail Emperor Augustus," I mocked, and then patted him on the back. "I know you'll make a great one."

"Can't make a much worse one, I suppose," he pondered. "Thank you for having my back. I'm sorry I couldn't have been upfront with you—it seemed like it would have just complicated things."

"It's okay, Auggie," Lydia interjected. "We understand." He came over and gave her a hug. Then he turned to me and gave me a hearty embrace. The pressure made the tourniquet around me loosen up a little, and blood soaked in onto his suit.

"Shit, sorry about that," he said as Lydia bent down to tighten it back up.

"It's fine—I can't feel a damn thing."

"Well, let's get you out of here and get you some help. Just have to do one thing first." He walked over to where his dad's body was and retrieved a tablet out of the desk. Then, out of nowhere, he pulled out his knife and cut off his dad's thumb. The blood flowed out onto the carpet, and he made his way back toward the door. As we moved back into the entryway of the mansion, the beginning of "Moonlight Sonata" was now playing softly from somewhere. August laughed. "Well, this song is pretty ominous. I promise this isn't some spooky foreshadowing of what will come under my leadership. We really did a great thing here today."

For the short time since I had known August I was absolutely positive that he was telling the truth. There are just some people in life where it is abundantly clear that their hearts are in the right place. August was one of them.

When we got to the bottom of the stairs, the two men in their three-piece suits opened the door for us again, and we walked right out. Everyone was still going about their business in an alarmingly calm manner. Once we got back to the door, I took one look back at the beautiful estate before August used his father's thumb to open up the tablet and swipe a couple times. The door opened.

The ghastly scene of blood entered my vision as the door slid to the ceiling. Turrets slowly rotated back and forth in the corners of the room. Bodies riddled with holes leaked blood onto the flawless white floors. The man who had planted the thermite would have been completely unrecognizable besides his wild black hair. As I stepped over body after body with the help of Lydia, the turrets retracted back into the walls. We slowly made our way past the chambers, the clinics, the farms, the houses, the shops, until we were back at the staircase that spiraled around the walls.

Walking up the stairs caused the dull pain in my stomach to become a little greater, which wouldn't normally have been alarming except for the fact that the pills were so strong I shouldn't be feeling anything at all. Lydia's face was full of alarm as well as she examined my stomach. August fiddled with the tablet again, and the gate inside the council chamber slid back to the ceiling, unpinning the bodies that were lodged underneath it with a sickening squelch. Inside the main hall of the capitol, the scene was the same as in the cryogenic chamber room. An impossible amount of bodies were scattered along everywhere you looked in the beautiful room. The width of the hall made it possible to weave around them, so at least we didn't have to cross over any of them.

Once we were outside, the early afternoon pierced my eyes. There were probably about fifty people gathered outside now, clapping as August emerged from the interior. I looked up into the windows of the surrounding buildings and saw hundreds of members of the Aristocracy looking nervously out. Some people were down on their knees with their hands behind their backs, pistols softly pressing against the backs of their necks. Hera and Rose ran up to approach August and gave him a hug, then did the same for me. Rose hugged Lydia, and Hera smiled at her. What a great little family reunion, I thought to myself, and then August began to speak.

"Hey guys," he said. "It looks like we might have won." What a speech. But the sentence was met with uproarious cheers. "Let them go," he told the people who had their guns pointed at the guards. Some of them were visibly sobbing as they stood up and stared in disbelief. "Gone are the days of brutality and slavery. Today marks the day that Arcadia became a city of peace and freedom. So, if the rest of the Empire has any problems with that, well, then they're just going to have to take it up with their new emperor."

August continued speaking while Rose whispered over to me. "Looks like you took one for the team."

"Sure did," I whispered back.

"I always knew that we could count on you."

"Sure you did," I laughed.

"Okay, maybe I had my doubts for a little while. But you proved yourself to be new-world material." She smiled.

"Only took a bullet to the stomach to do that," I replied. "Worth it." She grinned and gave me another hug.

"Thank you for helping protect my brother."

"Anytime," I smirked back.

"... And although we have an immense amount of rebuilding to do, with your help, I will be right there beside you in our quest to make Arcadia the greatest city the world has ever seen," August finished to another round of thunderous applause. We walked out into the street to find, behind the crowd, dozens of people writhing around in agony while others tried to address their wounds. Cars were now out driving themselves again, but there were no drones in the sky anymore. Likely all had been destroyed from the falls they took. The cars picked up the wounded and zoomed them off.

"We need to get you into one of those cars to get you to a hospital," Lydia told me.

"You take one and go help as many people as you can, I'll be right behind you." I smiled at her.

"We really did it, Louis." She had a couple tears in her eyes. "Who would have thought a couple of twenty-first-centuriers-like us would have had it in us?"

"We're stronger than we look." I smiled.

"Damn right."

"Now get out there and save all the people you can. They need you, I'll be fine."

"Okay," she conceded. "Stay safe, Louis. I love you."

"I love you too," I agreed, and brought her in for a long embrace, kissing her on the top of her head. Then she ran off to go help the people scattered about, bleeding out from their injuries.

Small tears were forming in the corners of August's eyes. "I hope you're not planning what I think you're planning."

"This is your world, August—I don't belong here," I told him.

"No," he protested. "This is our world. You helped create it just as much as the rest of us did. You have to be here to see what it turns into."

"No, I don't. Under your leadership, I already know what it will look like."

"We can easily save you though. Why?" A tear rolled down his cheeks.

"There's already more wounded than can be treated. Save my bed for someone else who really needs it. Like you said, only idiots try to live on past their pre-determined expiration dates." I smiled gently.

"That was just some bullshit I said."

"All your bullshit comes from a place of truth," I told him. "And trust me, there is a lot of bullshit that comes out of your mouth."

He smiled through the tears. "Well isn't this some shit," he concluded. "If that's truly what you want, I can't stop you. But I wish you would stay. I need good people around me to start rebuilding."

"It is. But, you already have good people around you." I looked at Rose and Hera—both wore dejected smiles.

"I've never met someone like you," Hera said as she hugged me and put her head on my shoulder. "Arcadia..." She paused. "No, the world will be missing a big piece without you here."

"Thank you," I told her as we parted from our hug.

"I'll make sure he doesn't get into too much trouble," Rose said as she hugged me and gestured her head toward August.

"Good luck with that," I replied.

"We'll miss you."

"I'll miss you guys too." I smiled. "Maybe we'll see each other again someday."

"I hope so," Hera said.

"I think you'll need a car for where you're going," August told me as he wiped at his eyes and fumbled around on his new tablet.

"Thank you," I told him.

"No." He shook his head. "Thank you, Louis. From the bottom of my heart and everyone else's here. Thank you." All of a sudden, a car zoomed up in front of us and the driver door hissed open.

"Take care of Lydia, would you?" I asked August. "She's just a kid."

"Of course," he said, and gave me another gentle hug this time. "I'll even let her call me Auggie."

"I appreciate it," I laughed as I went to the car. The three of them stood staring at me as I got in. All three raised their hands in farewell as the car took off. I looked back out the window at them, then sighed heavily as I turned around and watched in the rearview until they were out of sight, and became part of history.

EPILOGUE

Something drew me here. In the back of my mind, I knew there was something that I needed. It's weird how a gut feeling can often lead you to what you need most. It was a shame that the gut feeling was also accompanied by a hole through it. But what can you do? That's life. You gotta roll with the punches. Or bullets. I pulled the car up outside as it whirred to a stop. The building that August had found me, which felt like years ago but in reality was only a little over a month ago, stood in front of me. I slowly made my way up the stairs and into the same grimy room with the broken window August had thrown the chair through. Searching through the room, I came to a cabinet labeled *Personal Effects*. I opened the top drawer and saw some unfamiliar names, so I moved to the next one down. There was a file in it that had *King, Louis* on the tab. I pulled it out and opened it.

Laying it on the ground, I kneeled down next to it. Inside were a bunch of pictures of Violet and me. One of us standing in our doorway when we first moved into our house. Another of when we dressed up as Harry Potter and Ginny for Halloween. It made me laugh. As a small amount of blood started leaking out from under the tourniquet, I tried to tighten it back up a little. The Halloween that we had accidentally burned down a swinging bench we had just put together. It was wonderful. I was beaming when I saw the picture on the bridge I had fallen in love with her. And another identical photo that I had stored away in my shoe. The last picture was of Violet when she must have been about ten years older. She was sitting next to the cherry blossom tree, smiling, with a child sitting on her lap. Behind all the pictures was a letter engraved with *Louis* on it in Violet's handwriting. My heart felt more warmth than it had the entire time I had been in the future. She looked so happy in the picture, and it gave me a huge liberation from the unknown. Although I would never know exactly what happened in her life after I left it, I could see here that she wasn't alone, and that made all the difference. A strong feeling of pain entered my chest. But it was a good pain. A longing pain that allowed me to envision the mysteries of her life, and the beauty that could have been, and was likely there for her.

I grabbed the folder and struggled my way back to my feet. My head was feeling a little foggy by this point as I walked back out to the car, the folder tucked safely under my arm. Getting in, I drove the same route I had all those times before, for the final time. The sun was starting to get lower in the sky as I drove down the highway. A beautiful blend of orange, red, blue, and violet.

Pulling up onto the street in front of our old house, I looked around and recognized nothing. Everything had returned to the earth, save a couple chimneys still standing defiantly. The whole neighborhood was in ruins, but it was beautiful at the same time. I got out of the car and tucked the folder back under my arm to visit Violet and the cherry blossom tree for the last time.

Our initials were still carved into the side of it. It was astounding that the tree was still here; most of the species only live around half a century. But here ours was, standing defiantly and proud in a wasteland. A testament to what we had once built here. I sat down and leaned my back against the trunk. The slightly warm embrace from the setting sun sparkled on my face and all around me.

As I was sitting down, my tourniquet loosened up, and now blood was coming out freely. Not gushing, but a steady stream of warmth sliding down my stomach and into my lap. I pulled the letter out of the folder and spread the pictures around my side, glancing at them as I turned the letter over in my hand. Slowly, I slid my thumb through the slit on the back of it, causing the glue to crack apart. Resting it gently on my knee to avoid the blood obscuring any words, I began to read:

Hi Honey Bear,

There are so many things that I long to tell you. I wake up every morning to turn over to talk to you, and when you're not there it's like reliving a nightmare over and over again. But I tell you anyways, because I know wherever you are, you can still hear me. Even though you're a cute little popsicle now. I visit as often as I can, but as time goes on it's getting harder and harder. I know that you will understand. You have been the only one in my entire life who has truly gotten me. It's so hard to say goodbye, but I know this will never truly be a goodbye. We will always be there for each other in our hearts.

Whenever I visit, they tell me that there is no cure in sight for your tumor, but I still hold out hope. Pretty soon the age gap between us will be insurmountable, and even though our love for each other will never fade, neither of us want people to think I'm robbing the cradle. I turn 40 next week. Can you believe it? I envy you and your youth you little bastard. Kidding! But still, you look just as handsome as the day I met you. Our wedding photo still sits on your nightstand, and every time I look at it, you're here with me all over again.

I'm guessing if you're reading this it means you have seen the pictures too. Do you remember when we burned down that stupid little swing set we put together? Good riddance, I say, it made better kindling than anything. I miss you. I miss you so much every day it hurts. That's why I have to move on. Did you see the picture of the kid on my lap? Well turns out I am irresistible and had a whole line of suitors banging at my door once you left. Got me all knocked up, don't know whose it is. Sorry, sorry, mean joke!! I know my tone of voice doesn't come through in letters. But I'm guessing you've picked up on it by now. He's yours, Louis. By some miracle, we were able to have a baby with what you had frozen. I think we can both appreciate the dark comedy in that, since you're all frozen too and whatnot.

He's a wonderful child though, Louis. He reminds me so much of you. I wish you would have gotten the chance to meet him. Maybe someday. Although he might be older than you at that point. So weird. His little mannerisms are almost identical to yours. He even taps at his leg when he gets nervous. It's crazy. Like I'm looking at you when you were a child when I look into his eyes. Time really is a funny thing. Cruel, but funny. Maybe I'll end up freezing myself one day when I'm nice and old. It would be pretty fun to come and freak you out. I'll see you every day for the rest of my life

Louis, you're always in my thoughts and my dreams. I love you more than the moon loves the night. Whether it's in this life or somewhere else in the plane of existence, I'll see you again someday Honey Bear, that I promise.

I took a deep breath and wiped away at the corners of my eyes. "I'll see you again too Vi," I said as I smiled. I briefly thought about the beautiful life that Violet and our son had together, and that maybe he was still out there somewhere. But as the blood continued pouring out, that thought was soon replaced by the vision of Violet standing in front of me on the bridge I had proposed to her on all those years ago, and I could hear the soft whirring of the stream. She smiled. Looking into the perfect blue-green pools of her eyes, I knew that I was safe. I was home.

Printed in the USA
CPSIA information can be obtained
at www.ICGtesting.com
LVHW050150200524
780759LV00003B/252